When Seasons Change by Susan K. Do

Debbie and Rick Weaver each have their own ideas about how they want to enjoy their soon-to-be-empty nest. Debbie dreams of returning to college to complete her undergraduate degree or maybe even writing the next great American novel, while Rick thinks the two of them should fly the coop on the back of a new motorcycle. But nothing can prepare them for the news her doctor is about to deliver. . . .

Reunited by Kristy Dykes

After twenty-four years of marriage, Felicia Higgins asks her husband, Jake, to move out to give her time to think about their future. After all, he doesn't have a clue about bringing happiness to her romantic soul. At first, Jake is incensed. Why can't Felicia be happy? He's a good Christian man. What more could she want or need? Both discover some surprising things about each other—and marriage—in their journey to a second chance at love.

Love Is a Choice by Sally Laity

The wedding of their fourth—and youngest—daughter leaves Bess and Arthur Wright with a suddenly empty nest. Art is thrilled with this new freedom, but the silent house drives Bess into a depression that soon affects their own marriage. Even the new hobby she takes up increases the wedge between them. Will two people who once loved each other more than life find their way back to wedded bliss?

Wherever Love Takes Us by Carrie Turansky

Tessa Malone finds it difficult to trust her husband after a business failure rocks their marriage. Matt inherits a mountain lodge in Oregon and wants to move the family there and start a new business. Tessa can't imagine giving up her tea shop, Sweet Something, and the security of her life in Princeton. Matt and Tessa must decide how much they value their marriage and whose dream they will follow.

wedded bliss?

Published by Barbour Publishing, Inc., P.O. Box 719, Uhrichsville, OH 44683,
www.barbourbooks.com

*Our mission is to publish and distribute inspirational products offering exceptional
value and biblical encouragement to the masses.*

Member of the
Evangelical Christian
Publishers Association

Printed in the United States of America.

5 4 3 2 1

wedded bliss?

*Romance Needs Restored
During Four Silver
Wedding Anniversaries*

susan k. downs ● kristy dykes
sally laity ● carrie turansky

BARBOUR
PUBLISHING

when seasons change

by Susan K. Downs

Dedication

To my Pinkie-Promise Pals and my Spit-and-Polish critique team—the best buds a gal could ever hope to find. And to the love of my life, David. Together we've proven an empty nest gives more room for love to spread its wings!

God is our refuge and strength, an ever-present help in trouble.
Therefore we will not fear, though the earth give way
and the mountains fall into the heart of the sea,
though its waters roar and foam
and the mountains quake with their surging.

There is a river whose streams make glad the city of God,
the holy place where the Most High dwells.
God is within her, she will not fall;
God will help her at break of day.
Nations are in uproar, kingdoms fall;
he lifts his voice, the earth melts.

The LORD Almighty is with us;
the God of Jacob is our fortress.
PSALM 46:1–7 NIV

Chapter 1

Debbie Weaver considered herself a "roll with the punches" kind of gal, and she refused to let this latest blow score a TKO. She swallowed hard as she watched her son, Matt, carry an egg-crate foam mattress into the freshman dorm of Eastern Evangelical University. One more armload would do it. She handed out a lacrosse stick, baseball glove, and CD case to her daughter, then climbed from the back of the family van. "Looks like this is the end of Matt's stuff."

A sweat bead trickled down the side of Debbie's face, and she swiped at it with her T-shirt sleeve. The disgusting garment would need to be burned when she got home anyway. Her deodorant had failed her hours ago, thanks to the twin assaults of rural Pennsylvania's late-August heat and humidity added to the stress of parting with her oldest child and only son.

"Hey, the jerk is trying to steal my Flying Elephants CD!" The ball glove dangled from the lacrosse stick like a hobo's pack over seventeen-year-old Madison's shoulder while she leafed through the plastic sleeves of her brother's CD case. "I'd better see what else he's trying to swipe."

Everywhere Debbie looked, across the parking lot and around the grounds surrounding the dormitory, a menagerie of freshman boys and their families milled about them in various phases of unloading and moving into the dorm—definitely not the best stage for one of Melodrama Queen Madison's infamous scenes.

"Puh-leeze, Maddy!" Though Debbie spoke in a volume less than one tick above a whisper, her voice bore the definite tone of command. "Not here. Not now. Not in front of all these people. Don't you *dare* pick a fight with Matt right before we say good-bye!"

Her daughter responded with her trademark rolled eyes. "As if, Mom. Like I would throw a fit in front of all these hottie guys."

Debbie opened her mouth to chastise her daughter's blatant disrespect but ended up blowing out a puff of frustration instead. She didn't have the strength to do battle with a hormonal teenager right now. At this stage of the game, Debbie's own hormones had taken home-field advantage over her emotional state. Wrung out, not just emotionally but physically, she felt the need for a good long nap. If things went according to schedule, she planned to sleep away the five-hour drive home.

"Well, girls, I do believe our work here is done." Debbie's husband, Rick, snuck up behind them, and, ever the diplomat, he wedged himself in between mother and daughter, draping an arm over each of their shoulders. "All done but the payin' and the cryin', that is. I didn't think I'd ever get to the head of the line at the financial aid office. Finally got things squared away, though. Seems like we just finished paying off my graduate school loans, and we're in hock up to our ears again to that old hag Sallie Mae."

He tugged on Madison's long cocoa brown ponytail. "This time next year, I'll be going through all this rigmarole times *two* when you join your brother here."

"Uh, maybe. If I decide to come to EEU." Madison paused just long enough to glance at her dad, obviously gauging the impact of her words. "Lauren says she's going to Ohio State, and she really wants me to room with her."

Now it was Debbie's turn to roll her eyes. Madison knew all the right buttons to push, and she was jabbing every last one. Debbie didn't have anything against their home-state university, but three generations of the Weaver and Daniels families claimed Eastern Evangelical University as their alma mater. While she and Rick were high school sweethearts, both sets of their parents and grandparents had met and fallen in love on this campus. Rick had even managed to get Matt moved into the same freshman dorm room he had occupied.

Debbie regretted the fact that she'd had to quit college a year shy of graduation in order to work and put Rick through graduate school. She had appeased herself, though, with the knowledge that they would provide their children with every opportunity to carry on the family tradition as EEU alumni, no matter what the cost or the level of personal sacrifice.

Leave it to Madison to throw away a blessing with both

hands, and for no other reason than sheer stubbornness. Then again, her words were likely empty threats.

She knew their daughter's verbal sparring goaded Rick, too. She caught a glimpse of her husband out of the corner of her eye. Ripples coiled up and down the muscle in his right jawline—a reflex action that took over whenever he let pent-up irritation go unexpressed.

"Well, punkin, you've got a year to decide," Rick said, his voice flat. "Ah, look, here comes our college boy now."

At the sight of their six-foot-four baby boy, Debbie fought off a sledgehammer assault to her crystalline emotions. How had he grown up so fast?

By Debbie's internal calendar, it seemed as though only a year—maybe two—could have passed since she and Rick flew to Texas to meet their newborn son-to-be at the adoption agency. His birth mother sought Christian parents for her baby, and through a scenario orchestrated solely by God, a mutual acquaintance from the counseling center where Rick served his internship told the unwed teenager about them. When they got the initial call from the attorney inquiring as to whether or not they'd be interested in adopting, they had not yet begun the official application process, but they had been trying to start a family—with no success—and had been praying in earnest about what options they should explore. Since Rick was still in graduate school, they'd been pasta-every-day poor, but their parents sprang for the adoption expenses and legal fees.

Rick dropped his hold on Debbie's shoulder and stepped

toward their son. Debbie did a quick two-step to catch up with him, thankful Matt's approach provided them another saved-by-the-bell reprieve from Madison's latest round of provocation.

While neither she nor Rick could take any biological credit for the way Matt turned out, Debbie had to take full blame for passing along her own roller-coaster personality to her daughter. Three months after Matt came home to his forever family, Debbie learned she was pregnant, and the day after Matt's first birthday, she gave birth to Madison. Though they'd been open to the prospect of having more children, when it didn't happen, they'd been content with one of each.

Now, for the first time in a long time, Debbie found herself wishing they'd had a dozen kids instead of two. Then she wouldn't feel the impact of Matt's departure quite so hard. *Make that a dozen boys*, she thought, revising her wishful thinking. *Boys are so much easier to raise than girls.*

She was going to miss Matt's contagious smile, his hearty laughter filling the house. Matt always provided the counterbalance to his sister's caustic wit.

To look at him, no one would ever guess their adopted son's genes didn't swim in the same pool as his dad's. Standing face-to-face with his father, Matt mirrored the classic Weaver family features—dove gray eyes with those long, thick eyelashes the girls all envied, olive-toned and pimple-free skin, and thick mahogany hair. As Matt transitioned from the gangly adolescent stage into manhood, his adoptive father had been forced to share with his son the heartthrob role Rick had always held. If Debbie hadn't snagged Rick's attention in their high school days, when he was still all arms and legs and nose, she had no doubt she wouldn't have stood a chance at catching his eye, much less his heart, in later years. Even back then, she'd found it hard to believe that a senior would cast a second glance at a measly sophomore like her.

The recent laugh lines Rick had developed around his eyes and lips, along with the peppering of silver at his temples, only served to enhance his head-turning good looks, while on Debbie, such outward indicators of the years' toll made her look, well, just plain old.

Madison's future didn't bode well in this regard either. The poor girl had inherited not only Debbie's bent toward moodiness but also her short stature, unnoteworthy features, and drab brown hair—on which Debbie now spent a small fortune each month masking the hoary roots and coating with blond highlights. Maddy might have a perfect hourglass figure at seventeen, but if history repeated itself, in the years to come, she would likely also lay heir to her mother's tendency to carry a few extra pounds.

Poor girl. I really ought to cut her some slack. Debbie turned and sent her daughter a smile.

"What?" Madison mouthed, her eyebrows puckered and her eyes mere slits.

Debbie shrugged but kept her smile as she turned back to her son. "Matt, honey, are you sure you don't want us to help you set up your room? I don't understand why you won't at least let me come up and put the sheets on your bed."

"Come on, Mom, you don't want to be responsible for hanging a 'mama's boy' label on me right off the bat, do you? I can manage. Trust me." Matt retrieved his lacrosse stick and ball glove from his sister's shoulder and reached for his CD case.

Madison swung sideways, pulling the case out of his reach. She wagged a silver disc in the air. "You thought you could sneak this one by me, didn't you?"

Debbie tried to silence her daughter with one of *those* looks, but Maddy knew better than to glance her way.

Matt's mouth dropped open. "Oh, Maddy, I'm so sorry. I didn't realize I still had that. Let me look and see if I have any other CDs of yours." His words rang with genuine remorse.

"Don't bother," Madison snapped.

But from where she stood, Debbie could see the sparkle of mischief in Maddy's eyes. *The imp.*

"I already checked. Besides, I'm just trying to give you a hard time. You know me," she said, fluttering her big brown eyes over her shoulder at her older sibling. "I can't go without leaving you with one last bratty-little-sister memory." With her back still turned away from her brother, Maddy tucked the compact disc into an empty sleeve. Then she jerked her head toward her brother, stuck out her tongue at him, and giggled. "I'm kinda sick of the Flying Elephants anyway. I don't mind if you borrow this one until you come home for Thanksgiving if you want."

"Aw, thanks." Matt gave his sister's arm a playful jab before accepting the CD case from her.

Rick cleared his throat, and the rest of the family looked at him. "Look, I hate to break up this family lovefest, but there's no use postponing the inevitable. Son, I guess it's time we said good-bye. We've got a long drive ahead of us, and I think we'd better hit the road."

Wait! Debbie wanted to scream, a rush of last-minute instructions, advice, and mother-to-son sentiments bombarding her thoughts. *I'm not ready to leave him behind!* As much as she wanted to protest, she kept her objections to herself. She knew she had to act like a mature adult, despite the childish tantrum raging in her mind. "I'll have my cell phone on if you think of anything we might have forgotten. We can turn back if we have to—"

"Tell him good-bye, honey," Rick said, "and let's go. He'll be fine." He slapped his son on the back. "Matt's a big boy now." Most of the time, Debbie found Rick's psychologist voice soothing, but at the moment, the soft-spoken approach grated on her nerves like the squeal of brake pads gone bad.

"Come here." With open arms, Debbie waved her boy to her. "Or are you too embarrassed to give your mama a hug good-bye?" Matt leaned down, gathered her in his arms, and returned her squeeze.

"Dad's right, Mom. I'll be okay." His voice cracked on the last word.

"Uh-huh. I know. . . ." Debbie couldn't elaborate further. She planted one last kiss on his cheek, then turned and made a mad dash for the van.

Chapter 2

Rick passed another semitrailer, then signaled his move back into the right lane and reengaged the van's cruise control. For the last hundred miles of the Pennsylvania Turnpike, they'd ridden in silence, Madison with her earphones on, listening to her MP3 player, and Debbie fast asleep. He hadn't even bothered to turn on the radio or listen to a tape for fear it would keep his wife awake.

He copped another quick glance at Debbie, then focused his attention on the road. He worried about her. She hadn't been herself since—when? Maybe as far back as after they'd gotten home from their twenty-fifth-anniversary cruise in June? Ever since then, she seemed moodier than usual and exhausted all the time. Every meal, he watched her pick at her food.

If anyone were to ask his professional opinion as a psychologist, he would diagnose depression. He'd witnessed these same symptoms of lassitude in many of his forty-something clients when their children started leaving the nest. Still, he'd never expected Debbie to be the type to suffer from what he termed "midlife melancholy." She had experienced her share of mood swings over the past quarter century. Her personality type lent itself to such temperamental fluctuations, but nothing outside the realm of normal as far as he could tell. Until now.

He thought back over the clients he'd helped pull through such seasons of depression. Oftentimes, something as simple as a new hobby or special interest would focus attention away from the problem and lift their spirits until they were able to transition through their life change. He wondered what kind of new diversion Debbie might enjoy. Definitely not knitting or needlepoint. She already spent too much time sitting and concentrating on detailed work in her job as a proofreader for Barnhill Publishing. She loved her job, and it allowed her to work from home and set her own hours, but she'd said on many occasions that she wished she could spend more time out of the house. There were days she complained of feeling like a prisoner in their home. She needed something to get her out of her chair and enjoying the great outdoors.

He refused to acknowledge as much to Debbie, but he himself struggled with this whole concept of middle age and empty nest and growing old. He wasn't about to go off the deep end and have an affair or anything self-destructive like that. In his line of work, he'd witnessed, time and again, the devastation such trysts caused. Besides, he loved his wife now more than ever, and he'd never entertained any serious temptations to stray down an adulterous path. Why would he, with a wife as beautiful and talented as his? She embodied the perfect mate.

But he had been toying with the idea of a new recreational activity, something to make him feel young again. He knew just what would do the trick for him. . . .

Debbie shifted in her seat, and when Rick looked over at her, she offered him a sleepy-eyed, thin-lipped smile. "I haven't been much company for you, huh?" She stroked his sleeve. "I'm sorry."

"That's okay. I'm glad you were able to rest. You've put in some stressful days trying to get Matt ready for school." Rick pulled his concentration from the road as long as he dared and studied his wife's face. He frowned. "You look pale. Do you feel all right?"

"Um, well, I'm feeling a tad carsick, but that's the price I pay for falling asleep in a moving vehicle. I'll be fine." Debbie leaned forward and strained to read an approaching road sign. "Maybe we could pull off at the next rest stop so I can use the restroom and stretch my legs."

"You got it, babe." Rick winked at his wife. "Looks like a service area is coming up in three miles. Think you can last that long?"

She gave him a less than convincing nod. Then, clutching the armrests of her captain's seat with a white-knuckle grip, she rested her head against the leather upholstery.

A rumble on his left pulled Rick's attention to the side mirror, and he counted five full-dresser motorcycles in the passing lane getting ready to overtake them. The sun glinted off chrome as streaks of candy-apple red, classic black, and midnight blue flashed by. The loud exhausts on these moving works of art produced an awesome thunder roar, sending gooseflesh sweeping up his arms. His pulse drummed in his ears.

Rick admired each bike as they barreled past and even waved at a couple of the riders. He was a little surprised when they waved back. "Look, Deb, those guys have all got to be older than we are." He guessed the lead rider was closer to his dad's age.

"You must be ready for glasses, honey." Debbie peered around him, craning her neck. "Some of those guys aren't guys. They're girls—ladies. Women. Female, at least. . .I think."

They shared a laugh, and Rick glanced in the rearview mirror to see if Maddy was laughing, too, but she had fallen asleep.

"That could be you, you know—a Harley mama riding a Road King down the open highway." Rick shot Debbie a grin. "Why not? You're always looking to try something new."

"Yeah, right." Deb leaned back in her seat.

"I'm serious. I think you should look into taking a safety course and getting your license. We could do it together." Rick pressed down on the van's accelerator to keep pace with the pack of bikers. They sported Michigan plates. He wondered where they'd been and if they were heading home. "I've kept up the motorcycle endorsement on my license since high school days, but I could use a refresher class. It'd be fun. Tomorrow will give us a good test for whether we like it or not."

"Tomorrow?" Deb lifted her head just long enough to ask the question.

"You know, the big Biker Sunday special service at church?

The motorcycle parade through downtown after worship? You missed out on it last year. Wasn't that when you were down in Florida helping your folks move into their condo? Anyway, I decided then I wouldn't be left sitting on the sidelines again while everyone else had a blast."

Debbie gave one of her infamous sighs. "All I know about Biker Sunday is that I have to wear black jeans and a T-shirt and tie my hair up in a bandanna in order to sing in the choir. I'm stretching my limits to sing 'Born to Be God's Child' to the tune of 'Born to Be Wild.' You're not suggesting I actually get on one of those death traps, are you?"

Rick chuckled. He loved his wife's sense of humor.

"You're kidding, right? I told you, didn't I? About the rental?" One peek at Deb and he could tell he was drawing blanks. Rick cringed. He hated when he forgot to tell things like this to her. As a marriage and family counselor, he was expected to be an expert at communicating with his mate. "Pastor Steele arranged with the local dealer to rent bikes at a discount to the ministerial staff, and he included our counseling center staff in on the deal. I signed us up and paid several weeks ago. I thought for sure I mentioned it to you. I didn't? I guess it just slipped my mind. As Maddy would say, 'My bad.'"

"Oh, Rick, I don't know. . . ." She broke off her sentence and pointed to the turnoff for the rest area. "Don't forget I need to stop." She sucked in a deep breath. "I'm afraid I'm going to be sick."

Debbie splashed water on her face and patted it dry with a

swath of trucker-grade paper toweling. She squinted into the polished chrome that served as a mirror. A sweaty old lady stared back at her.

Next week, she would turn forty-four. She dreaded the approaching event, for more than one reason. As she did every year, she'd scheduled her yearly physical with Dr. Peterson on the day before her birthday. But she didn't need a doctor to tell her what her body already screamed. She could tick off a list of the classic symptoms and self-diagnose her malady: perimenopause. According to what she'd read on the Web, she bore all the signs—the hot flashes, sleepless nights, mood swings, missed cycles, and general malaise. Betrayed by her body at a time when she needed to feel her best.

A young mother with babe in arms entered the facility and struggled to open up the wall-mounted changing table. Debbie stepped over and offered her assistance. "You've got a beautiful baby there," she said as she unhooked the strap that held the device in place.

"Thanks," the young woman replied, an aura of veneration haloing the Madonna as she looked at her child. "Her dad and I sure think so, but then again we're prejudiced."

"Enjoy her. They grow up too fast." Like a whomp upside her head with a two-by-four, a dread realization battered Debbie's thoughts. She hurried out of the restroom before she did something crazy, like bawl in front of a perfect stranger. Until just this minute, she'd never really stopped to consider the finality of menopause's effects. The "change of life" meant she faced the end of even the remotest prospect of revisiting those happy baby days, the days of diaper bags and bottles, toothless grins and slobbery kisses, Frankenstein-style first steps.

By most standards, she'd be considered smack-dab in the middle of middle age. Her hormones, however, must not have consulted the right charts. She seemed to recall that her mother had gone through the change of life earlier than the average woman did. Someday when she found the stamina to talk about it without crying, she'd have to ask her. She felt herself rolling, tumbling, hurtling over the dark side of that dreaded hill and into the abyss of old age.

Debbie quarried the bottom of her purse for change to buy a soda pop, thinking a Sprite or 7-Up might help to settle her stomach. Instead of the loose coins she expected to harvest, she recognized the feel of a roll of quarters. She'd meant to leave the cache with Matt so he would have no excuse not to do his laundry. Oh well. As Rick had been so quick to point out, their son was on his own now.

She pushed a few of the coins into her palm and fed them into the vending machine, then made her selection and waited for the plastic bottle to thump down the chute.

With her beverage in hand, she skulked down the walkway toward the parked van. She could see Rick, his arm draped over the open door next to the seat Maddy occupied. He appeared to be talking to their daughter or, more likely, teasing her.

Rick claimed one of his missions in life was to keep Maddy from taking herself too seriously. Debbie wondered if he'd also make light of her present troubles. Like the cobbler's children in need of shoes or the plumber's wife with a clogged sink, sometimes she felt the counselor had little patience to listen to the miseries of his own kin. She didn't fault him, though. He worked long, hard hours, and as much as she hated to admit it, he was right when he insinuated her troubles were mild compared to most of the messes he dealt with on a day-to-day basis. His work stresses accounted for part of the reason she hadn't found the courage to talk to him about her aging anxieties or her physical woes. Not yet. She tried her best to carry on the status quo, acting as though everything was fine, but she knew he suspected something amiss. She could feel him psychoanalyzing her at every turn. She could only guess what diagnosis he'd pinned on her or what act of psycho-surgery he would try to use as a cure for what ailed her.

In some sick way, she wasn't ready for him to make it all better just yet or, even worse, pooh-pooh away her hurt. She wanted to nurse her troubles awhile longer. She felt the need to stew and pout. And, truth be told, Rick had problems enough coming to grips with his own aging issues. She didn't want to burden him with hers.

Not only had her body petered out on her, but her son had left home, her daughter forever slashed away at her last nerve, and now her husband showed signs of a full-blown midlife crisis of his own, whether he wanted to accept the truth or not. The very idea sucked the breath right out of her, and she blamed his Harley-drooling for her latest hot flash.

Rick's behavior mystified her. It was *so* not like him to go nuts over machines like he had those motorcycles.

Last year when their ancient family station wagon died,

she'd balked at the idea of buying a minivan. She much preferred to go with something sporty and red this time around, or at least an SUV. Ever-practical Rick, on the other hand, never even concerned himself over what kind of car he drove. He saw their vehicles as transportation, nothing more.

As she approached the van, Rick straightened. At first, Debbie thought he must have seen her coming and would hop into the driver's seat and start the engine to head out again. Instead, he turned to the highway behind them and, shading his eyes from the August sun, scanned the open road.

Another pack of motorcycles roared past. The racket they made as they lumbered down the highway hadn't even registered on her sonar, but Rick's ears had perked up at the first ground-shaking *boom* from their exhaust pipes—long before they came into view.

Who was he trying to kid? He couldn't possibly think she'd bought his line when he insinuated he thought a motorcycle would do *her* good. She thought back to the black-leather-clad female riders who'd passed them on the turnpike and shuddered. Uh-uh. Definitely not her look.

He'd pulled this same sort of stunt before, although on a much smaller scale—like the time when Rick's feet hurt, so for Christmas, he gave her a fancy foot massager. The behavior had a name, but she couldn't remember what—transference or projection or some such psychobabble tag.

She suspected the same principle applied when he took her to the Caribbean for their silver anniversary. He'd been the one who wanted to go on a cruise, not her—although she had to confess she'd loved every minute of it once they finally got away.

He was a psychologist, after all. Couldn't he hear his own cry for help? A proverb that Jesus quoted came to mind: *"Physician, heal thyself."* She figured the phrase applied to psychologists, too. To her way of thinking, an old guy on a motorcycle always meant one thing: A Harley symbolized an aging man's pathetic attempt to recapture his youth, salving his aging issues with power and speed. She might not have a college degree, much less a Ph.D., but even she could figure that out. She'd once heard a leathery-skinned old coot refer to his bike as a "geezer glide." At least that guy hadn't been afraid to face the facts.

"Hey." Debbie sidled up beside her husband and rubbed his shirtsleeve. Without flinching, Rick kept his eyes trained on the motorcade.

"Earth to Rick." She bumped against him with her hip, adding a little extra *oomph* to her shove. This time, he startled and looked at her as though surprised to see her standing at his side. She waved her open palm in front of his face and grinned. "Is my new motorcycle maniac about ready to hit the road?"

"Oh, yeah, sure. I'm just enjoying the scenery." He dropped his hand to his side and pivoted back toward the van. "Motorcycle maniac, huh?" His eyes twinkled as he returned her hip bump. "Funny, very funny." By the time Debbie made it around to her side and climbed in, Rick had already clicked his seat belt into place and turned the key in the ignition. While he waited for her to buckle up, he used his fingers as drumsticks and the dashboard as a drum and accompanied his own vocal solo. "Get your motor running. Head out on the highway." He belted the words of the sixties rebel theme song at the top of his lungs.

"Dad! Do you mind? You're drowning out my tunes." Maddy voiced her protest and flopped back in her seat.

Rick looked at Debbie and shrugged, the joy and exuberance leeched from his face. "Sorry. Guess I did get a little carried away."

Debbie watched her husband as he backed the van out of the parking space and steered onto the turnpike access ramp. In all likelihood, Maddy didn't have a clue what she'd done. With her self-centered words, the child had humbled her father, put him in his place—at least the place she thought he should occupy.

For a moment, Debbie had seen a spark of the old Rick—the Rick who saw life as one big adventure. The Rick who wanted everyone to share his enthusiasm and joy in living. With his hair hanging in his face from his rock-and-roll outburst, he looked like the twenty-year-old she'd married over a quarter century ago.

Her criticisms of her husband, the grumblings she'd been harboring minutes earlier, returned to haunt her now.

Her heart stirred the embers of a fire she'd allowed to bank over the years. Love burst into flames. She took her husband for granted most of the time, but the Lord had blessed her with a good man with whom to live out her years. She never questioned his faithfulness and devotion to her or the kids.

So what if he chose to manage his midlife crisis by riding off into the sunset on a motorcycle? She could think of any number of more damaging ways he could placate a sagging ego in the autumn season of his life.

She could rail against his ideas or she could play along. If she didn't fight him on this, he might just give up the obsession as fast as he'd been overcome by it. Maybe a day on a rental would do the trick. For Rick's sake, she could suffer through a short ride, if that's what it took to make him happy again.

Debbie pictured herself on the back of a big ol' Hog, her arms clutched around Rick's waist, the wind whipping her hair—but she refused to let her mind's eye capture the image of her wide thighs in chaps.

"Rick, this motorcycle you've rented—are you sure there's a seat on the back big enough to hold me?"

Chapter 3

Debbie circled the black and silver behemoth in their driveway, shaking her head all the while. "I don't know, Rick. Are you sure you can drive this thing without killing us both?" The rented motorcycle seemed much larger than the ones she'd seen on the turnpike yesterday, despite Rick's insistence otherwise. The very thought of climbing onto such a colossal machine and expecting two tires to keep them upright made her woozy. Debbie turned her face toward the sun and filled her lungs with fresh air.

Well, if she had to pick a day to die, today would be a good one, she supposed. The good Lord had provided one of those warm and cloudless-blue-sky August mornings Debbie liked to store in her memory to keep her sane through the long Ohio winters—a day that hinted of what heaven must be like.

"Honey, I promise I'll be careful, and I'll keep to the speed limit. You know I'd never unduly risk your safety or do anything to hurt you." Rick held out a helmet at arm's length and urged Debbie to take it, but she wasn't buying into his smooth-talking sales job just yet. She kept her arms folded across her midriff and sent him a calculating squint. The sight of her husband decked out in borrowed helmet, fancy gloves, and black leather riding regalia would have had her in stitches if terror hadn't frozen her features in place.

"I'm telling you, babe, it's the same as getting back on a bicycle after not having ridden for years." Rick's voice and countenance radiated zeal. "The steering, the balance, the throttle, the brakes—it all came back to me in a flash. I had the hang of this puppy by the time I'd gone around the parking lot a few times."

This puppy? You think of this monstrosity as a puppy? Looks more like an attack Doberman to me! Debbie watched Rick as his gaze darted from the motorcycle to her and back again. *You're the one with puppy dog eyes, my dear. How can I tell you no? Oh, but how can I say yes?*

Rick seemed to read her vacillating thoughts, and his words tumbled out of his mouth at warp speed. "You've only got to ride the three miles to church, and there's no traffic this early on a Sunday. . . ."

Debbie kept her granite expression, and desperation began to edge Rick's voice. "Tell you what," he said. "I'll make a pact with you. If you go as far as the church with me and decide you're too scared to ride in the parade, you can come home with Maddy in her car. Deal?" He waggled his eyebrows and, in silent pleading, offered her the helmet again.

She didn't like her survival odds with either option. Maddy's battered Ford advertised the teen's less-than-stellar driving skills.

But since Rick had left their van at the motorcycle dealership parking lot when he picked up the bike, her choices were severely limited. She accepted the proffered headgear like she would a dead-mouse offering from their cat, Jinx.

"Deal—I guess. But you're gonna owe me big-time for this one, buddy-boy."

"You'll love it. You'll see." A grin as huge as Texas spread across Rick's face. "Now let me give you a rundown on things bikers riding two-up need to watch out for. . . ." He threw his leg over the bike and settled into his seat, then donned a pair of mirrored sunglasses. "First, wait for me to start the engine and right the bike. I'll tell you when I'm ready for you to climb on board. Always mount from the left so you don't risk touching a hot exhaust pipe. . . ."

Debbie nodded as she did a quick mental left/right quiz. She could remember *left* because that was the side of her head where the throbbing had commenced.

"Once you're aboard, you can rest your feet on these floorboards and put your arms around my waist to hold on." He paused and leaned toward her. "And should you feel so inclined, I wouldn't mind if you hugged a little tighter every now and then." Even though she couldn't see his eyes, she knew by his snicker that he had charmed himself. His moment of levity passed as quickly as it came, however, and he returned to his directives. "When we go to turn, I'll try to warn you ahead of time so you can watch over my shoulder in the direction we're going to take."

Debbie thought she'd done a decent job of masking her

fear until she caught sight of her reflection in Rick's sunglasses. She used his mirrored lenses to aid in retooling her wild-eyed horror into one of her infamous Mona Lisa smirks.

"You don't need to do anything special as far as leaning is concerned. Lean naturally with me. Don't shift your weight. Just relax and follow my lead."

Relax. Yeah. Right. If Rick thought his litany of riding safety tips eased her fears, he had another thing coming. Already the knot in Debbie's stomach was so tight she'd lost all feeling below her waist.

"Our goal is to move as one, just like in marriage." Rick lifted his glasses and gave her a wink, then laughed. "I'm starting to sound like Matt's old karate instructor—I feel like I should break out in a chant. Humm—become as one with the bike—humm."

"Listen, Rick," Debbie said, tilting her head to one side. "You may be pressing your luck with the oneness thing." She slipped on her sunglasses and swung the helmet up over her hair. "Maybe you should be happy with my reluctant cooperation at this point." She cinched the helmet strap tight beneath her chin and tugged on the hem of her jean jacket. "I have to admit, though, if our marriage survives this little adventure, we can probably survive anything."

Debbie watched as Rick went through the routine of starting the engine, but he aborted the start-up and eased the bike back onto the kickstand when Maddy came out of the house and through the open garage door.

The weekly battle Debbie waged to get her daughter to dress

in proper church attire had suffered a severe setback when Pastor Steele asked all the regular attendees to come dressed "casual" in order to make their biker guests feel at home and comfortable. Still, Maddy's garb looked more *slob* than *biker*, with holey-kneed jeans and her brother's black-turned-gray, threadbare Little League T-shirt. Debbie thought for sure Maddy had dug the garment out of the Goodwill donation bag.

"Hey, Maddy," Rick called out. "Do you know why motor-cycles can't stand up by themselves?"

She rolled her eyes but humored him with, "No, Dad. Why?"

"Because they're two-tired," he quipped. "Get it? Too tired."

"Ha-ha. Very funny." In typical Maddy form, she refused to condescend to a real laugh. She turned to Debbie.

"Mom, you aren't serious about going through with this, are you?"

Was that panic in the girl's voice?

"I'll be fine, sweetheart." Debbie tried not to let her shock over her daughter's concern show. "Don't worry. Your father is a very conscientious driver."

"Yeah, so, promise me you'll keep your helmet on at all times," Maddy said, fidgeting with the keys on her key ring.

"Of course." Not once had Debbie really considered Maddy's feelings in all this. If her daughter felt concern for her parents' safety, maybe they should reconsider this whole cockamamy idea. After all, Maddy had said good-bye to her only sibling just yesterday. She might be struggling with issues of grief and loss, even though she would never come right out and admit her insecurities. Debbie wondered if Rick was thinking the same thing. If only they could find a moment to discuss the situation in private.

"Madison, honey—" Debbie fought for the right words to say to back out of the bike ride without hurting Rick's feelings, while being discreet yet sensitive to her daughter's needs. Before she could settle on the appropriate tack to take, Maddy piped up again.

"Jessica says there'll be TV and newspaper reporters there. I'd die if any of my friends from school were to recognize you in tomorrow's paper or on the evening news."

Debbie's sympathies dissolved like a salt-sprinkled slug. She should have known Maddy's embarrassment factor trumped any concerns for her mother's safety.

"I see." Debbie swallowed hard, trying to keep down an anger bubble that threatened to burst to the surface. Actually, she had to admit she was more than a little embarrassed herself, showing up at church in such a ridiculous fashion. She wondered what Rose would say. Debbie had been so consumed with getting Matt off to college that she hadn't even discussed this whole Biker Sunday fiasco with her best friend and soprano section seatmate. "Would you have me wear the helmet while I'm singing in the choir, too?"

"Oh, Mom, don't be silly." Maddy leaned against the crumpled fender of her rust-on-white Focus. She made a weak attempt to flick her bangs away from her eyes, but they fell back down to their original shaggy-dog position before she could drop her hand to her side. "Say, Jess asked me over to her place after worship, so I won't be doing that picnic thing with you guys on the church lawn. We're cutting out as soon as the service is done." She took another swipe at her bangs.

Debbie made a mental note to schedule her daughter a haircut appointment. "Don't leave church without checking in with me first. I may need you to drop me back here at the house before you go over to Jess's. And no arguing," she added before Maddy could inject her standard protest. "I'm not sure if I'll be going along in the parade or not."

Rick cleared his throat and tapped his watch face. "If we don't get a move on, we'll miss the whole shebang." He waved to Maddy. "See you at church, punkin," he said.

"You ready, Deb?" He turned the ignition knob, pushed the starter button, and the engine roared to life.

She took in a deep breath and blew it out again, then barked over the din, "Ready as I'll ever be, I guess." She figured they'd better get the noisy contraption out of the neighborhood before someone lodged a formal complaint.

"Saddle up, then," Rick replied. "I'm ready for you to climb aboard."

While Debbie eased herself onto the seat behind her husband, Maddy pulled her car out of the driveway and disappeared down the street. For once, Debbie didn't really blame her daughter for wanting to put as much distance as possible between her and the old 'rents.

True to his word, Rick puttered down the street below the speed limit. At least that's what the speedometer registered when Debbie checked it over Rick's shoulder—a hair under twenty-five miles per hour. But when she watched the ground flash past beneath her feet, she felt like they must be traveling at the speed of light.

At the first stoplight they came to, Rick twisted in his seat and looked at her. "You doing okay back there?" he asked. Debbie was surprised at how well she could hear him over the idling bike. He didn't even need to shout. Not quite.

"Yeah, okay," she answered. "I'm keeping my eyes closed when we're moving, though. My stomach turns somersaults when I watch the road. I probably shouldn't have eaten that bowl of Lucky Charms for breakfast."

A look of chagrin washed over Rick's face. "I'm sorry, babe. I forgot to tell you. Don't look straight down. Keep your gaze fixed on the horizon instead of the ground beneath your feet." He gave her helmet a gentle tap with his. "Look where you're heading, not where you've been—good advice for life as well as motorcycling."

"I'll try that, then, O sage biker dude." She responded to his helmet tap with one of her own. "But if your advice doesn't work to settle my stomach, I'll be using this helmet for more than a brain bucket." She spoke with a smile in her voice to downplay the sincerity behind her caution.

"You're a good sport to go along with this, Deb. I appreciate it more than you'll ever know." The thin-lipped smile he tacked on to the end of his appreciation speech broke into a full-fledged grin. "And, might I add, you look mighty cute back there, even if you are a little green around the gills." Rick's words bathed away her current misery. The fact that he'd noticed enough to comment made her sacrifice worthwhile. However, she thought his remarks about her cuteness pushed the envelope off the table and onto the floor.

"I hope you're having at least a little bit of fun."

Debbie hesitated, then nodded toward the traffic signal. *Saved by the green light.* "The light's changed, and your flattery will get you nowhere. Get this thing in gear and let's go." She gave his helmet one more loving head conk before he turned and clicked his foot shifter from neutral into first.

By the time they reached Church Street, a flood of other motorcycles had engulfed their bike in a swelling tide. Clusters of people stood alongside the roadway holding poster-board signs with messages like WELCOME, GOD LOVES BIKERS, HONK IF YOU LOVE JESUS, and BE BLESSED! Everyone shouted and waved. When they turned into the parking lot, the welcoming committee became a gauntlet of greeters lining each side of the drive.

Contemporary Christian music blared from mammoth loudspeakers set up on the church lawn as Rick followed the parking attendants' waving flashlights and pulled the bike into a sliver of empty space on the massive paved lot. Deb resisted the urge to kiss the ground when she dismounted the bike. With such wobbly legs, she might never get back up. However, while they stowed their riding paraphernalia in the saddlebags, she had to admit to herself—and herself alone—that the ride wasn't all *that* bad.

Excitement saturated the air as wave after wave of motorcycles kept rolling into the parking lot. Deb clutched Rick's hand, and together they followed the signs to the tables where volunteers registered the guests. Included in the registration paperwork was a liability waiver, which required a signature from both driver and passenger if they planned to participate in the parade.

"Just because I sign this doesn't mean I have to ride in the parade, does it?" She waved the release form in the air. One look at Rick's downcast eyes made Deb sorry she'd asked the question. She blurted out the first excuse she could conjure. "Don't worry, hon. I plan on going as long as I'm still feeling all right, but you know how flu-ish I've felt lately, so I thought I'd better make sure before I commit."

He smiled, obviously pacified by her explanation. "You're not obligated to go. They just want to make sure you won't sue if something happens to you during a church-sponsored event."

"Never." She rushed to erase the streaming video of catastrophic possibilities that played through her mind. "But if anything happens to me, you'll have to answer to my mother, and if that prospect doesn't scare you into caution, nothing will." Debbie cringed as she recalled the phone conversation she'd had with her mother the night before. She'd intentionally kept quiet about the news of their impending motorcycle ride. If her dear, sweet mama ever caught wind of today's plans, there'd be no end to the badgering and nay-saying Debbie would be forced to listen to concerning the dangers of motorcycling. It was her mother, after all, who refused to allow Deb even one ride on Rick's putt-putt motor scooter back in their high school days—and her mother who birthed the biker phobia she fought today.

Rick draped his arm across Deb's shoulders and led her toward the sanctuary entrance, but Debbie stopped in her tracks and looked up at her husband.

"Look, let's make a pact." Deb crooked her little finger. "If we make it through today unscathed, this whole motorcycle escapade will be our little secret—no soul-baring to my folks." She didn't need to elaborate. She knew Rick read between the lines. "Pinkie promise?"

"You can count on me." He intertwined his little finger with Deb's. "Mum's the word as far as I'm concerned."

They bypassed the line to get a free T-shirt. Debbie had gotten her shirt after choir practice on Wednesday, and Rick didn't want to take one until he was sure there were enough for all the guests. If she'd gotten a bigger size, she would have just given hers to him. She didn't know when she'd ever wear the thing again. The day's date and the words BIKER SUNDAY were emblazoned on the front, along with the church's logo. On the back was a drawing of an eagle in flight surrounded by the words of Isaiah 40:31, "They shall mount up with wings as eagles. . . ."

Deb heard a familiar voice calling her name, and she searched the mingling crowd for her friend Rose Reynolds.

"Yo, girl," a voice called over Debbie's shoulder. "We're both going to be late for choir if we don't hurry, and that's not good, considering my husband's the director."

When Debbie spun around to greet Rose, she gasped to

find that some biker chick had stolen her best friend's native West Virginia drawl. "*Where* did you find that getup?"

Rose spun a pirouette to model her outfit—replete with leather chaps and vest and a black bandanna covering her hair. "Like it? I call it my alter ego look," she said with a curtsy. "My backyard neighbor rides, and she loaned me a few things from her wardrobe. She promised me she'd come today. I can't wait to introduce you."

Rick slid his arm off Debbie's shoulders and stepped away. "You gals run on to choir. Honey, I'll catch up with you after church. Meet me at the bike. That's as good a meeting place as any."

Deb nodded her consent and let Rose lead her away. As she wove through the milling crowd behind her friend-gone-wild, a growing certainty overcame her. Surely she would awaken any moment now to discover this had all been one very strange dream. Maybe the strain of sending Matt off to college had pushed her over the edge and left her delusional. Would the weirdness ever end?

When the guest speaker stepped onto the platform to deliver his sermon, his tough-guy persona didn't do much to raise the needle on Debbie's expectation meter. He epitomized Debbie's preconceived ideas of the classic biker rebel, riding with his gang from town to town, boozing it up, and terrorizing the local citizenry with a corrupt brand of outlaw justice. With his ponytail down his back, full beard, and jaundiced skin, Brady Matson looked like he'd walked in from drug rehab or a prison cell. In fact, he admitted to the crowd that it was while doing time in the federal penitentiary that he heard about the new life he could find in Christ.

Her post in the choir loft afforded Debbie an ideal observation deck for studying the atypical preacher and unusual church crowd. She watched the speaker on the jumbo projection screen at the back of the sanctuary while studying the faces of his audience.

The congregation—biker guests and regular churchgoers alike—sat in rapt attention as the speaker shared how, until he became a Christian five years ago, evil ruled his every thought and action. Not until he turned his back on his sins, repented, and accepted the new life Christ offered did he find true happiness.

At the close of his talk, Brother Matson extended an invitation for those who wanted to find their own fresh start to come forward so he could pray with them. From all across the sanctuary, men and women stepped into the aisles and walked to the front. Debbie guessed they numbered fifty or so. Rose gripped Deb's hand and whispered, "My neighbor's coming to pray!"

As Debbie watched the tender scene unfold, a spirit of conviction gripped her heart; a fresh realization sprang up. Beneath each gruff and rather frightening exterior lived a human being with fears and failures and struggles and deep hurts. No matter how tough their facade, each individual bore his or her own painful burdens and life challenges. They came to this place with needs and questions for which they searched for answers. And each one represented a soul for whom Christ died. Maybe she had gotten these biker types wrong, had jumped to conclusions about this crowd. . . .

Of course, she was still far from ready to buy a bike and hit the open highway as Rick fantasized. But depending on how this parade ride went, she might not object too vehemently if he were to rent a motorcycle for Biker Sunday again next year.

Chapter 4

At ten o'clock sharp on Monday morning, Rick pulled into the parking lot of the motorcycle dealership to drop off their rental. They were just opening the overhead doors when he drove around back to the return bay. A scruffy grease monkey in a bright orange jumpsuit motioned for him to drive on into the garage. The scents of oil and chrome greeted Rick when he dismounted, and he breathed in the pleasing smells.

He hated for the fun to end. He could have dropped off the bike at any time yesterday evening or earlier this morning and left the key in the drop box, but he wanted to take advantage of every last minute of riding time he could get. Thankfully he wasn't due at the office until eleven, so he didn't have to rush the return. Since he worked late into the evening every Monday, he always tried to keep his morning schedule clear. Most Mondays, he took Debbie for blueberry pancakes at FlapJacks, but she'd begged off this morning, saying she would rather sleep than eat. The poor girl looked beat, and he bore the lion's share of the responsibility for her condition after the regimen he put her through yesterday afternoon.

He'd tried to express a befitting modicum of disappointment over her decision to stay home rather than join him for breakfast, but in truth he relished the idea of skipping the weekly routine this once. He gladly forwent his favorite morning fare in exchange for a sunrise ride around the lake. Since no one was around to protest, he'd even dared to leave the helmet in the saddlebag so he could bask in the crisp morning air and let the wind lash through his hair.

Throughout his morning ride and all the way over to the dealership, Rick had replayed in his mind the events of yesterday. He didn't see how the day could have gone any better. Debbie not only rode with him in the parade, but Rose talked her into extending their afternoon ride and joining three other pastoral staff couples on an impromptu tour of Amish country.

The very fact that she agreed to go along nearly caused him to drop the bike. Rick knew the ins and outs of Deb's personality as well as his own, but yesterday, whether dealing with midlife perplexities or missing her absent son, she had behaved totally out of character.

As long as he'd known her, Debbie never agreed to spur-of-the-moment suggestions. If pushed for an answer in a hurry, the answer was always no. She needed to think things through, take possession of an idea before she ever agreed to any change of plans. So Rick sat up and took notice when she went along with such an outlandish—by her way of thinking—proposal.

Not only had Debbie gone along, but Rick believed she'd thoroughly enjoyed herself, even though she would never admit to as much. In fact, every time he caught a glimpse of her in his rearview mirror, he noted her smile. If he hadn't warned her to watch out for bugs, she probably would have been wearing an all-out toothy grin.

No, she didn't need to come right out and say so. He'd stumbled across enough clues to this woman of mystery to know—Debbie Weaver liked her first venture into the motor-cycling world.

"She's a real beaut," Rick said as he handed the keys to the waiting serviceman. He noted the name WES embroidered on the fella's left lapel.

With a featherlight touch, Rick stroked the gas tank. "And she rides like a dream. Wish I could keep her." He took one last walk around the bike, admiring the pure artistry of the machine.

"Far as I know, she's for sale. Most all our rentals are." Wes the Mechanic paused to crack his gum and knead the back of his neck with his grease-blackened fingers. "Ya oughta step on over to the sales floor and talk to Stanley. He could fix you up with financing so's you'd be ridin' outta here for lunch."

"Right," Rick huffed. "Don't I wish. Someday, though. Maybe."

"No time like the present. None of us are getting any younger. You know what they say. Carpe diem—seize the day."

Rick had to bite the inside of his lip to keep from laughing out loud. The picture didn't match the audio—a down-home good ol' boy spouting Latin. "I don't think I'll be buying a bike today, but speaking of not getting younger, my wife's birthday is this week. Maybe she'd like some memento, a shirt or a jacket or something, to remind her of the fun we had yesterday."

"They've got a decent sale going on up front. Check it out." Wes used his jumpsuit sleeve to buff out a smudge on the bike's windshield.

"I believe that's just what I'm going to do." Without thinking, Rick extended his hand. The mechanic rubbed his right palm on his pant leg before accepting the handshake. "Name's Rick, by the way. Rick Weaver. Who knows, maybe I'll be seeing you again one of these days."

"Nice ta meet ya, Rick. I'm Wes. Been workin' here at Independence for nigh onto twenty years now, and if experience tells me anything, I figure I'll be seeing you again sooner rather than later." He balled his fist and threw a mock punch at Rick's bicep. "I can tell you've got the itch."

Rick fought a sudden urge to scratch. "I'm not sure I can afford your cure, Doc."

"Like I say, talk to Stanley." Wes pointed to the glass doors leading to the sales floor. "You might be surprised how little dough you need to get you onto one of our used bikes."

"Thanks. I'll keep that in mind." Rick left his new friend to his work and ventured into the showroom. He walked through the various merchandise displays, which peddled a full gamut of products for the motorcycle enthusiast—from every conceivable bike accessory and chrome doodad to baby clothes and toys. In one corner, the clearance rack held an assortment of leather jackets, each one black. He searched for one he thought might fit Debbie and held up the coat to examine it, then checked the price. After a quick scan of the store to make sure no one was watching him, he buried his face in the sleeve and inhaled his all-time favorite cowhide smell. *This might do.* He draped the hanger over his arm and headed to the counter to ask about their return policy for sale items, just in case the coat didn't fit. But like the Sirens in Homer's *Odyssey*, several rows of display bikes beckoned him, lured him, tempted him beyond resistance into waylaying his journey. Their hypnotic effect caused even the healthiest of adult males to drool, Rick included. For the sake of his sanity, he forced himself to offer little more than cursory adulation to the new models. Despite their beauty, the hefty price tags dangling from their handlebars stripped away much of their luster and enticement.

However, one particular sweetheart in the pre-owned section seemed to call his name. A year older but the same model as the bike they'd rented, this one had custom pipes, a pearl white paint job with intricate red and black pinstriping, and a cushy passenger seat that looked to be as big as his recliner. The one complaint Debbie verbalized at the end of their ride yesterday centered on the saddle-sore condition of her backside. She could ride forever on a throne like this.

He studied the price tag and winced. But once the initial sticker shock wore off, Rick convinced himself, what with the modifications and add-ons, this bike had to be worth a whole lot more. According to the list of features on the tag, she sported a modified V-twin, bored out to 103 cubic inches, with a tricked-out cam and six-speed tranny. Besides, it was much cheaper than any of the brand-new ones.

He knew there was no way. Still. . .

Wouldn't Deb be floored!

Since he had surprised her in June with the twenty-fifth-anniversary cruise, he doubted she expected anything elaborate for her birthday this year. He could just imagine the look on her face if she were to find something like this tied up with a huge bow and parked in the garage come her big day.

"Can I help answer any questions?" A burly guy stepped into Rick's daydream and yanked him back to reality. Dressed in khakis and a polo shirt sporting the dealership logo, with his long hair tied back in a ponytail, he looked like a man confident enough to be a Stanley.

"I'm just browsing, really. But maybe you could go over a few of the specs on this bike here. . . ."

Debbie riffled through the footlocker at the end of Matt's bed in search of his lacrosse mouth guard. She couldn't keep from slamming the lid shut when she found the offending item.

Here it was Thursday—a whole five days since they'd said their good-byes—and he hadn't bothered to call once until now. This morning, Deb was even starting to wonder if her son would think to call tomorrow and wish her a happy birthday. She still had her doubts.

She'd lost count of the number of times she almost caved and picked up the phone to call Matt. Rick insisted she refrain.

He said they needed to give the boy space, let him set the ground rules for this new phase of their parent/child relationship. She knew she should be grateful for her son's independence. And deep down, in that logical, left-brain side of her thoughts, she believed she was. But in that warm and cozy place, where she acted on emotion before analyzing why or what was best, she ached with missing her son.

So when she first saw Matt's cell phone number pop up on the caller ID, her heart flip-flopped. Finally, the boy remembered his roots. She imagined him deathly homesick, calling to beg his dear ol' mom and dad to let him come home. She would talk him down from his freshman-blues ledge and convince him to tough it out. Yet deep down in her heart of maternal hearts, she would smile, knowing the apron strings held strong.

Instead, he stated from the get-go that he didn't have time to talk—that he had to rush to be on time for class—but that he needed his mouth guard, and, "Mom, could you please dig it out of my footlocker and mail it off today?"

Nary a single "I miss you" or "I love you." She may have even imagined the postscript "Thanks" he mumbled right before the call went dead.

Debbie scanned her son's room. Only the skeletal remains of his lesser-valued trophies, keepsakes, and childhood memories graced the walls and bookshelves.

In a matter of days, her net worth as Matt's mother had degenerated to the fetch-and-retrieve stage.

Her role in Maddy's life ranked somewhere between nag and fashion cop.

And Rick's leap off the deep end of this motorcycle fascination left Debbie floundering for ways to rescue her sanity, as well as his.

She carried the mouth guard into her office and searched her supplies for an envelope that would hold the awkward-shaped object. Her best option left a perfect space for a package of peanut M&M's, Matt's favorite. Maybe she could pick up a pack at the store on her way to the post office. She needed to buy fiber supplements and vitamins, too.

An involuntary sigh lifted Debbie's chest. She could do without this "growing older" business, thank you very much. If she had the option, she'd skip right over her birthday this year.

Considering the way Rick had been acting this week, she stood a good chance he would forget the occasion anyway. She almost hoped he did. Then she could use the spousal oversight as leverage to gain support for her decision.

The thought of her secret project sent a rash of chills down her spine. Maybe while she was sending off a package to EEU, she should include a request to the academic dean's office asking for a copy of her decades-old transcript to be sent to the registrar's office at their local Smidley State extension campus.

The seedlings for this crazy idea of hers first took root on Sunday, while they were parading through the streets of downtown on that bike. At the corner of Market and Main, they passed a billboard advertising a degree-completion program at the local branch of one of the state's universities. The moment she saw the graphic of a middle-aged woman in cap and gown, bells and whistles went off in her head. That billboard was meant for her. She'd spent the rest of the afternoon dreaming about her return to academia. She broke into a smile every time she envisioned herself wearing that mortarboard, clutching her diploma in hand.

Her family didn't need her anymore. The time had come for her to do something for herself. She was going back to school.

Debbie picked up the Smidley State brochure from off the top of her stack of incoming mail. This week, whenever Rick pored over motorcycle magazines or surfed the Internet for biker Web sites, she'd been doing a little research of her own.

The tuition costs at the state school fell far below what they were shelling out for Matt's education at EEU, and while she wouldn't earn her degree from their beloved institution, the local school would accept almost all of her credit hours for the classes she'd taken eons ago. If she pushed herself, in two years' time she would be able to lay legitimate claim to the title of college graduate. To sweeten the deal even further, when she called to find out about the program, she learned she could major in creative writing. Writing! There couldn't be a program more tailor-made to her interests and needs. Rather than using her skills to nitpick the work of other authors, she would soon have the education she needed to try her hand at writing the next great American novel.

With her new dream came renewed energy. She had felt like her old self these past couple of days. That's the way it always seemed to go—after feeling rotten for weeks, right before her trip to the doctor, she would start feeling fine.

Debbie checked her watch. She had to get a move on if she hoped to mail a package off to Matt before her two o'clock appointment.

Chapter 5

"Come in, Debra. Have a seat." Dr. Peterson rose from his desk chair when his nurse ushered Debbie into his private office. At his urging, she settled into the navy wingback chair on the other side of his desk while he returned to his seat. The leather squeaked when she fidgeted to find a semicomfortable position. At least she didn't have to perch on an examination table wearing a paper gown to greet him.

Among the many things she appreciated about Dr. Peterson was his practice of meeting with the patient in his private office to discuss any health concerns or questions before showing her into an examination room for a physical. This way seemed much less demeaning. More personal. Even though she knew, as a liability precaution against any malpractice accusations, the clinic used a security camera to record these one-on-one conversation sessions—just as Rick did with his counselees.

"I see here on your chart that it's been a year since I last saw you." He glanced at an open manila folder on his desk, then looked back at Debbie over the top of his bifocals. "Hardly seems possible. I would have sworn we did your last physical a month or so ago. The years fly by, don't they? Each one faster than the one before. And to think, this time next year, I'll be retiring."

"Retiring?" His very allusion to her needing to find a new doctor depressed her to no end. She couldn't let herself think about saying farewell to another important person in her life, not if she wanted to keep a rein on her tears. "You can't possibly be old enough for that. You look far too young."

Dr. Peterson chuckled. "I'm well on the other side of sixty, but thanks for the offhanded compliment."

"Really?" In stark contrast to the havoc time had wrought on her appearance, the years had proven kind to the good doctor. To her, the sexagenarian looked the same today as he had some two and a half decades earlier, when Debbie scheduled her first appointment with him.

"So tell me, how's the family?" Dr. Peterson removed his glasses and tapped his chin with one of the earpieces. "What are the kids now? Fifteen? Sixteen?"

"No, Madison is a high school senior. You delivered her seventeen years ago this past July, and Matthew is a college freshman." Without warning, the floodgates opened wide to Debbie's tears. She could no more dam their flow than she could plug Niagara Falls.

While she sobbed, Dr. Peterson got up from his chair and came around to sit on the corner of his desk opposite her. He offered her a box of tissues. Then he waited. And waited. And waited for the storm waters to recede. Deb's sobs finally tapered to hiccups, then sniffles, until she managed to put a voice to her emotions. "I–I'm s–s–s–sorry, D–d–doctor," Deb stuttered. She drew in a ragged breath and waited a moment longer before she tried to speak again.

"I feel like such an ingrate, considering how God's blessed me in so many, many ways." She dabbed at her nose with a fistful of sodden tissues. Then, in a torrent as rapid as her tears, she let her woebegone words spill from the well of her soul. "I don't know what's come over me. I've been so emotional lately. I cry at rent-a-car commercials and bookstore grand openings." She let out a watery laugh. "I think a lot of it has to do with this haywire time of my life. Everything is hitting me all at once. This time last year, I was in the process of moving my parents into a senior citizens village down in Florida, and next year at this time I'll have a totally empty nest." Debbie shook her head and sighed. "On one hand, I hate the very thought, but then on the other hand, Maddy and I seem to bicker and fuss at one another constantly, so maybe some distance between the two of us will do us both good. Silly as it might sound, I'm also thinking now might be a good time to pursue my dream of finishing my own education."

The doctor left his roosting spot on the desk's edge and eased into the empty wingback chair next to Deb's. "I don't think that sounds silly at all. In fact, I think you've come across a great idea. What does Rick think about your going back to school?"

"Rick." She harrumphed. "I haven't found the right time to discuss my idea with Rick yet. He's got too many other things on his mind."

Debbie leaned forward in her chair and leveled her gaze at the doctor. "Dr. Peterson, I know you don't deal with men as patients, but since you are one, maybe you could explain to me why a sensible, intelligent, and responsible man like my husband, who is a trained mental-health professional to boot, is bound and determined to act like a crazy teenager again. Is there something physical going on with Rick and this midlife crisis business? Should I be insisting he see a doctor?" She shook her head. "Out of the blue—well, not out of the blue, since he did it for a function at church. Still, he didn't discuss his harebrained idea with me first—he went out and rented a motorcycle last Sunday. Can you believe that? A motorcycle."

In an almost imperceptible lilt, the doctor's eyebrows quirked when she mentioned "motorcycle." He tried to mask his curiosity by deepening his frown, accompanied by a swallow and a nod, but he hadn't worked his facial magic fast enough. Debbie knew the truth. She could see the questions rolling around in his mouth like marbles, threatening to spill forth. Debbie admired her doctor, but at that particular moment, she felt like smacking him upside the head. Instead, she raced to shift the focus back onto her own issues before he could zero in on the hackneyed topic of men and their fixation with motorized bikes.

Deb cleared her throat. "I'm telling you, I didn't mind turning forty nearly as much as I mind turning forty-four. Forty was still close enough to my thirties not to hurt. Now I just feel, I don't know. . . ." She looked at the aged physician and caught herself before she said the word *old*. If she felt the effect of advancing years, she could only imagine what her close-to-retiring doctor felt. She didn't want to go away with guilt over having offended Dr. Peterson heaped on top of all her other miseries.

"Let's just say I feel as though my body is betraying me when, for sanity's sake, I really need to be on top of my game physically." She let out another heavy sigh.

"Over the past couple of months, I've about convinced myself that I'm going through the change. I show all the signs."

"Um, I see," Dr. Peterson said.

Debbie took his brief response as an urging to continue. "Rick took me on a cruise to celebrate our twenty-fifth anniversary in June, so at first I thought my symptoms were due to the excitement over the trip and the stress related to all those little details that needed attention before we could leave town. Then when we got home, our schedule turned even wackier for the rest of the summer, what with Matt's graduation party and helping him get ready for college."

He sure keeps it hot in here.

She shoveled the blizzard of wadded tissues from her lap and tossed the squishy ball into a trash can by the side of the doctor's desk. Then, pulling a fresh sheet from the box, she proceeded to dab at her forehead. "I keep telling myself it's nothing to worry about, that every woman's body goes through this time of life sooner or later, and that when I came in to see you, you would confirm my suspicions and maybe talk to me about the possibility of hormone therapy."

Debbie rolled yet another tissue into a ball and wiped her

sweaty palms while she spoke. "But yesterday, I was surfing on the Web and came across an article that detailed the symptoms of ovarian cancer. Ever since then, I've had this anxiety niggling at the back of my mind. Maybe I've got a more serious problem than I originally thought."

The doctor opened his mouth to speak, but Debbie stayed him with a lift of her hand. "I know, I know, I should have called you long ago, but I already had this appointment scheduled, and until yesterday, I didn't figure I had any urgent needs. I'm so glad I'm here now, though, so you can set my mind at ease."

"Let's not jump to any conclusion yet, Debra." The physician's tone carried more sympathy than chiding; his countenance bore a patience acquired throughout a lifelong career of treating emotionally fraught women. "Chances are, you are right in your original diagnosis of perimenopause, but we won't know for sure until I've had a chance to run a few tests and examine you."

He scooted forward in his chair and stretched across his desk to pull her chart toward him. Then he scratched a few lines in a blank space at the end of the top page. "I'm sure this isn't what you want to hear, but you really are not too young to experience menopausal symptoms. While the average age is fifty-two, menopause can occur in women in their thirties." He stood and picked up the handset of his desk phone. "Like I said, though. . ." He paused and cupped his hand over the receiver. "Excuse me just a moment," he said to Debbie, then he removed his muffler and spoke into the phone. "Send Paige in to show Mrs. Weaver to the lab, please."

Dr. Peterson returned the handset to its cradle and resumed his address to Debbie as though he'd never left off. "As far as the various relational and stress issues you're facing, I'd be happy to refer you to a good counselor. However, your husband could likely direct you in that regard better than I can."

He closed Debbie's chart and tapped the folder's spine against his open palm. "Let's check out what's going on with you physically, though. Maybe we can find ways to help you better navigate through this spot of rough water. We'll run a few tests, check your thyroid and your hormone levels and such, see if there's something there that we can address. I hazard to predict that if we can get your hormones on an even keel, the whole world will look better to you." A knock sounded at the office door, and on the doctor's command to come in, a way-too-young-and-perky blond in a lab coat entered the room.

Debbie endured the routine battery of pricks, jabs, prods, samples, and humiliations the same as she did every year, spending most of the half hour or so of the testing and examination with her eyes closed, as she couldn't bear the sight of needles or the embarrassment of the gynecological exam. She had to smile at the banter between Dr. Peterson and his nurse throughout the delicate procedure, though. She saw right past their discussion of Paige's baby's latest new tooth to their true intent—to employ banter as a means of setting the patient at ease. After Dr. Peterson's reassurances at the outset of her visit, however, her anxiety gauge registered a significant decrease compared to her explosive levels upon arrival. Only when the doctor clucked his tongue at one point during her exam did her apprehension spike.

Per the doctor's instructions, she finished dressing and waited for him to return for a wrap-up of his preliminary findings. She fully expected him to come bearing a prescription for hormone replacement therapy. While she knew there were cons as well as pros to the treatment, after enduring a summer of these symptoms, she would, without question, try any remedy her doctor recommended.

"Mrs. Weaver?" asked Nurse Paige as she opened the door a crack.

"Yes?"

"When you're ready, Dr. Peterson would like to see you back in his private office."

A shot of fear sliced through Deb as she crossed the examination room and opened the door. "I'm ready now," she said, grabbing up her purse. *Whatever he has to say, the news can't be good,* she thought. *This isn't standard operating procedure.* But she pasted on her best Mona Lisa impression and presented herself to the nurse. She traveled the long corridor behind Nurse Paige and waited while her presence was announced. Debbie lectured herself about the dangers of jumping to conclusions, but despite her best admonitions, she couldn't shake a feeling of impending doom.

Dr. Peterson sat poring over what looked to Debbie to be a printout of lab results.

This is going to be bad. She watched him remove his bifocals and draw in a deep breath. One look at the good doctor and she knew. *I've got some kind of growth or tumor.* She refused to entertain the *C* word. He offered her a thin-lipped smile, one of those fake little smirks meant to reassure her because there was something big she was about to need reassurance for. She reclaimed the seat where she'd had her earlier meltdown and clutched the armrests in a death grip. The jewel-toned colors and heavy furniture of the room had always appealed to her as being strong and masculine. Now the dignified setting reminded her more of a funeral parlor than a doctor's office.

Help me, Lord. Please help me make it through whatever I'm about to face.

"Mrs. Weaver. . ." He stumbled on the formality and started again while Deb told herself to breathe.

"Debra, let me begin by saying, I believe your general physical condition is good, and given time, you'll be feeling right as rain. You're going to be fine. Just fine."

Somehow she didn't find comfort in his optimistic assertions. His gaze settled on her for a nanosecond before he glanced away.

"I found what I believe may be the cause of your various symptoms. I have to agree with your lay diagnosis of a hormone imbalance. However. . ." Dr. Peterson cleared his throat and shot Deb another fleeting glance. "However, the root cause isn't menopause."

At this point, Debbie wanted to climb across his aircraft-carrier-sized desk and pull the words right out of his throat.

Instead, she sucked in another deep breath and told herself to stay calm. She focused on the doctor's hands, which he scrubbed together, fisted, unfisted, and then scrubbed together again.

"I'm sorry. I know I'm not being very forthright, but I'm trying to be sensitive to your current emotional state." He picked up his bifocals from the desk and began to drum them against the lab reports. "I suppose I just ought to come out with it. I've never been one to pull punches with my patients before."

Debbie edged forward in her seat and urged him on with a nod. He scoured his lips and clean-shaven chin with one hand, then appeared to shake himself out of his nervousness. He looked Debbie straight in the eye and held her gaze.

"Mrs. Weaver—Debra." Dr. Peterson broke out in a grin. "You, my dear, are going to be a mother again."

Chapter 6

Rick leaned over his daughter's blanketed form and gave her a nudge. "Maddy, honey, wake up," he rasped. "You need to get ready for school, and I need to ask a favor of you."

She moaned.

Rick answered with another prod to her shoulder, followed by a shake. "Come on, sweetie pie. Please. It's your mother's birthday, and I need you to help make this day special for her."

"Dad!" she hissed, poking her head from beneath her covers like a turtle venturing out of its shell. "You are so mean!" Maddy scrunched her eyes and squinted at her clock radio. "My alarm won't go off for another half hour. Come back then." She dropped back onto her pillow and yanked the bedspread back over her head.

"I wouldn't bother you if it weren't important. I'm a firm believer in letting sleeping dogs and sleeping children lie." Rick ratcheted the intensity of his jabs. "But this won't wait. Sit up so I know you're listening to me."

"I can hear you just fine." Her muffled words filtered through the quilting. "What do you need?"

"I want you to plan on leaving the house early enough to drop me off at my office on your way to school. I'm going to leave the van here so your mom can go to lunch with Rose."

A groan issued forth from the dark recesses.

"Don't worry. You won't need to pick me up. I'll get another ride home." Rick straightened to his full height and pushed back his shoulders to work out the kinks of his early-morning-stiff muscles. When no further protests appeared forthcoming, he turned to leave Madison's room but decided to add a postscript to his commands before his daughter slipped back into a fully comatose state. "No stomping around and waking up your mom this morning, either. I don't want anything to spoil her big day."

"Yeah, yeah."

He couldn't hold Maddy accountable for her curt responses, considering the predawn hour. Even so, her perpetual smart-aleck attitude made him sigh.

Rick reached for the doorknob but froze in his tracks when Maddy threw the covers away from her head and sat up in bed.

"Hey, Dad, is Mom okay?"

Her words slugged him hard in the breadbasket, and he swallowed a gulp of air. If even Maddy—who lived in that teenage universe where all other planets revolved around her as the sun—if even *Maddy* noticed a difference in Deb, his concerns must be legit. Debbie seemed more despondent than ever after her annual physical yesterday, but she refused to discuss the visit, other than to say the doctor had given her a clean bill of health.

"Far as I know, she's fine," he said, trying his best to mask his alarm. "Why do you ask?" Rick moved back to Maddy's bedside and sat on the mattress's edge.

"She's acting—I dunno, different." Madison shrugged. "Mopey. Kinda depressed." Rick studied his daughter's expression and tried to read the extent of her concern. In her present half-awake/half-asleep state, wearing pink pj's, her right cheek pocked with blanket nubbles, she looked so childlike and innocent—shades of the Madison he knew ten years ago.

"She hasn't been on my case lately. Not like she usually is." Maddy stroked the worn fur of her bedtime snuggly, Mr. Rabbie. "I hate to admit it to you." She paused her caressing long enough to meet her father's gaze. "But I don't think it's because I deserve better treatment."

Madison snuffled a quick laugh. "I'm not complaining or anything, you understand, but she's sorta freaking me out."

"I appreciate your interest in your mother's well-being, Maddy. I really do," he said, patting her on the arm. "She could use your prayers, I'm sure. But I don't think you should be overly concerned about her. She's just going through a rough patch, what with Matt leaving home and her turning another year older and all. Once this birthday business is over, I imagine we'll see the return of the dear old mother you know and love."

"You better not let her hear you calling her old." Maddy

poked him in the chest. "And I sure hope you aren't doing anything goofy for her birthday like you did for her fortieth. Over-the-hill humor might not go over so good with her right now."

"No, never again. I learned my lesson on that one." He winced. Even if he had meant it as a joke, giving Debbie the deed to a burial plot wasn't such a brainy idea. "I think she's gonna love what I'm getting her this year."

Maddy wiped the sleep from her eyes. "Whatcha gettin' her?"

"That's for me to know and you—not." He laughed and sent her a wink. "Not until this evening, anyway. You're the queen of Can't-Keep-a-Secret. I'm not about to tell you. You'll know when your mother knows."

"Daaad!" She climbed onto her knees and snuggled into him. "I'm not some punky little kid anymore. I won't spill the beans. Besides, I'll be at school all day. I couldn't spoil your surprise even if I wanted to." She fluttered her long brown lashes and waved her clutched hands in front of him.

"Nope. Uh-uh. Don't even try those feminine wiles on me. Not this time. My lips are sealed." He tousled her already bedraggled hair and stood to leave. "And don't even bother trying to guess. You'd just be wasting your time."

Debbie sent one hand out from her blanket cocoon and fumbled for the clanging phone. She pulled the receiver in under the covers with her. "Heaw-woh," she bleated in her best Elmer Fudd impersonation.

"Happy birthday, girlfriend!" Rose's voice tolled through the fog of sleep.

"Um, thanks," she answered on autopilot, her eyes still closed.

"You aren't still in bed, are you? Oh, if I woke you up from a birthday sleep-in, I feel just horrible."

"No problem," Debbie muttered as she snailed her way toward daylight and looked at her clock. The numbers 10:47 screamed at her in neon green. "I had to get up to answer the phone anyway."

Rose groaned over the phone line. "Old joke and definitely not funny, but I'll let it slide since it's your special day. Say, are we still on for lunch? You're not sick or anything, are you?"

"I'm fine. And yes, we're still on. I'm not about to pass up a free meal." The last thing Debbie wanted to do today was spend an afternoon acting perky and cheerful, as though this were just another run-of-the-mill birthday. Out of loyalty to her husband, she couldn't tell Rose her secret until she first broke the news to Rick, but to pull off such a masquerade with her best friend would require hard work. She prayed she was up to the task.

"I know this is a ratty thing to do to the guest of honor, but can you pick me up?" Rose asked. "Trevor needed to take my car in for servicing, so I'm sans wheels today."

"Sure." Debbie swung her legs to the floor and stood. "I think I can, anyway." She shuffled to the bedroom window and separated the slats of the miniblinds to look out. From this particular angle, she couldn't tell if their van was parked in the driveway or not. "I need to check to make sure Rick left me the van like he said he would. His plan was contingent on getting Maddy to take him to work."

"Call me back right away if we need to make other arrangements. If I don't hear from you, I'll be ready when you swing by at, oh, shall we say twelve o'clock sharp?"

"It's a date. See you then."

Debbie nearly tripped on the dragging hems of her sweatpants as she trundled into the kitchen and over to the coffeepot. She touched the half-full coffee decanter. Cold.

After filling a mug with the brew, she set the microwave to cook for two minutes. Each second seemed to take forever to tick off the timer while her body screamed for caffeine.

As she waited for the countdown to zero, Debbie spied an envelope on the kitchen table bearing her name. She recognized Rick's scrawl. She sat down, nested her chin in her hands, and began to read.

Happy birthday, honey!

You were sleeping so peacefully, I hated to wake you. Hope you were able to stay in bed as long as you wanted. You deserve the chance to rest.

As promised, I've left the van for you to use to go to lunch with Rose. The keys are on the hook. Enjoy your special day. We'll celebrate big-time tonight when I get home!

All my love,
Rick

P.S. Don't bother trying to find where I've hidden your present. I've learned better than to leave surprises in the house. ☺

Debbie sighed. The poor man probably wouldn't feel much like celebrating once she sprang her own little birthday surprise on him. She pushed back from the table and paced three round-trips across the kitchen floor, chewing on her thumbnail the whole way.

Someone had left the morning paper strewn across the kitchen counter. Debbie scanned the headlines. As far as she could tell, nothing had happened to wipe out her axis-tilting news of yesterday. She didn't wake up to find that the doctor's announcement had all been a dream—a nightmare—although she'd allowed herself plenty of sleep time for such a possibility to occur. She hadn't imagined the whole ordeal. Nor had Rick admitted to corroborating with Dr. Peterson to play one of his demented birthday jokes on her.

The microwave dinged, and Debbie pulled out the steaming mug and slurped a swallow. She knew she ought to cut her caffeine intake, but after the trauma of yesterday and a rough night's sleep, she needed this one cup. She needed it badly.

Last evening she couldn't bring herself to share her news with Rick. Not yet. She needed time to come to terms with the reality of it all first. She also needed to think through her revelation strategy before she spilled the "baby" beans, so that she didn't send her husband into shock or cardiac arrest. She had watched him carefully, though, when he asked how her checkup had gone. He hadn't displayed any of the symptoms he usually bore when he was up to mischief, not the slightest hint of a twinkle in his eye. Rick could never deceive her, even in fun. At least not for long. His eyes always spoke the truth.

She looked down at her baggy nightclothes and padded frame. So far as she could tell, she was still pregnant. At this precise moment, she was barefoot, too. Barefoot and pregnant and, as of twelve o'clock midnight, an old lady of forty-four.

Forty-four.

Pregnant.

Pregnant and forty-four.

Happy Birthday to me! Whoopee! She circled her index finger in the air. *Bring on the cake so I can blow out the candles and make a—*

"Be careful what you wish for"—she could hear her mother's voice repeating the well-worn adage—*"because your wish just might come true."*

With her mug nested between both hands, Debbie ambled across the room and gazed out the breakfast nook's bay window, which looked out over their backyard. The wind pushed the swings on the kids' old jungle gym in the far corner of the lawn.

Was it only a week ago she'd been lamenting to herself about being too old to bear more children? She groaned when she recalled her conversation with the young mother at the turnpike rest stop. Debbie had gotten all weepy when she thought she'd never know the joy of cuddling another child of her own. Surely that couldn't be construed as a wish, could it?

If so, she deserved to have her mind washed out with soap.

Deb carried her mug to the sink and poured out the dregs. All this thinking about babies made her yawn and stretch. Babies meant no sleep. Maybe she ought to call Rose and cancel and go back to bed while she still had the chance. Too bad she couldn't bank a few years' rest. She yawned and stretched again.

After years of longing and wanting and praying and hoping for another child, today she could see no good reason to get excited. Having a baby at this stage of the game looked a lot more like work than fun, not to mention the long-haul investment of the eighteen years needed to raise another child.

She laid her hand on her poochy abdomen. Here she'd thought she suffered from middle-age spread. She shook her head.

Hard as she tried, she couldn't sort out her feelings concerning this seeming impossibility that had now come true. They ran the gamut—surprise, shock, amazement, fear. Numb. Mostly numb. One feeling she hadn't found yet, however, was joy. No matter how hard she tried to talk herself into being happy about her news, bemusement at this absurd twist on life's road seemed the most she could manage at this point. How could she possibly be pregnant after all these years?

Well, she knew how.

This was all Rick's fault—Rick and his romantic notions of how to celebrate a twenty-fifth anniversary. The best she figured, she'd gotten pregnant while they were on the cruise.

When many of his peers needed the aid of a pill, her man

still had the get-up-and-go of a young buck half his age. She could hear her macho husband now, bragging about this tangible proof of his virility. She smiled in spite of her sour mood.

Though she laid all the blame at Rick's feet, she wondered why God would allow such a thing to happen to her. She'd trusted the Lord with every aspect of her life. He'd never let her down yet. But at this particular moment, she wondered if He and Rick shared the same definition of funny.

Visions of diapers and spit-up, playpens and squeaky toys bounced through Deb's head. She couldn't have a baby. Not now. As much as she'd bellyached about the prospect of facing an empty nest, the longer she thought about the possibilities, the closer she'd come to seeing the benefits: More time for herself. The chance to devote more attention to Rick. The opportunity to go back to school—or whatever else she chose to do.

Having a baby now meant they'd be retirement age by the time they'd have the house to themselves. What a cruel upbringing for a child to be raised as virtually an only child and giving him or her senior citizens for parents, with siblings old enough to look like Mom and Dad. Debbie winced to think of the prospect of being mistaken for a grandmother to her own offspring or, worse yet, seen by their child as an embarrassment to be endured when they attended school functions together as a family.

And there were no promises they'd have a healthy child.

After Dr. Peterson delivered his pronouncement, he felt it necessary to detail the risks of carrying a child at her age, not the least being the higher percentage of Down's syndrome babies born to older moms—a one in five chance. He recommended running tests right away in case they found substantial reasons to, as he put it, "terminate the pregnancy." She dismissed the suggestion out of hand. She saw no need to risk the dangers of amniocentesis, nor did she see the need to consult with Rick to know what his answer would be. On this issue, they would be of one accord. The fetus she carried within her was a living human being. If there was something wrong with this baby, she didn't know how she could possibly cope; however, she refused to entertain abortion as an option. God would have to give her grace to face whatever challenges might come.

The phone rang again, and Debbie checked the caller ID on the kitchen extension. Her parents' number popped onto the small screen. She sighed. Another situation where she'd have to hide her inner turmoil and act as if nothing were wrong.

If she managed to pull off an entire conversation with her mother without setting off Mom's maternal alarms, she deserved the lead role in the community theater's next play. She considered not answering but shook off the temptation and reached for the phone.

Chapter 7

Rick thundered into the neighborhood astride the White Stallion—the name he'd tentatively dubbed their new bike. Of course, he would let the birthday girl have final say in what moniker would stick. When he reached the top of their street, he cut the engine and coasted in silence to their driveway. If things worked out according to plan, Rose would keep Deb busy until at least three thirty or four o'clock, but he didn't want to spoil the surprise if she happened to come home early.

He dismounted and circled the motorized steed. What had he done?

Buyer's remorse hit him hard before he pulled out of the dealer's lot, and he'd suffered from a classic case of cognitive dissonance all the way home. He cringed to think this might end up being another one of his way-out-in-left-field gift ideas. Rick patted the thick leather seat. No, if nothing else, Debbie would love the weekend getaways for two he already had in the works—and she could always use the leather jacket for more than just motorcycle rides.

Rick flipped open his cell phone and punched speed-dial number eight to call fellow Grace Church staff member Trevor Reynolds. Rick knew he could count on Trevor and his wife, Rose, to work in cahoots with him to pull off the arrangements for Debbie's birthday gift. While Rose kept Debbie occupied at a surprise party with a gaggle of her friends from church, Trevor had dropped Rick off at the dealership, then gone to the store to pick up a balloon bouquet to tie to the bike's handlebars.

"Coast is clear. Swing on by."

"I'll be right there. I'm only a couple of blocks away." Trevor's voice crackled through the phone. "We'll need to make our handoff snappy. I was on the phone with Rose when you beeped in. The party's broken up and Debbie's on her way home. She just left our place, so you've got ten minutes max to get everything ready."

"Ten-four, good buddy." Rick resorted to the use of CB lingo, since he didn't yet know if bikers had their own special vernacular. As he snapped his phone shut, Maddy swung into the drive. She climbed out of her car, shaking her head.

"Insinuating Mom needs to reclaim her youth, huh? I thought you weren't going to play any gags on her this year," Maddy said as she drew closer, still wagging her head from side to side.

"This is no gag." Rick bumped into his daughter's shoulder with his and sent her book bag sliding down her arm. "I wouldn't tease her with something as big as this. I'm crushed that you think

I'd be so cruel." While he tried to make light of her remarks, he didn't like the rock wedged in his gut by her words.

Maddy's head kept shaking back and forth like a toy dog in the back of a '67 Bel Air. She appeared to be speechless, but Rick knew the condition would soon pass. He hurried to explain while the explaining was good.

"Your mom's name will be on the title, and I've signed her up for lessons so she can learn to ride by herself. She's going to love it. Stick around and see for yourself. She'll be home any minute now."

"I wouldn't miss this show for all the chocolate in Hershey, Pennsylvania," she said, hiking her book bag back onto her shoulder. "Let me dump my stuff and grab a pop, and I'll be right back."

By the time Maddy returned, soft drink can in hand, Trevor had made his balloon delivery and Rick was putting the finishing touches on his gift presentation. He bungeed the two helmets to the luggage rack, then rested the wrapped and beribboned package that contained the leather coat against the spokes of the motorcycle's front wheel. Next, he propped the certificate for Deb's riding lessons on the seat.

"Don't you think you've gone a little overboard, Dad?" Maddy untangled a couple of balloon strings. "Are you sure we can afford all this? We could pay for my first year of college with what you've sunk into a silly bike."

He choked at the way Maddy bandied the *we* word about. He didn't see her making any contributions to her college fund.

Rick tried his best to keep his cool while he racked his brain for a smart comeback. The teen had no concept of a motorcycle's true worth, but he found himself at a loss for words to explain how its value went far beyond mere dollars and cents. Before he could respond, though, he heard the familiar ping and rattle of the family van.

"Here she comes." He patted his jacket pockets in search of the digital camera. "I want to capture the look on your mom's face the moment she sees the bike. Be careful not to block my shot." He walked up the driveway toward the incoming van, waving his arms. The glare of the afternoon sun on the van's tinted windows veiled Debbie's face from his view.

"Surprise!" he yelled before the vehicle came to a complete stop. Rick began knocking on the window to get Debbie to open her door. He centered the camera's viewfinder and prepared to snap a few shots as soon as she exited the van. "Happy birthday, Harley mama! Come and check out your new wheels." He walked backward, motioning for her to follow him.

Her mouth dropped open. Her eyes bugged out. Deb's face registered absolute shock.

Rick clicked off a photo round. He hoped the digital images captured the full essence of his wife's stunned expression. His gift had elicited an even better response than he'd hoped for—and more than justified the expense.

"So what do you think, hon? Are you floored?" Rick picked up the envelope from the bike's seat and offered it to Deb with one hand while cranking off another series of pictures with the other. "She's all yours. I already signed you up for lessons, and you'll be riding this pony solo before you know it." He lowered the camera and sent Maddy a wink. The teen shook her head, rolled her gaze heavenward, then toasted him with her pop can.

Deb covered her mouth with one hand as though suppressing a squeal.

"Hurry and open your other presents, then I'll take us for a spin."

A tear slid down Debbie's cheek and disappeared behind her palm. Another quickly followed in its track. Rick froze at the sight, unable to decipher if her crying expressed sorrow or ecstasy.

Debbie lowered her hand from her face. Unmistakable pain twisted her features and reddened her eyes.

"I knew she wouldn't like it," Maddy muttered under her breath. Rick scowled at his daughter as he moved past her on his way to Debbie's side.

He slipped the camera back into his pocket and tried to take Deb in his arms, but she stiffened and pulled away.

"Richard Jefferson Weaver." She spat his name with more venom than his mother ever had when he got into trouble as a boy. "You're not about to get me back on a motorcycle after what you've done."

Her pronouncement sent Rick into a panic. He scoured his memory to think what horrible act he might have committed against his wife to bring on such fury.

He needn't have bothered taxing his brain. Debbie volunteered the nature of his crime with a verbal slap that sent him reeling.

"I'm pregnant, thanks to you."

Rick stumbled back. "W—w—what?" He pushed his heart back in his chest with the palm of his hand. "What are you saying?" Blackness seeped into his vision and he saw stars. He forced himself to gulp for air before he collapsed onto the concrete drive.

"Ew, how did that happen?" Maddy interjected.

"Be quiet, Maddy!" He and Debbie dismissed their daughter's comment in unison, and Rick returned his full attention to his wife.

"Pregnant? We're pregnant? You must be kidding, right?" He tried to search Debbie's face for a confirmation to his question, but she'd buried her head in her hands. "Tell me you're kidding. You can't possibly be pregnant; I mean, we're too old."

"Well, excuse me," Debbie hissed. She fisted her hands at her side and stomped her foot. "Evidently my biological clock didn't get that memo. This is no joke. Do you see me laughing?"

Rick lowered his head and rubbed the back of his neck. "Wow!" He twisted the toe of his boot against the pavement. "Pregnant, huh?" The concept would take some getting used to. He sent Debbie another glance. This time, she met his gaze. The icy rage in her eyes melted, and her shoulders slumped.

"Look, I'm sorry." She offered a weak smile. "I'm sorry for blowing up like that. This isn't how I'd hoped to tell you. My emotions got the better of me. After spending my day trying to keep a lid on this little bombshell, here I exploded all over you."

Rick pulled her back into his embrace, and this time,

instead of resisting, she wrapped her arms around him and tipped her head back, inviting his kiss.

"So that's it—a little kissy-kissy and everything's fine?" Without warning, a second tempest broadsided him from the starboard, Maddy-side. "Well, it's not fine as far as I'm concerned."

He felt Debbie tense in his arms. She burrowed her head in his chest. But Maddy didn't catch the glare he threw his daughter's way.

"I've had it with you guys, always trying to act like you're a couple of college kids or something. Why don't you both just grow up? How could you do this to me?" Softer than a whisper, Rick heard Debbie sniffle and felt her swipe at her nose with the back of her hand.

"Maddy, stop—" Rick tried to interrupt, but she continued her tirade.

"Don't you know how stupid our family will look to all my friends? You're old enough to be grandparents, you know."

Rick could feel his blood pressure rise a point with every word his daughter spewed. "Maddy, I said—"

The teen was on a roll. There was no muzzling her.

"Everyone will just assume this baby is mine—that I had a child out of wedlock—and I'll be the object of pity at school. I'll never go out in public with you again!"

Debbie pulled away from Rick and raced through the garage into the house, slamming the door behind her. Rick watched her go, then he turned and faced his daughter head-on, his hands on his hips and fire burning in his chest.

"That's enough, Madison. I want you to go to your room and stay there until I say you can come out. I'll be in to talk with you when I'm good and ready and not a moment before. We all need some time to cool off and come to grips with this news."

She stormed past him, and mimicking her mother's force and velocity, she slammed the door when she went inside.

Rick stood frozen in place, scrubbing at the back of his neck and trying to get his thoughts around all that had just transpired. As he stared at the bike, his most precious gift gone bad, a big, fat *aha* moment hit him right between the eyes.

Chapter 8

Debbie was too busy nursing her hurt to care when Rick announced, from the other side of the bathroom door, that he needed to leave for a while but he'd "be back in just a bit and we can talk things through then." An hour later, though, when she'd managed to pull herself together, she wondered if he had decided to keep on riding down the highway after he roared off into the sunset on that new motorcycle of his.

She peeked into Maddy's bedroom and found her asleep on her bed, curled in a fetal position and still wearing her stereo headphones. Debbie eased the door closed and padded back downstairs to the living room. As hard as she tried to sit and wait patiently for her husband's return, she found herself rising, time and again, to peer out the living room window, looking up and down the street in search of Rick.

She returned to the sofa and picked up her Bible, which she'd left open to yesterday's devotional reading reference. She thought she'd drawn the appropriate conclusions when her study guide gave Ecclesiastes 3:1 as the Old Testament scripture verse for the day: "There is a time for everything, and a season for every activity under heaven." Before her big news event of yesterday afternoon, she thought the Lord was telling her she needed to grow old gracefully and enjoy the autumn of her life. Now she wasn't sure what lessons the Lord wanted to teach her through this verse, or what spiritual truth He wanted her to grasp by sending a little blast of Indian summer her way.

At what sounded like a car door slam, Debbie set her Bible aside and hurried to look out the window again. By the time she got there, however, the street was clear. She figured it must have been one of the neighbors getting home from work.

"You looking for me?"

Debbie threw herself into Rick's arms. He must have slipped in through the garage. "I was starting to worry. You were gone an awfully long time."

"I'm sorry if I had you scared, babe." He hugged her tight and kissed her hair. "I needed to set a few things straight, seeing as how I'm going to be a daddy again." He held her at arm's length, shook his head, and grinned, then pulled her back into his embrace. His warm breath brushed her forehead as he spoke. "The Lord and I had a long talk while I was gone. He showed me just how selfish I've been lately. I realize I've not been sensitive to you and your needs."

Rick stepped back and took Debbie's hands in his. "I need to ask you to forgive me for being so self-absorbed. I honestly had myself convinced that I was buying that motorcycle to make you happy." He winced. "And I call myself a counselor. What a dope, huh?"

"No, not at all." Debbie squeezed his hands. "I'm the one who should apologize for my selfishness." She offered him a crooked smile. "While you were gone, I was thinking—and, well. . ." She paused and drew a breath, reevaluating her decision one last time before she made a verbal commitment. "Rick, I want you to keep the bike. You seem to get such a kick out of riding. I'd hate to see you nail the coffin shut on your dream. There's no reason why you can't enjoy motorcycling even if I can't join you for a few more years."

"Whoa, whoa, whoa." He released his grip and waved his hands in front of her face. "Stop right there." His smile softened his rebuke. "My mind's made up. No use arguing with me. It's too late now, anyway. While I was gone, I returned the bike to the dealer. When I explained our situation, he took it back without even charging a restocking fee, then I called Trevor and had him come pick me up and bring me home." He chuckled. "I don't have any business riding a motorcycle when we're going to have another little dependent underfoot, relying on me to provide for her needs. Besides, I won't need a bike to keep me young if I'm chasing a toddler around."

Despite Rick's cheerful expression, Debbie's heart sank. "You say that now, but let's see if you're singing the same tune after walking the floor all night with a colicky baby in your arms." She plopped down on the sofa, and Rick followed suit, sitting sideways on the cushion next to her.

Debbie crossed and uncrossed her arms, then picked at a

hangnail before finding the courage to look her husband in the eye. "I don't know if I can do this baby thing again, Rick," she said with a sigh. "Just thinking about all the work that goes into raising a child leaves me flat-out exhausted." She dropped her head to his shoulder and sighed again, emptying her lungs with a long puff.

Rick covered Debbie's hands with his. "I know it won't be easy. Babies never are, even for parents half our age who still have the energy of their youth."

With a featherlight touch, he stroked the backs of her hands with his thumbs. "I have to admit, when you first broke the news, I was pretty floored—and not just because you didn't like your birthday present, either." He dipped his head and looked at her, teasing in his eyes. "But now that the shock has worn off, the idea is growing on me. To tell you the truth, I'm starting to get pumped."

Debbie studied Rick's face. She saw nothing but earnestness there. Her heart swelled with love for this man. His words soothed the deep, troubled spots of her soul.

"We've always said children are a gift from God, but I have a feeling God intends this child to be an extra-special blessing to us in the second half of our lives. Besides, since the Lord has seen fit to entrust you with the care of another of His precious lambs, I believe He's confirming what I've known all along—you are a great mother, in a day and age when great mothers are hard to come by. And if having a dad who adores his kids counts for anything, I think this little one's gonna be mighty blessed. Just think, we'll have an opportunity that few couples ever have. Now that we're older and wiser, we get a second chance to correct all the mistakes we made with Matt and Maddy when we were still amateurs in this parenting business."

"But Maddy—you heard her." The memory of their daughter's biting discourse caused tears to well in Debbie's eyes. "She sees us as an embarrassment. And who knows what Matt will think."

"Don't worry about the kids. They'll come around. Remember how, when Maddy was ten, she would always pester us about giving her a baby brother or sister? Her prayers are just being answered a little later than expected is all. Knowing that daughter of ours, we'll have a struggle on our hands trying to keep her from toting that baby brother or sister around everywhere she goes." He rested his hand on Debbie's abdomen and grinned.

She studied Rick's face. "Are you sure you don't mind giving up the bike?"

"I promise you, I'm not bummed in the least. I only ask one little favor of you. If it's a girl, let me name her Marley."

"Marley?" Debbie shrugged. "Sure, I think it's cute. But why Marley, other than to carry on the 'M' tradition of Matthew and Madison?"

Perhaps the evening sun was playing light tricks on Debbie's eyes, but she thought sure she saw her husband blush.

"Since I'm giving up my chance at a bike, this baby will be my Harley instead; and the contraction of My Harley is—"

"Marley!" Debbie broke in, then laughed.

Debbie wrapped her arms around Rick's neck. "I don't know if I can survive another teenage daughter." She faked a shudder.

"Ah, but I think you and I produce such beautiful baby girls," Rick said, nuzzling up to Deb's neck.

She giggled and scrunched against his ticklish whiskers. "Don't think you are fooling me. I know the real reason you're all excited about becoming a dad for the third time. You're proving to the world that you're a manly man, even if you are past your prime."

Rick tipped his head back and bayed at the moon. Then, scooping Debbie into his arms, he kissed her with the same passion that got them into this predicament back in June.

SUSAN K. DOWNS
When she isn't writing, Susan works as a freelance fiction editor. She and her minister husband raised five children and recently became the enthusiastic grandparents of two delightful grandchildren. Whenever the weather is fair and they can break away from their duties and responsibilities, Susan and her husband enjoy a Harley ride along the old Erie Canal routes and Amish buggy trails of eastern Ohio. Read more about Susan's writing/editing ministry, family, and latest motorcycle adventure at her Web site: www.susankdowns.com.

reunited

by Kristy Dykes

Dedication

To my hero husband, Milton, who is my collaborator in the
deepest sense of the word—he's believed in me, supported me,
and cheered me on in my calling to inspirational writing.

Let us run with endurance the race that God has set before us. . . .
Don't become weary and give up.
HEBREWS 12:1, 3 NLT

Chapter 1

*T*onight I'm asking Jake to move out.

Felicia Higgins wheeled her SUV into the garage, thinking about what she intended to do this evening. She put the gearshift in PARK, pressed the garage door remote, and reached for two book bags full of term papers that needed grading.

"Jake, I'd like you to move out temporarily to give me time to think," she said, preparing her speech just like she prepared lesson plans for her English classes at Palmdale Middle School.

A pang hit her in the heart. Hurt? Despair? Guilt?

No matter.

She was stuck in a routine, unfulfilling marriage, and she had to do something about it.

Now.

That's what her teacher friend Stacy often told her. Before she met Stacy, she thought this was her lot in life—staying married to Jake Higgins—something she had to endure. But not anymore.

"You deserve better than you're getting, Felicia," Stacy had said repeatedly. "You're too good for Jake. Why, I wouldn't let a man treat me the way he treats you. It's ridiculous. Aloof and indifferent, to put names on his behavior. He's a moron. He's got a good thing going—you—and he doesn't even know it."

Stacy always ended her diatribe the same way. "My first husband was just like Jake, Felicia. But Darren, my second husband—he's so different. He's attentive, and he's interested in me, and—and he likes to do all the things I do, and, well, he's everything I could ever want in a man. I'm so happy, and you deserve to be happy, too."

Felicia took a deep breath. "Yes, I—I want to be happy. That's all I've ever wanted in my marriage." Forcing herself to put her somber thoughts behind her, she got out of her vehicle and made her way toward the door.

Inside the house, she put down her heavy book bags, then she breezed out the front door and got the mail. In minutes, she had the mail sorted and boneless chicken breasts browning, seasoned just right. Tonight for supper, it would be chicken Parmesan and fettuccine with her special homemade sauce. Accompanying the chicken dish would be island salad with romaine lettuce and strawberries from Plant City, plus Italian bread slices buttered and broiled and dotted with parsley. For dessert, it would be Jake's favorite, later in the evening when he was watching "sportswhatever," her homemade chocolate chip cookies, which she kept on hand at all times.

She glanced at the clock. If she hurried, she could spend an hour in her backyard garden before supper. Her impatiens were long and leggy, and they needed pruning so spring growth could make them full and pretty again and profuse with colorful blossoms.

Chicken breasts browned, she pulled the pan off the burner and covered it. She would make her sauce and boil the fettuccine right before serving time.

She started to set the kitchen table but then decided not to. Jake would insist on eating on trays in front of the TV when he found out their son, Curtis, wouldn't be home for supper.

She let out an angry sigh. "I guess that's what we'll do. Jake always gets his way." Supper time was the only opportunity for conversation in their house, it seemed, and with Curtis away so much, it had pretty much degenerated to a few grunts from Jake during the evening news.

She hurried out the French doors, then stood on the flagstone patio in the pleasant Florida sun, scanning her garden, admiring it, feeling proud. Nature had given her a massive laurel oak tree. She had provided the rest through "blood, sweat, toil, and tears," as Sir Winston Churchill had put it.

"Ahh." Beauty abounded in her beloved backyard. Impatiens in delicious hues circling the oak. A thick carpet of St. Augustine grass. Stepping-stones leading to an exquisite English garden. A white gazebo. An orange tree dotted with oranges and thick with white blossoms that smelled like heavenly sachet.

"Pure eye candy, my garden. And soul candy, too." She breathed in deeply of the heady scent, smiling. With central Florida's year-round growing season, she experienced soul candy every day of the year—a refreshing tonic for her aching heart.

"Too bad my marriage can't provide the same thing." Woodenly she made her way to the cottage-style potting shed.

Tonight she would talk to Jake about the weighty matters facing them. She simply needed a break from unconcerned, indifferent, and unromantic Jake Higgins. She thought he was her Prince Charming when they married over twenty-four years ago. She thought he was Mr. Perfect when they dated. She thought he was the answer to the prayer she'd prayed in her teenage years. *Lord, send me a Christian mate.*

Though he was a Christian, she really didn't know Jake back then. But she *had* loved him. It would be unreasonable to think any other way. From the get-go, there had been an attraction between them—a strong one—and then love. The trouble was, their love was now dead. Was their marriage dead, too? She thought so.

She pulled on garden gloves, attached her knee pads, and knelt near the impatiens bed.

Hold stalk. Clip. Toss in pail.

Hold stalk. Clip. Toss in pail.

On she worked, but her mind was a million miles away.

She remembered Jake on their wedding day, both of them starry-eyed and in love, as the proverbial saying went. They were salt and pepper: she blond, he raven-haired—a striking couple, people said. Of course she didn't realize how much of a sports nut he was and how he would glue himself to the TV every evening of their lives.

For twenty-four long years.

She didn't know they would turn out to be salt and pepper in life—complete opposites with nothing in common. When she married him, she didn't know he would quit doing the things that were important to her, like going to the symphony, or attending a flower show, or even taking a simple walk through the mall or along the seashore—all the things they did while dating.

She didn't know there would be arguments—discussions, Jake called them—that usually turned into pouting sessions, she being the pouter, he liked to remind her. No, she didn't know back then that their marriage for the most part would be characterized by lots of time spent apart. They were simply two unconnected people.

As a teenager looking for the perfect mate, she thought marriage to a Christian man, your soul mate, meant pleasant togetherness in all things, a skip through daisy-dotted fields with your very best friend, hands entwined, hearts melded together in sweet wedded bliss.

"Humph, was I in for a rude awakening. Ouch!" She yanked off her left glove and squeezed her finger where the pruning clippers had grabbed it.

"Oww," she said in her characteristic quiet way. She released her hold on her finger and examined it.

"At least I didn't cut it." But an angry red mark was there, below her fingernail.

"What's the matter with me?" She hadn't done something like this in years. She was always careful when handling garden tools, always mindful. She paid attention and took proper care. She had studied gardening manuals by the armloads, knew just what to do for every chore, from pruning, to hoeing, to clipping branches, to properly lifting heavy bags of mulch, to achieving different colors with hydrangeas, to you-name-it.

Still rubbing her sore finger, she glanced at her watch, then gathered her things and stood up. "Guess I'll go finish supper. Jake arrived home from the office twenty-six minutes ago, and he's been in his recliner exactly twenty-two minutes. He'll be starving to death by now, as usual. And bellowing about it, too."

❋

Jake Higgins pulled his car into the garage beside his wife's SUV. He smiled. Felicia would be in her backyard garden, working with her flowers. He could see her in his mind's eye, bent over the bed that circled the giant oak tree, clipping her—pansies? Geraniums? Whatever.

He was glad gardening was her hobby. Some women were gadabouts, going all over town running up huge charge bills. Not Felicia. For the most part, except for that one trip she'd made to England a few years ago with the church women, she was a homebody. She worked in the yard, cooked sumptuous meals, made scrapbooks full of family photos, graded English papers, and prepared for her Sunday school lessons.

"You lucky man, you." With a touch of a button on the garage remote, he let the garage door down, reached for his briefcase, and headed for the kitchen.

"Umm." He breathed in the delicious scent as he stepped

inside. He glanced at the stove top, saw the saucepan, and lifted the lid. Chicken. What recipe was Felicia cooking tonight? Whatever it was, he knew it would be good. Everything she cooked was fabulous.

He set down his briefcase and thumbed through the mail on the counter, appreciative that Felicia had already gone through it and culled the junk. In her organized way, she always sorted the mail for him, bills in one stack, letters in another, magazines in a third stack, catalogs in a fourth. He picked up the bills, headed down the hall, and put them in the study with the rest of the bills that he planned to tackle tonight.

He knew Felicia would take care of the remainder of the mail pronto in her usual efficient way. She was neat and tidy, and he loved that about her. She kept the house as clean as a whistle, everything in its place. Of course, he was that way, too. But when they first got married, he was a slob, stemming from college dorm living. Gradually he'd come to be more like her, and now he wanted things organized and in order just like she did. Her good points had rubbed off on him—in more ways than one—and he was thankful for her.

He thought of their many years together. Didn't she say the other day that their next anniversary was their twenty-fifth? Yes, that was right. In a few months. How would they celebrate the milestone event? Some couples had formal receptions. Some took trips. His secretary and her husband had celebrated their twenty-fifth last year by going on a cruise. She'd already taken her two-week vacation to be with her baby granddaughter during surgery, and when Jake found out about her looming anniversary, he'd insisted she take an extra week of vacation for the cruise.

"A twenty-fifth anniversary only comes once in a lifetime," he'd told his secretary. "Just consider it a reward—you keep me organized here at the office, and I appreciate that."

Would Felicia enjoy going on a cruise? The kids wouldn't have the time or expertise to put on a formal reception—Cara, a brand-new schoolteacher living two hours away, and Curtis, a senior in college living at home but mostly gone, what with his classes and work schedule.

Jake made his way up the hall. He and Felicia would probably take a special trip to celebrate. Paris, perhaps? That sounded nice.

In the family room, he plopped into his leather recliner and clicked on his big-screen TV.

The newscaster reminded him of Felicia. Blond. Blue eyes. Elegant clothing. Slim figure. He was proud of Felicia. She worked hard to stay in shape. He did, too, though it was a challenge, what with her cooking. He worked out regularly—either at the gym at lunchtime or on his treadmill in the evenings. Treadmills and TV went together like he and Felicia did—you couldn't have one without the other.

A commercial came on showing a family at dinnertime, a chicken dish in the center of the table.

He smiled. It wouldn't be long, and his family would be gathered at the table, devouring Felicia's fabulous food.

He sighed, relishing the thought, then slipped into his regular before-dinner nap.

Chapter 2

"J ake, dinner's ready."

Jake stirred from his nap, hearing Felicia's sweet voice wafting through the room, smelling a bevy of enticing aromas.

"Wash up and come to the kitchen. It's just us this evening. Curtis is working again tonight."

Jake let the recliner footrest down, stood, yawned, and headed for the powder room off the hall. "He won't be here? Then let's eat on TV trays, okay? I don't want to miss the news."

❈

Minutes later, he made his way back into the family room, saw two TV trays facing the TV, both formally set and laden with food. Being careful not to bump his tray, he slipped behind it and sat down in his recliner, then pulled the tray toward him.

"Here's your iced tea." Felicia came into the room carrying two tall glasses of iced tea, fresh lime slices wedged on the sides.

"Thanks." He reached for his glass and set it on the end table beside his recliner, his eyes never leaving the TV screen. He hit the MUTE button, then bowed his head. "Lord, thank You for this food. Bless it to our bodies and our bodies to Your service. In Jesus' name we pray. Amen." He turned the sound on, and the newscaster's voice filled the room.

Felicia sat down and pulled her tray forward. "Jake, I need to talk to you."

The newscaster continued talking, reporting about the traffic accident on the bridge, then a robbery, then a kidnapping, all in Tampa, Florida, forty miles from the idyllic central Florida town where they lived.

"Jake?"

"Hmm?"

"Can we talk during the next commercial?"

"Sure." He was practically wolfing down her food, it was so good. He slowed his eating, his manners kicking in. A commercial came on, and he pressed the MUTE button and looked over at her. "This is fabulous. Better than Carrabba's. New recipe?" He forked a piece of chicken and popped it into his mouth, then ate a few bites of the delicious salad with the sliced strawberries and slivered almonds. "Yum-yum for my tum."

He dabbed at his mouth with his napkin. "Felicia? You hear me? I asked if this was a new recipe." His eyes were on the TV. There was that commercial again, the one with the family around the dinner table. What they were eating couldn't possibly compare with Felicia's dinner. With his fork, he made a *ting-ting* sound on the edge of his plate to get Felicia's attention. Was she daydreaming? "What's the name of this chicken dish?"

"Nothing fancy. Chicken Parmesan is all."

"And wow, is it good."

"Thanks. I found the recipe in *Southern Life*. There's something I need to tell you—"

"Shh. News is back on."

Fifteen minutes later, plus a second helping, Jake set aside his TV tray and reclined all the way back, letting out a loud, contented sigh. A commercial was on, and so was the MUTE button. He rubbed his stomach. "I'm going to have to run an extra twenty minutes tonight to work off some of this. Wow. You've got to be the best cook in Camden County."

Felicia stood and in short order had their dishes scraped and stacked. She headed for the kitchen, her hands full.

"I take that back. You're the best cook in the world, Felicia."

"And the best wife," she said over her shoulder.

Felicia made her way to the kitchen. She had almost added, "But not for long," in response to Jake's telling her she was the best cook in the world. But she thought better of it. If she was going to deliver her edict tonight, she needed to do it in the right way. No jabs. No slurs. No arguments. Forthright all the way.

Twenty-five minutes later, the kitchen cleaned and the dishwasher humming softly, Felicia knew this was the time to talk to Jake.

She entered the family room just as the top-of-the-hour commercials were over. Good timing. News was done. Now she could have his full attention. "Jake—"

"Let's—play—*Wheel of Fortune*," came the announcer's voice.

"Jake, can I talk to you now?"

"In a minute. Come watch *Wheel of Fortune* with me. You're as addicted to it as I am."

She charged across the room, picked up the remote from the arm of his recliner, and hit the POWER button.

"What are you doing?" Jake looked up at her, surprise in his eyes, then irritation.

"We're going to talk, that's what."

"Is something wrong with Cara? Curtis?"

"No. Something's wrong with our marriage."

He hit the foot lever and shot forward into a sitting position.

"I'd like you to come into the living room with me. Now." She worked at keeping her tone staid and serious instead of her usual kitten-soft. "I need to talk to you."

"Sure, Felicia." He stood up. "I don't know what's gotten into you. You're acting different somehow. You know I don't have a problem talking with you. All you have to do is ask."

Minutes later, they were both seated in the living room, her in a wing chair, him on the camelback sofa at the end nearest her.

"I'm not going to beat around the bush, Jake. I'm—"

"Of course not. What's on your mind?" He tapped on his bottom lip. "I know. I bet you want to go on that trip to Israel with the church women."

She glared at him. First it was the TV. Now it was his

big mouth. Couldn't he shut up so she could talk? She took a deep breath, shocked at her rude thinking. She wasn't usually so aggressive.

His eyebrows drew together. "Is something bothering you?"

"Can I have five minutes of your time without your interrupting me?"

"Uh—of course." His voice had a soft quality to it. A worried one?

"Promise me I can talk without your saying a word. Until I—"

"Sure."

"You just did what I asked you not to do."

"What's that?"

"You cut me off before I finished what I needed to say. Jake Higgins, look at me." She inched forward and looked straight into his eyes. "I have some things that need saying. Will—you—promise—not—to—say—anything, not—to—interrupt—until—I'm—through?"

"I promise."

She leaned back, looked down at the flowered rug that covered the hardwood floors, and studied the medallion at the center. "When we got married twenty-four years ago, I loved you. And I believe you loved me. I'm not stupid enough to think otherwise. Obviously there was an attraction. We wound up together. But we were wrong for each other. I knew it on our honeymoon—"

"You what?"

She glared at him again, setting her mouth in the grimmest line she could muster.

"I'm sorry." He clasped his hands together, his knuckles popping. "I won't say another word."

She waited a long moment, trying to get her thoughts back on track. This was hard. Harder than she thought it would be, especially with the contrite look on his face. He looked like a little boy who'd been caught with his hand in the cookie jar. But this was no time to be sympathetic toward him. She'd done that for twenty-four years. It was time to be strong. For her own sake.

She moistened her lips and took another deep breath. "Marriage should be a togetherness, a blending of two people. A person should feel like her mate is her best friend. Sometimes I feel like you're a stranger. You don't know me. Not really. And I don't know you. We're as different as night and day, poles apart, as different as lightning and—and—a lightning bug."

With her toe, she traced the floral designs on the rug. "You're loud, and I'm quiet. You love sports, and I hate them." On she went, naming their differences, one, then another, then another, for close to five minutes.

"Like I said, I found this out on our honeymoon. I guess I was too naive to realize it before we married. But on our honeymoon, I was so hurt when you. . ."

A sob caught at the back of her throat, but she pushed it down. She quickly recounted an experience on their honeymoon that had deeply hurt her, something that had to do with his brash and brawny ways and her shy, quiet manner. On their third day as man and wife, when it had occurred, she had tried to tell him how hurt she had been, but he had brushed her off.

"I soon learned to ignore my feelings. After all, I was taught that marriage is for life, forever and ever, same as you were taught. The day of our wedding, Mom said to me, 'You've made your bed; now lie in it.' You and I both know what that means. It means 'Don't come back home crying to Mom and Dad after you're married.' It means sticking with it and making the best of it. So that's what I did. . . ."

He opened his mouth as if to say something, then promptly closed it.

"I longed for—for. . . Oh, I—it's hard to put this into words. I don't know. I wanted companionship. . .and contentment. . .and—and comfort, but I never felt like I was getting any of those things. I felt so alone, so unloved." She stopped abruptly, pushing down another sob.

"But before I tell you what I really want to say, I need to say something positive. During some of our years together, I *have* gotten something out of the relationship. I can remember loving you so much it hurt at times. I can remember being so happy I could burst. So I want to assure you that our marriage hasn't been a farce. We've had some good times, Jake, some really good times, especially after the kids came along. You're a good father."

Memories assailed her. "We had fun on family outings. And I loved our summer vacations, even though we didn't plan them out like I wanted. We'd take off in the van for two weeks, crossing the country and going anywhere we pleased and eating anything we liked, and you'd sing at the top of your lungs with Cara and Curtis as we clocked off the miles. I remember that year when we went white-water rafting in the mountains, and you rented a one-man raft as well as a family raft, and you and Curtis took turns swapping places the whole way, and you two had water fights with those oars and splashed the daylights out of Cara and me until we were so cold from that freezing water we thought our blood would freeze over. I think I loved our family outings so much because I felt like I had *some* of your attention during those times. . . ." Her voice trailed off.

"All through the years, I tried to be a good wife to you. And I guess in your own way, you tried to be a good husband to me, or what you thought was a good husband. And in the bedroom department. . ." She paused, feeling almost shy, and that was an odd feeling to experience after being married to someone for nearly twenty-five years. "Well, I'll just say that thankfully we never had problems there. We always seemed to work around our issues when it came to those times."

She stopped, suddenly tired. "But we've grown apart. And the chasm gets wider every day. There's no denying it. And it's so wide at this point, I don't think it can ever close back up. I'm looking at you and reading surprise on your face. But frankly, Jake, that surprises *me*. You had to know something wasn't right. You had to know this thing was coming to a head. You're a smart man. You own your own insurance agency. You're no dummy."

She paused and took a breath. "Maybe you ignored our

problems." She let out a *tsk*. "Yes, of course that's what you've been doing. You've always done that. But you have to admit that you knew something was afoot when I asked you to go for counseling last month. Too bad you turned me down—over and over, I might add. Last month, I believed that was the solution to our problems. But I don't think that way anymore. There might be only one solution. I won't say the *D* word at this point. What I *will* say is this: Will you move out for a while so I can think things through?"

She was almost panting from her long monologue. Her throat felt like cotton from talking so long. She jumped up. "I need some water."

She ran to the kitchen, filled a glass from the water dispenser on the refrigerator, filled another one for Jake—always thinking about Jake—returned to the living room, and handed one to him. She sat down and guzzled the water, then set the glass on a coaster.

"Aren't you going to say anything?" She picked up her glass, took another long swallow, set it back down, and waited. Her eyes roamed the room. Above the shiny ebony piano hung a classic studio portrait of Cara as a senior in college. In six weeks, a similar portrait of Curtis would hang by its side. And in a few years, portraits of two bride-and-groom couples would hang on the opposite wall when Cara and Curtis each married. Who knew? It might be soon. At least for Cara. She was getting serious with her young man.

"In six weeks. . ." Felicia looked at Cara's portrait again. "Curtis will graduate from college. The kids are grown now.

All these years, they were the glue that held us together. Once glue no longer sticks, things fall apart. That's what's happening to us. So we've got to make some plans, to see that everything's done properly and in order."

Still Jake didn't speak. But a dark, brooding look came over him.

"I repeat my question. Will you move out for a while so I can think things through?"

"Yes."

"You will?" She hadn't expected to win the battle so quickly and smoothly. She'd expected him to—to explode? If not explode, then certainly to be his brash, brawny self. She never expected him to say a simple yes.

"I'll be out by the end of the month."

She made mental calculations. Less than a week.

"Meanwhile, I'll sleep in the guest room." Jake got up and left the room.

She sat there, feeling as bad as she'd ever felt in her life. Even worse than when her father died from liver cancer last year. And they'd been as close as any father and daughter could be.

Chapter 3

You're too late, you big oaf. And too stubborn." Jake placed his T-shirts and underwear in the suitcase on the island cabinet in the large master closet.

"I should've been a better husband." He realized his errors and shortcomings—*after* Felicia asked him to move out. All of his pleading and promising the last few days had fallen on deaf ears.

"I'll try to be more attentive to you," he had promised. "I'll even go shopping with you." He hated that thought, though he didn't let her know it. "What if I work in your garden with you occasionally? Would you like that?"

But she had been intent on getting what she called "think time" away from him.

Surreally, he gathered his neckties from the rack and looped them around the tops of suit hangers, then placed stacks of casual clothes in the suitcase beside the underwear and T-shirts.

Who would've thought just a week ago, on the night Felicia

cooked her new chicken Parmesan recipe, that he'd be moving out of their home? The beautiful home he'd designed to their custom specifications. Felicia had wanted to buy one of those old houses downtown and remodel it, but he knew that was ridiculous and had told her so.

"They want a ton for those run-down hovels," he'd told her, "and then you have to remodel them. You end up investing a fortune."

This way—building a brand-new house—Felicia got the kind of closets she wanted and a cook's dream kitchen, and he got his exercise room and a third garage and a lake out back, plus a lot of other amenities. The resale value would be fantastic if or when they built another house.

Only now, I won't have any of those amenities. For a while, anyway. Felicia had asked him to move out for a month or two. She wouldn't say what would happen after that. If she—no, he wouldn't let his mind roam to the *D* word. It was too painful.

He couldn't believe this was happening to them—a couple who had been raised in the church, the pair who tried to put God first in their lives. Who did she think she was, to do this to him? To them? To their children? What was wrong with her? Why couldn't she be happy? He knew a dozen women who would give their eyeteeth to be in Felicia's shoes. He might not be Mr. Romeo or Mr. Husband Extraordinaire, but he was—what was he?

"I'm Jake Higgins, Mr. Easygoing, a don't-bother-me-and-I-won't-bother-you type of guy. But I'm someone you can count on. My track record proves that. And I'm a Christian—since my teenage years." A little chanting ditty from his teenage years ran across his mind, and he smiled.

"We don't drink, and we don't chew," he said, singsong style, "and we don't go with the girls who do."

He placed his shoes in a bag: black lace-ups, cordovan tassel loafers, brown slip-ons, casual deck shoes, pair after pair of all types. "I was Mr. Nice Guy, Mr. Keep Your Nose Clean Guy." He snorted. "And look where it got me."

He jerked open his sock drawer, scooped up a handful of balled-up socks, and threw them like grenades into the suitcase, some of them bouncing out. "Okay, Miss Felicia Fancy-Pants. I'll use your tactics. Out of sight, out of mind. That's just fine with me."

Chapter 4

Today Felicia was going to prune her hedges and fertilize them with Milorganite. The granular fertilizer wouldn't burn even the most tender shrub or flower, yet it would make her garden flourish. She had this whole glorious Saturday to spend in her backyard. She wouldn't have to stop to prepare lunch or dinner for Jake. She wouldn't have to grocery shop. She hadn't cooked in a week. She felt carefree and relaxed, like the ball and chain had been taken off. She was a woman in command, independent and able to make her own decisions, and it felt good.

She pruned a long row of shrubs with the electric clippers, then connected her new spiral water hose to the spigot and placed it near the hedge. She went back to the potting shed and scooped the milorganite into two buckets, then returned.

Scoop, pour on shrub, water thoroughly.

Scoop, pour on shrub, water thoroughly.

Azaleas, ligustrum, synensis, boxwood, schilling, Indian

hawthorne: All would see healthy new growth shortly, and that pleased her.

On she worked, thinking about the pleasant evening ahead. She was going to dinner and a literary reading with her teacher friend Stacy. An author was in town, a big event for their community, and she looked forward to hearing him read from his book and make comments on it. Tomorrow afternoon, she would do the laundry, what little there was. With Jake gone, it took awhile to accumulate enough to wash.

"Jake gone." That sounded good to her. He'd been gone over two weeks now. A peace had settled over her in the absence of disagreements, disappointments, and frustration.

Except for Curtis's disappointment—devastation, really. She could tell he'd taken this hard. She could read her son even though he wasn't a talker. He was a chip off the old block, just like her, quiet and reflective. Cara, on the other hand, was like her father, boisterous and outgoing. Neither Curtis nor Cara liked what she'd done—asking Jake to move out. And Cara had let her know it in no uncertain terms. But it simply couldn't be helped. It was something she had to do.

She had planned to do a lot of thinking once Jake was gone. But it hadn't happened. Life had been too full lately. There'd been the three-day spring teachers' convention she'd attended in Tallahassee. She'd never gone before, since Jake never wanted her to leave him. Then there was her annual field trip with her schoolkids to see the off-Broadway production of *Romeo and Juliet* in Tampa. That required lots of planning and fine-tuning. Then, last week the school principal asked her to take on some extra duties.

But she would find time, soon, to do some serious think-ing about Jake. She had to. Things had to be sorted out in her mind before she could proceed with plans for her future, whatever they turned out to be.

"Only the Lord knows." She said the pat statement with-out even thinking, out of habit, she supposed. But after she said it, she felt guilty. There was something else she hadn't thought much about these last two weeks—the Lord. She hadn't even been to church, totally unlike her.

She'd been raised in the church by devout Christian par-ents. They had taught her the ways of righteousness as firmly as they'd taught her to brush her teeth and do her chores and mind her manners at all times.

"Always do what's right, no matter what the other person does," her mother used to say. "That applies to marriage, too," her mother always added.

Bent over a boxwood, Felicia felt a near-physical pain hit her.

That applies to marriage, too?

The fertilizer scoop still in her hand, she stood up to her full height and took a deep breath, feeling shaky.

She certainly hadn't done what was right concerning her marriage, putting Jake out like this and considering breaking up their union.

She hurled the scoop to the ground, wanting to take her frus-tration out on someone, some*thing*. Her bottom lip trembled, and her eyes blurred with tears. Why did she have to be the one who was required to do right when Jake seemed to be getting off scot-free? He could come home every day, a delicious dinner awaiting him, then spend the rest of the evening in his recliner or on the treadmill, not having three minutes of conversation with her. He could sail through life taking no interest in what was important to her, yet expect her to meet his every need.

"It's just not fair." She kicked at the plastic scoop on the ground. Maybe she was too nice. The brilliant spring sun moved behind a cloud, and the play of shadows made her look up.

"Lord, I tried. I really did. But Jake wouldn't budge an inch." She had begged Jake to go to marriage counseling, but he said no—he would never stoop to that. It would be too degrading, he'd said. After all, he was a church leader. They could work out their problems—what few they had, he'd told her—between themselves.

Through her mind passed her list of complaints against Jake, and she had a mental picture of a long scroll filled with tiny writing.

"I tried to be the best wife in the world, but it didn't work." The sun came out in full strength, forcing her to look away from the sky. "Lord, where are You? Do You even care about me? About us?"

The heavens seemed like brass, unyielding, and that made her sadder still. Here she was, experiencing her lowest moment, and it seemed God was nowhere to be found.

Finished with her fertilizing, she shut off the water and disconnected the hose, gathered up her supplies, and headed for the potting shed in the backyard.

Then a thought hit her like the proverbial ton of bricks. *It's not God's fault. It's Jake's fault.*

Jake had been too stubborn, too brash, too dense, or whatever it was, to listen to the cries of her heart.

"Yes, this is Jake's fault, pure and simple." She scowled, and it felt good. She scowled harder, her mouth set in a grim line.

"Things are going to change around here. All my adult life, it's been *Jake* time and then *Cara* time and then *Curtis* time. Well, it's *Felicia* time now." Her spirit resolute, she put her supplies in the shed, then headed for the kitchen for a short break from her gardening. A glass of sweet iced tea sounded like the perfect thing for her parched soul.

Chapter 5

This is humiliating. Jake glanced around the church office, chomping at the bit. He was waiting for Margaret, the pastor's secretary, to tell him he could go into the pastor's office. He sat there, hoping against hope that he wouldn't see anyone he knew. But that was unlikely. The church was large, and the office was a busy place, what with the big staff and assistants and volunteers coming through at any given moment. But if the pastor didn't keep him waiting too long, perhaps he could avoid being seen.

He'd been here many times for meetings with the pastor and leaders, giving his expertise on business matters as requested by the pastor. Usually he would sail past the sofa he was now sitting on and head straight for the plush, paneled boardroom.

But he'd never been here to get. . .personal marital advice. The thought made him. . .angry. Okay. He admitted it. As angry as a bull with a flag in his face. It was all Felicia's fault. He still couldn't get over what had happened to him. He still couldn't get over the fact that he was living in one of those rent-by-the-week motel rooms. He was away from his leather recliner and his big-screen TV and his treadmill and his PWC tied to the dock and his—

"Jake, I said the pastor's ready to see you."

He shot to his feet, feeling disoriented for a moment. Then he focused on Margaret and her pleasant, though puzzled, expression.

"Follow me, and I'll take you back."

He followed Margaret down the hall, saw her open the pastor's door and gesture to go inside.

In moments, he was seated in the chair that faced the pastor's desk, greetings done with, and the door firmly closed. Was the door soundproof? He hoped so.

"I've never felt so foolish in all my life," he began. He, Jake Higgins, church leader and role model, had been put out of his house by his wife, forced to face public embarrassment in the church. . . .

It was more than he could bear.

An hour later, ranting done and a long session of counseling behind him, Jake was on his knees in the pastor's office, pouring out his heart to God.

"Lord," he prayed aloud, "if You'll help me get Felicia back, I'll—I'll—oh, God, forgive me for that, even. Forgive me for seeking Your hand and not Your face. Lord, I seek *You*, the Almighty, the King of kings. I ask You to help me live for You victoriously, with the right spirit, my heart in tune with Yours.

Forgive me for being such a louse. Forgive me for being uncaring toward Felicia, even though I didn't realize I was doing it. Forgive me for being an insensitive clod."

He continued praying. "Lord, if I ever get her back, help me to be the husband she needs. And if I don't get her back. . ." A sob rolled up his throat and shook his being. "If she won't reconcile with me, then—then help me to bear it with grace."

Ten minutes later, praying completely done—with a fervency that shocked even him—Jake hugged his pastor as they stood near the door. "You're a real friend, Rod. I'll never forget this day, and your kindness and understanding, and your wise counsel."

"I consider you a friend, too, Jake. I'm glad I could help. You've been a blessing to me personally and to the church. I'll be praying for you. Let go and let God, okay? You know? Some of the things we talked about?"

"Right."

" 'Commit thy way unto the Lord; trust also in him—' "

" 'And he shall bring *it* to pass.' " Jake smiled as he finished Psalm 37:5, the verse his pastor had quoted.

"Bring *what* to pass, Jake?"

Jake smiled more broadly. "What I'm contending with. That's what you told me when you explained the verse."

The pastor nodded. "I just wanted to remind you. Remember, Jake, the secret is, let the Lord bring it about—not you."

"Oh, I will, Rod. This thing's too big for me. I've *got* to have God's help. I'm trusting in Him from here on out."

�֎

Jake drove straight to the florist. "I'd like to order that bouquet." He pointed to a round floral arrangement in the florist's pictorial album. "I want flowers delivered every day at noon to Felicia Higgins at Palmdale Middle School." He gave the address. "That's my wife, and she's in the teachers' lounge every day at noon."

"That's our large posy. It's a mixed arrangement with a lace doily at the base. The bouquet sits in a crystal dish."

"I think she'll like it."

"You want it just like that?" The young clerk paused in her writing on the order pad and pointed at the picture. "Any changes on any of the flowers?"

He racked his brain. Felicia loved all kinds of flowers. She was a master gardener. What flowers would impress her the most?

"The large posy has daisies, carnations, and five sweetheart roses. And greenery, of course."

"Sweetheart roses?" A memory kicked in. "Make the entire thing with sweetheart roses. And make them pink." Those were what Felicia loved when they were dating. He had sent her one or two bouquets of pink sweetheart roses, even though he was a college student watching his money. Through the years, he'd sent her a few bouquets here and there for special occasions, but never pink sweetheart roses. Frankly, he'd forgotten they were her favorite. Until now. For some reason, that tidbit popped into his mind.

He was thankful for this little memory jog. He hoped to

dredge up some more of Felicia's favorite things. He had a lot of strategies waiting in the wings. If one tactic failed, it would be on to the next one.

"Sir, did you hear me? I said that'll be expensive. Sweetheart roses every day—"

"Doesn't matter. She's worth it. And more."

"O–kay." The clerk dragged out the word, putting equal accent on each syllable. "How would you like to pay? Cash? Credit?"

Later, as Jake drove toward his stale motel room that overlooked a grease-stained parking lot, he felt light in heart. "I'll be loving you, always," he sang. The song was one of their wedding songs years ago. "With a love that's true, always."

He grew somber, a heaviness stealing over him. "The question is, Felicia, will you love me for always? With a love that's true? I hope so. How I hope so."

Chapter 6

"There's a bouquet in the office for you, Felicia. Again. How many does that make now?" A giggle, then a door clicking shut.

At the sound of her name, Felicia jumped to her feet in the teachers' lounge and headed for the school office. Forget that she'd had a hard-and-fast morning of teaching English and listening to students murder lines of poetry as they tried to quote them. Forget that all she wanted to do for her twenty-minute break was curl up on the Naughahyde sofa and let her mind rest, maybe even catch a quick catnap, what she'd wanted to do every day during break for a week now.

Only it hadn't worked out that way. Every day—for five days in a row—her name had been called smack-dab in the middle of her reverie, and she'd hurried to the office to get a bouquet from Jake.

Though she loved pink sweetheart roses, she didn't like these bouquets—because they were from Jake. *And* because she had asked him to give her space. That was the whole reason she'd asked him to move out. She needed a break from him. But this was just like him, horning in, trying to take over, insisting on doing things his way, manipulating her.

Plus, the bouquets were publicly embarrassing to her. The whole office staff was atwitter over the beautiful flowers she was receiving—daily.

"What's the special occasion?" they'd asked. "Did you achieve something significant?"

And worse. "Did your husband do something wrong and he's making amends?" Giggles. Rolled eyes.

And worse still. "Oh, how lucky you are to have such a wonderful, thoughtful husband."

If they only knew. He wasn't wonderful, and he wasn't thoughtful. That was the problem. Otherwise, she and Jake wouldn't be in this fix. He was just—Jake.

Now she entered the office door, keeping her eyes downcast, not wanting to be teased again. Fortunately, only one secretary was there, and she was on the phone.

Felicia scooped up the bouquet and headed to her SUV, where she'd taken the other flower arrangements as soon as they'd been delivered. Practical-minded, she had headed to the hospital every day after school and delivered the expensive posies, asking the nurses to give them to patients who had no bouquets. She didn't have the heart to throw beautiful flowers in the garbage.

She let out an exasperated sigh. Jake was now controlling how she spent her afternoons, forcing her to head to the hospital.

"Give me a break, Jake." She didn't even crack a smile at her little rhyme. Instead, she opened the car door and secured the posy on the floorboard, books on each side to keep it from tipping, then slammed the door and hurried back to her classroom.

Felicia sorted through her mail and flicked the pink envelope to the side. A week had passed since she'd told Curtis to tell his dad to quit sending the bouquets. A day after the bouquets stopped, she started receiving pink cards in pink envelopes in the mail, for a total of five now, all expressing a man's love for his sweetheart.

"Give me a break, Jake." She repeated her little rhyme as she picked up the pink envelope, wondering whether to open it or not.

"If I open it, I get irritated. If I throw it away, I feel guilty. I can't win either way."

She looked at the card a long time, then made the decision to toss it. She also made another decision. She would telephone Jake tonight and ask him to call off his dogs.

"Jake, you're making a mistake. Go jump in the lake."

"You think this is cute, don't you?" She tried to keep the venom out of her voice, but it was hard. "Sending me all those bouquets and now all these cards?"

She and Jake had been talking a full five minutes, and she couldn't seem to get through to him. That was one of the main problems in their marriage.

She paced back and forth, the phone in her hand as he went on and on. She was confused. He talked ninety miles a minute—except when she *wanted* him to talk. Dinner conversation? Forget it. After-dinner conversation? Forget it. Weekend conversation? Forget it. But then, at other times, like right now, and like the night she had asked him to move out, he wanted to take over and yak his head off. To her way of thinking, his talking at times like this seemed to be a matter of control. Clear and simple. His control. And she was tired of it.

"You just don't get it, do you?" She felt like hanging up on him but refrained, her manners too ingrained. "I don't want to hear from you for—for—a while, Jake. Do you under-stand me?"

She was so upset she was shaking.

He apologized—to his credit—and promised not to contact her again.

She breathed a sigh of relief as she said a hasty good-bye, then hung up the phone. She leaned against the kitchen counter, her breath coming in nips and tucks. Tomorrow she would have the peace she'd been seeking all along. There would be no bouquets and no cards. She wouldn't have to think about Jake Higgins for—a while. Forever?

That thought was like water on a wilting plant. She was now free, totally free.

Chapter 7

Jake got out of his car and made his way across the road to the Christian bookstore. He could've bought books on marriage at the church bookstore, any number of them. The store in the lobby of the church was large and had lots of titles to offer.

But that would be too embarrassing. Somebody might ask him why he was buying books on marriage. People at church had been asking where Felicia was. He'd shrugged them off without fibbing. But if they saw him buying marriage books, they might put two and two together.

Instead, he would buy the books here. He'd never been in this store, and the clerk didn't know him.

Inside, he scanned the directional signs, saw that the marriage section was in the middle of the store, and made his way to it. He picked up a book, read the front cover, the back, the table of contents, then put it back on the shelf. He picked up the next one; did the same. He'd never heard of the authors. He'd never felt the need to read Christian marriage books. Until now.

After looking at nine titles, he was perplexed. Which ones were the best? No matter. He'd buy a hundred, if that's what it took.

He stacked up eleven books, some hardback, some paperback, and made his way to the checkout, contemplative about this, his latest tactic. There was more than one way to skin a cat, or in this case, to win back his woman.

Knowledge was the key, he had decided last night after he talked with Felicia. He would bone up on marriage material. He would change his ways. And he would let her *know* he'd changed his ways. And then he would get her back.

This was his new plan, his best plan. As soon as he read the books and altered his ways, he would write Felicia a long letter and tell her what he'd done. And all would be well.

He glanced at his watch as he plopped the books on the counter. Five thirty. He was a speed-reader. He could probably get through at least one book tonight, maybe two. But he wouldn't slough them off. He would be diligent about it. He would take notes in a notebook and study those notes. He would try to find out what made women tick. They were such odd creatures. Felicia had it all, or at least he thought she did. She had a Christian husband, a nice home, a fulfilling career, hobbies she enjoyed, and children she was proud of. So what was wrong with her? What more could she ask for?

He looked at the stack of books. Well, tonight he would find out. And he would mend his ways, since that was apparently what it would take to mend his marriage.

And then everything would be fine.

Chapter 8

Felicia nearly flipped out when she saw the fat white envelope in the mailbox. She drew it out and stared down at the return address.

Jake. Just as she suspected.

"What's he trying to pull now?" She retrieved the rest of the mail and sauntered into the house. In the kitchen, she sorted through the mail and set Jake's letter aside, feeling a mite shaky. What did he want to tell her?

It had been five weeks since Jake had moved out. She thought about the bouquets she had received, one per day for an entire week, recalled the pink cards he sent, also one per day for another whole week.

She fixed herself a glass of iced tea. These past few weeks had been like heaven. Well, sort of. She'd found time to think and reflect. That was good. And she'd done things she hadn't been able to do with Jake here. Like going on a couple of weekend trips with girlfriends without a care in the world. That was good, too. Jake always wanted her *around*, he'd said,

128

though why, she didn't know. He wanted to be engrossed in his sports channels and her busy with her scrapbooking or gardening or paper grading. That was his idea of a pleasant evening at home. He didn't want to talk and share his life with her, yet he didn't want her gone. The man didn't have a clue.

She decided to go out to her gazebo and read his letter. Iced tea glass in hand, she picked up the bulging envelope, then spotted her Bible on the antique bookshelf in the corner of the kitchen. She felt a stab of guilt. She hadn't been to church in a while, hadn't even read her Bible. That was so unlike her. She'd gone to church and read her Bible her entire life.

Without thinking why, she scooped up her Bible and headed out the French doors. Just holding it gave her a sense of comfort.

Comfort? Why did she need comfort? Life was fine.

Wasn't it?

She fathomed her innermost feelings as she situated herself on the wrought iron demibench inside the charming white gazebo. She was alone, really alone—for the first time in her adult life. Oh, Curtis was in and out, passing through like a ship in the night between his classes and work schedule. So that didn't really count.

Alone? But she'd been alone with Jake *here*.

She felt confused. And then it hit her. It was a spiritual void she was feeling. She was AWOL, what she'd heard some female speaker say on TV.

Alone without the Lord. Her? Yes, she had to admit it.

She took a sip of her iced tea and set it down on the

wrought-iron table. She opened her Bible, turned to the ribbon in Hebrews where their pastor had preached from last. Or at least the last time she'd heard him preach—a long time ago. She read the highlighted areas in Hebrews 12:1 and 3. She always highlighted scriptures as her pastor preached.

"Let us run with endurance the race that God has set before us. . . . Don't become weary and give up."

A brisk breeze seemed to come out of nowhere. It rustled the leaves in the oak tree with a ferociousness. Then all was still as before.

"Don't become weary," the Lord seemed to whisper. His voice seemed to float down through the branches of the oak, waft over to the gazebo, and swirl inside it. His voice continued on, hitting her heart as surely as if it were an arrow hitting a bull's-eye. *"Don't give up."*

She didn't say anything for a long time, just sat there soaking up what she knew to be the voice of the Lord.

" 'Let us run with endurance the race that God has set before us,' " she read in the marked pages of her Bible. " 'Don't become weary and give up.' "

But wasn't that verse referring to a person's faith? Not a marriage. She'd heard that scripture all her life as an exhortation to fight the good fight of faith, as the apostle Paul put it.

Deep down, though, her heart—*and God?*—was telling her that this scripture referred to her marriage, right now, this very moment.

"Felicia," she said to herself sternly, "you know there's no biblical reason for divorce. There's no adultery, no abuse, and no abandonment. You've simply given up."

And that can't be.

A tear escaped, followed by a deluge. Long moments passed. She unfolded the damp paper napkin around her tea glass and dabbed away her tears.

Her soul in turmoil, she ripped off the end of the envelope, scanned the thick letter Jake had written, and counted seven single-spaced typed pages.

She started at the beginning. Thirty minutes later, she put his letter down, more troubled than the day she had asked him to move out.

Her eyes misted over, but she willed herself not to cry.

Chapter 9

Jake raised the tennis ball high in the air and whacked it with all his might. How dare Felicia not respond to his letter! To his heartfelt plea for them to reconcile. . . To his promise that he would alter his ways. . . To his vow that he would treat her like the queen of his heart, forever and always, as one author so sentimentally put it. . .

How dare she not contact him in some way—if not to answer his letter, then at least to have the courtesy to let him know she'd received it.

He whacked another ball, and it sailed over the wall of the practice court. A second ball lost. He had restrained himself from calling and asking if she'd received his letter. He had even restrained himself from asking Curtis to be the go-between, what he'd done in the past.

Women. You can't live with them, and you can't live without them.

The cutesy adage popped into his head, but this time it didn't make him want to laugh like the first time he heard it.

It made him want to—whack another ball?

Sweat dotting his face under the hot midmorning sun, he decided this was a good time to quit or at least to take a break.

He walked to his sports bag under the shade of a giant palm tree, whipped out a towel, and wiped his face and neck. He pulled out a bottle of water that felt tepid to the touch and guzzled it down.

"Jake!"

Jake whirled around and saw Rod, his pastor, approaching.

"How are you doing today?" Dressed in athletic garb, Rod held a tennis racket and a sports bag. Another man stood some yards away, on another court, apparently Rod's tennis partner.

Jake felt sheepish. Though he'd attended church these past five weeks since Felicia put him out, he'd had no personal contact with Rod since their appointment. Because the church was large, their paths simply hadn't crossed.

"I thought you were going to come talk with me again. That's what you said."

Jake knew what Rod was referring to. During the first— and only—counseling session with Rod, Jake had promised he would come in weekly to get help for his marriage.

"But then as the weeks passed, I figured if you wanted to talk, you knew where to find me."

"I–I've been busy." Jake kicked at the clay court.

"Well, if you ever need to unload, I'm here for you. You know that."

A lightbulb went on in Jake's head. "I—I hate to ask you

this. . . . It's an imposition, but I'm—well, I'm at the end of my rope—"

"Wait." Rod held up his hand, traffic-cop style. "I'll be right back." He turned and sprinted toward his tennis partner. In minutes he was back. "It's all taken care of. Let's go have a cold soft drink at Louie's, okay?" He looked down at his watch. "Can you meet me there in ten minutes?"

"Five, my friend."

Five minutes later, Jake pulled into the parking lot of Louie's Sandwich Shop. He got out and made his way inside, saw Rod in a vinyl booth, and joined him.

"How's it been going?" Rod steepled his hands on the table. "I've been praying for you. And Felicia. I haven't seen her in a long time."

"We're a mess. Or at least I am. I guess it wouldn't be fair to speak for her. But for myself, I feel so. . . So—"

"Angry? Confused? Irritated? Whipped?"

"Yes to all of the above."

"That's normal."

"It is? I thought I was some kind of freak. My emotions seesaw. One minute, I love her like all get-out. The next minute, I could shake her. I've tried all kinds of things to get her back, but she ignores me. That makes me mad."

He listed all the things he'd done, counting on his fingers. The sweetheart roses. The pink cards of endearment. His recruitment of Curtis to relay messages. His purchase of books on marriage. His voracious studying. The letter in which he poured out his heart to her.

Jake slowly shook his head. "I've done everything I know to do, but apparently it isn't good enough."

The waitress set two tall soft drinks on the table.

"I ordered before you got here." Rod took a drink of his cola. "You like diet, right?"

"Right."

"So you've done everything you know to do?"

"Yes. I can't think of one more thing. I've racked my brain until it's sore."

"You're forgetting something."

"I don't think so. Women like attention. At least that's what the marriage books say. You know, tenderness. I've tried everything, but she won't budge." He went back over his list. "I've thrown pride to the wind and humbled myself to her. I've—"

"I, I, I."

"What?"

"I, I, I."

Jake looked down at the table, moved his glass to the side, then traced the water ring. *I, I, I?* Slowly it sank in, what Rod was saying. *I haven't relied on the Lord.* He'd been brash and brawny, what Felicia accused him of. He'd gone his own way, not the Lord's. And he had utterly failed.

"Remember what we talked about in my office?"

Jake's throat felt dry as he thought about the things Rod had told him during their appointment.

"Don't you think it's time to give the Lord a chance to work?"

"I was only trying to help things along."

"The Lord's big enough to do it on His own."

"I thought I was doing the right thing."

"Jake, sometimes that's exactly what the Lord wants you to do—your part while He does His. For instance, your reading all those books on marriage was a good move, an excellent one. You were on the right track with that. But when you bombarded her with the roses and the cards and then the letter, well, can't you see? She withdrew from you even further. Like I said, sometimes men should do things like sending flowers and cards. I'm not saying that's bad. In fact, that's good, for the most part. But in this case, after you told me the issues with Felicia, I felt in my heart that you should wait on God and give Him a chance to work in her heart."

Jake shrugged his shoulders. "I guess you're right."

"Ja–ke."

"Okay, okay. Tell me what to do, then."

"Pray. P-r-a-y," Rod spelled. "And not like the last time you prayed."

"What do you mean?"

"You got down on your knees in my office and prayed and asked God to help you. Then you put your plan into action, right? With no thought of waiting on God. Am I correct?"

Jake winced. "Felicia always accused me of being brash and brawny. Okay. This time I'm going to truly give it to God."

"First Peter 5:7 says, 'Casting all your care upon him; for he careth for you,'" Rod quoted. "Mind if I say a quiet prayer?" He gestured around him. "This place is empty. Mind if I lead us in prayer? Right here?"

"I wouldn't care if every booth was full. I need the prayer."
Jake grinned. "And you need the practice."

Rod didn't laugh at the old preacher cliché as he normally
would've. Instead, he bowed his head.

Fifteen minutes later, Jake whistled as he drove back to his
rent-by-the-week motel. He hadn't whistled in a long time.
He found himself whistling an old hymn.

"Trust and obey. . . ."

Chapter 10

Felicia sat at the end of the aisle in the big auditorium, waiting for "Pomp and Circumstance" to begin. Curtis was finally graduating, and she was proud of him—and for him. The Christian college he had attended would adequately prepare him for a life of ministry. In fact, he'd already been offered a position as a youth pastor and accepted it.

To her right were her parents, from out of town, and beyond them were Cara and her fiancé, Justin—they'd become engaged last month. Felicia hoped they would have a happy marriage.

A happy marriage? A sad pang hit her in the heart. *What I've never been able to achieve.*

Past her parents' seats were Jake's parents, also from out of town, and past them was Jake. Behind them were some siblings and spouses of hers and Jake's. Curtis's graduation had turned into a big family affair, and she was grateful for their support. After the graduation exercises, Jake planned to take everyone out to an elegant restaurant to celebrate.

When she first learned of Jake's dinner plans, she had refused to be a part. She simply didn't want the contact with him. She was still weighing her options concerning their marriage, still thinking—brooding, really, she had to admit.

But when she found out how many family members were coming—and from so far away—she had relented. She couldn't disappoint Curtis. This was his big day, and he'd worked hard to see this come about. She vowed to do all she could to make the occasion memorable for him.

One way she had made it memorable was to have the entire family at her house before the graduation for hors d'oeuvres and punch. It had been hard deciding to do it, then planning it, then pulling it off, given her circumstances. But she did it successfully. When Jake stepped into the house after six weeks of being away, well, she couldn't even describe how it affected her. It was. . .bittersweet?

Fortunately, the entire family had shown respect for her and her feelings, even though privately they didn't like the fact that she'd asked Jake to move out, or so Cara told her. They'd not said a word about the separation during the party, though, and just carried on in conversation and joviality as if she and Jake were still a couple.

"There's Curtis," Jake boomed now.

Felicia looked at the long line of graduating seniors filing down the aisle, clad in black caps and gowns. She spotted Curtis, and her heart swelled with motherly pride.

After preliminaries, the guest speaker was introduced, a man with a string of degrees behind his name who had written several books and was president of a seminary.

He stepped to the podium and greeted the audience. "Tonight I'd like to read from Hebrews 12, verses 1 and 3. 'Let us run with endurance the race that God has set before us. Don't become weary and give up.' That's the New Living Translation. The New International Version puts verse 1 this way: 'Let us throw off everything that hinders and the sin that so easily entangles, and let us run with perseverance the race marked out for us.' Shall we bow our heads in prayer?"

For twenty minutes, the speaker—an accomplished pulpiteer—hammered home his subject with aplomb. "Running the Race" was his topic. He talked about the graduating seniors' race through high school, then college, and how they hadn't given up but had achieved victory. He spoke about the race that was now before them, and he challenged them to continue and not become weary. Endurance, he said, was what it would take. Second, he said it would take choosing to put aside hindrances and sins that ensnared. Third would be to stay true to the course God had set before them. He touched on the many races the graduating seniors would run throughout life, from their faith to their careers to their marriages.

Marriage? Felicia fanned her face with her program. Was it hot in here? Or was it just her? Marriage? Why'd the guest speaker have to bring up that subject? Why couldn't he stick to faith and careers for these seniors? That was what was most appropriate for young people on the threshold of adult life.

She shifted in her seat, running her finger under the pearls at her neck. This was hitting too close to home. Why did the speaker have to focus on hindrances? And sins? And the race that *God* had set? Was it sin that had caused her to ask Jake to move out? Was sin behind her thinking about the *D* word? Certainly it was a hindrance of some kind. But sin?

She fanned her neck again. She knew the answer to her next question before she even asked it, and that made her fan harder. Had *God* set hers and Jake's race of marriage?

"What therefore God hath joined together, let not man put asunder." Matthew 19:6 was like a giant gong going off in her head.

Then the guest speaker's key verse repeated itself in her mind.

"Let us run with endurance the race that God has set before us. . . . Don't become weary and give up."

Ever since she'd read this scripture in her gazebo—the day she received Jake's letter—it had come to her mind repeatedly, morning, noon, and night. She simply couldn't get away from it. It haunted her—no, taunted her. Why did the speaker have to use *this* scripture, of all the scriptures in the Bible?

"Because I'm trying to get through to you," the Lord seemed to whisper. *"Please heed My voice, Felicia."*

Her program slipped out of her hand and floated to the floor.

Felicia hurried down the aisle in the throng of people. She was supposed to meet Cara and Justin on the front steps of the auditorium. They were riding with her to the restaurant.

"Felicia!"

She paused, turned, and saw Jake. He was about ten people behind her.

He waved her black sweater in the air. "You forgot this."

She saw the rest of the family far ahead of her, nearly to the lobby. But she'd do Jake the courtesy of waiting for him. She figured Cara and Justin wouldn't mind waiting a few extra minutes for her. She stepped into a long row of seats. From her peripheral vision, she watched Jake approach her. She didn't want to look at him straight on.

He caught up to her and joined her in the row of seats. "Here." He held out her sweater.

"Thanks." She took the sweater from him, still averting her eyes. She had hoped she wouldn't come face-to-face with him this evening, especially the two of them alone. Now, that very thing had happened.

"You must've forgotten it." He gestured. "Your sweater."

"I—I did. It got so hot during the ceremony, I didn't need to use it—"

"Hot? Cara was so cold I had to give her my jacket."

Felicia remembered the things she thought about during the ceremony. She looked down, making a production of folding her sweater just right across her forearm.

"Felicia?"

She tugged at the folded sweater, working on pulling one end so it hung just right. She pulled the sweater the other way, toward her wrist, so it lined up with her watchband.

"Felicia, you—"

A cowbell sounded in the crowd.

She looked up at Jake quickly, their gazes locking. She felt flustered.

His eyes seemed to caress her. "You—you look beautiful tonight. Stunning, in fact."

The cowbell sounded again.

She looked away. "Th–thank you." Her voice was so soft, she wasn't sure he'd heard her.

"What did you say?" He leaned closer, nearly touching her.

She could smell his minty breath from the close proximity. And his cologne. She pushed memories away, telling them they had no place in her heart. "Thank you, Jake. That's kind of you."

"I appreciate your giving Curtis the party at the house. It was better than any party you've ever thrown. And that's saying a lot, because you're good at it. You're the queen of party-throwers."

"I'm. . .glad I did it." She touched her sweater. "Thanks." She mumbled something about needing to hurry, brushed past him, and joined the rush of people making their way to the lobby.

All the way down the long aisle, she couldn't help thinking about Jake. He had been. . .tender?

Jake drove to the restaurant, singing in his heart the old hymn he'd sung or whistled for days now.

Trust and obey. . . .

That's all he could do. Trust. He had tried to strike up a conversation with Felicia in the auditorium, but she had been mum except for a couple of sentences.

"Commit thy way unto the Lord," he recited in his head.

"Trust also in him; and he shall bring it to pass."

Oh, she looked beautiful tonight, with her skinny black dress and gleaming pearls and black hosiery and spiky high heels. Her blond hair was in some sort of updo. A French twist, didn't they call it? Nice. Of course, he preferred her hair soft and swingy. With a little thrill, he remembered all the times he'd run his fingers through it, wished he could have done it as he stood there talking to her tonight.

She looked like she was sent down from heaven.

Oh, Felicia, please come back to me.

Felicia sat at the long table in Chalet Renee with their family members and some of Curtis's friends, orders taken, the blessing offered, the salads eaten. Jake was directly across from her. It couldn't be helped. When they arrived at the restaurant, she went to the restroom, and by the time she got to the table, it was the only seat left.

Three waiters working together set the entrées in front of them, lobster and shrimp for Felicia and several others. Some had blackened grouper or stuffed flounder.

"This seafood was caught not far from here." Jake good-naturedly elbowed his brother. "Don't you wish you lived in Florida, little brother? Instead of Kansas?"

His brother elbowed him back. "Not in the summer, thank you very much."

"What do you mean?" A twinkle formed in Jake's eyes. "Down here, it's 72 degrees year-round—72 in our cars, 72 in our houses, 72 at the office. . . ."

His brother laughed, as did the others at the table.

"Your garden is beautiful, Felicia," said her sister-in-law, Charlotte. "I didn't get to tell you earlier when we were out there enjoying the hors d'oeuvres this afternoon."

"Thanks, Charlotte." Felicia dipped a piece of lobster in melted butter.

"You must work out there all the time. It looks like something right out of a gardening magazine. Your flowers—they're gorgeous. I've never seen so many varieties in a backyard. Reminds me of the Biltmore House in North Carolina. You must really like gardening."

Felicia nodded. "I do. I've enjoyed working with flowers since I was a teenager. That's when my gardening hobby started."

"You must know everything there is to know about flowers, from the looks of things."

"Well, not everything. But through the years, I've tried to read as many books as I could on gardening. When something's important to you, you invest as much time and energy and thought into it as you can."

"You're a master, all right."

"I work at it. Hard."

"That's apparent."

❋

As Jake watched Felicia climb into her SUV, the question came to him. He had to ask her. He bounded toward her and stopped at her vehicle. "Felicia?"

Seated behind the steering wheel with the door open, she glanced his way. "Yes?"

He took in her appearance again. Wow, she looked beautiful tonight. Her black dress was riding high on her thighs—he couldn't help noticing. He was a man, wasn't he? And she'd kicked off her high heels, and he could see her red toenails through her sheer black hosiery. Wow. . .

"Jake?"

He tried to collect his thoughts. What was it he wanted to ask her?

She turned the key in the ignition.

Now I remember. "Felicia—"

"I need to be going. Cara and Justin are riding with Curtis and his friends, and they're all headed to the house, and I told them I'd pop some popcorn and make fudge for them. I think they're going to rent a movie."

Jake nodded somberly. "I wanted to ask you a question. If you have a minute."

She looked toward the front of the restaurant. "Curtis is still inside, so I'm safe. But I need to hurry."

He took a deep breath. "Do you. . ." Okay, he would blurt it out. "Do you like me at least as much as you like your begonias?" He watched her carefully as her expression changed. Was she exasperated with him? *Oh no. Now I've done it.*

Her eyebrows drew together like she was in deep thought. Then she smiled and burst into bright, bubbly laughter. She laughed and laughed.

He joined in with her laughter, not because what he said was funny but because her laughter was so contagious.

She held her ribs, still belly chuckling. Mascara smears

dotted her cheeks, and she dabbed at them.

He was puzzled.

"Oh, Jake." She wound her laughter down.

"I. . ." He looked at the ground. Women. What a mystery. He looked back up at her.

"It's just that this is the first time we've laughed together in eons."

"Well, do you?"

"Do I what?"

"Do you like me at least as much as you like your begonias?"

She looked like she was going to go into her hyena fit again. But then her expression grew serious. "Yes."

"That *was* a yes, wasn't it?" He was smiling. From ear to ear.

She nodded, twinkles dancing in her eyes.

Later, as he made his way toward his motel, he whistled an old tune.

I'm getting married in the morning. . . .

Funny that Jake should mention begonias. She knew he meant flowers in general, because he didn't know a begonia from a daisy.

Begonias? She'd never planted them. For some reason, they'd never appealed to her.

She laughed again at what had just happened between them. *Oh, Jake.*

Chapter 11

Sitting in the quaint tearoom with Kate, her friend from church and coteacher in Sunday school, Felicia took a bite of her chicken salad.

"I'm glad we could get together, Felicia." Kate dabbed at her lips with her linen napkin. "I've missed you so much."

"I've missed you, too, Kate."

"I would've called, but I wanted to respect your privacy. Curtis told me you wanted time away from everyone to think things through."

"I did. But I believe I'm ready to return to church now."

"That's good news. The kids in our Sunday school class keep asking where you are."

"I shouldn't have left so abruptly. I—I. . ."

"No need to explain. The important thing is, you're headed in the right direction."

"You're a real friend, Kate. And one who's guided by the Lord. I'm thankful for you."

"You'll find some answers soon. I have a good feeling."

Later, as Felicia left the restaurant, she clung to Kate's positive words.

❀

Felicia propped her pillows against the headboard and reached for the little book Kate had given her that day at lunch. *Never Let It End: Poems of a Lifelong Love* by Ruth Bell Graham.

"I saw it in the Christian bookstore," Kate had told her, "and, well, I bought it for you."

Felicia opened the little book. She couldn't sleep, so she might as well read. A half hour later, she was on her knees beside her bed, hands folded and tears in her eyes.

"I've been so selfish, Lord," she prayed. "Please forgive me. And I've been so wrong. I looked to Jake for my happiness all these years when I should've been looking to You."

For long minutes, she poured her heart out to God. Then she felt peace flood her soul. She climbed back into bed.

"Lord, concerning Jake and our marriage, I—I'm open to—to—whatever You bring about."

Chapter 12

H ello?"

"Hi, Felicia. This is Jake. How are you? Having a good afternoon?"

"Yes, I am. I just planted some begonias."

"Like the ones under the oak tree?"

"No. Those are impatiens. Impatiens have to have shade, but begonias can take the full sun."

"Oh."

"I put in a new begonia bed by the lamppost in the front yard." Ever since he'd asked her if she liked him at least as much as she liked begonias, she'd been thinking about planting some. Though they weren't her favorite flower, they were hale and hardy. And she had to admit they produced lots of color—for a long time. They would withstand the summer sun and endure for the entire growing season.

"Did you dig out the grass by yourself? That St. Augustine floratam can be a doozy to deal with. It's as thick as all get-out."

"No. Curtis did it for me." She was surprised that Jake was asking about her gardening. He was showing interest in the things she cared about? Nice.

"Good. What'd you edge it with?"

"Cedar strips, the kind that are joined by wire. They were easy to put in."

"What color flowers did you plant?"

"Pink and white."

"Sounds nice." He paused. "I saw you at church this morning."

"As of today, I'm back. I taught my class with Kate, and then I sat with her in the service."

"I'm glad you're back."

"Thanks, Jake."

"I was wondering. . . Would you. . .go to dinner with me tonight? After the evening service? Since we get out before eight o'clock, that would give us a couple of hours maybe. I know you like to get to bed early on a school night, but I was wondering—"

"I'll go."

"You will?"

"Yes."

"Yahoo!"

She laughed, and he did, too.

"I'll see you after church tonight," he said. "By the information desk? Is that a convenient place to meet?"

"Sounds like a good plan to me."

"A *very* good plan."

"Where to?"

Felicia did a double take at Jake where he sat behind the wheel. *You're asking me? You're considering my feelings? What a change.*

"What if we drive over to Florida Springs? That suit you? I haven't been there in a long time, but they have a new restaurant. It's Greek. I read about it in the paper. That okay with you? If not, we'll go anywhere you want. What do you think?"

"The Greek restaurant sounds good."

Mile after mile they talked, with him asking her questions about her school and classes, her gardening, and more, then listening as she answered.

You're different, Jake.

They pulled into the little town of Florida Springs, then into the parking lot of a fancy Greek restaurant. Only it was closed.

"Ax that." Jake wheeled back onto the road. "Now what?"

"We can drive around and look."

"Maybe we should drive back to Palmdale."

"I'm kind of hungry."

"Me, too. We'll find something over here in Small Town, USA. Look." He pointed. "There's a pizza place. Feel like pizza?"

"No."

"Me neither. Barbecue?" He gestured to his right.

"Um. Not really. I was thinking about veggies. And maybe a salad."

152

"There." He tipped his head sideways. "Hodges Family Buffet. How's that sound?"

"Perfect."

"I'm envisioning broccoli and black-eyed peas and corn and carrots and all kinds of vegetables."

"Right up my alley."

"I know."

Felicia was enjoying his. . .wooing. An old-fashioned word, but it fit—his tenderness and attention and small courtesies like letting her decide where they'd eat.

After they parked, he opened her car door and touched her elbow as they walked toward the restaurant. "This restaurant must have some kind of good eating, from the looks of the crowd."

She nodded. Down the sidewalk snaked a line of people, at least twenty-five or thirty.

The whole time they waited, they talked. She warmed to the flow of conversation between them. Occasionally she would glance up at him. He reminded her of a wet-behind-the-ears boy in love with his ready smile, his playful looks, and his easy banter. And she reminded herself of. . .a teenager. . .who was enjoying her first brush with love?

"Felicia? Did you hear me?"

"You caught me daydreaming."

"I said we're almost to the door."

"Oh."

The hostess came out of the restaurant and turned to Jake. "Are you a party of two?"

Jake nodded.

"You're next. Please wait here while I escort the party in front of you to their table. I'll be right back."

"Thanks."

The hostess turned and headed back inside, gesturing to the party ahead to follow her.

The entrance clear now, Felicia spotted a sign by the door of the restaurant. It struck her so funny she broke out into loud, spontaneous laughter. She couldn't help herself.

"What're you laughing at?" Jake started laughing, too. Hard.

She pointed at the sign. MANAGEMENT WILL NOT BE RESPONSIBLE FOR BROKEN TEETH.

She laughed so hard, tears came to her eyes. "I'm envisioning pecan hulls in the pie. What about you?"

"Metal in the meat loaf?"

She dabbed at her eyes, knowing her mascara must be trailing.

"Maybe we should leave."

"I'm too hungry. I'll take the risk."

"I'll take the risk with you." He looked straight into her eyes, his voice husky.

She broke their intense stare, knowing exactly what he was talking about. *Risk*. It didn't have anything to do with food.

Chapter 13

T hanks for taking me to the home and patio show, Jake."
Felicia glanced across the table at him. They'd had a
full day of looking at everything to do with homes and
gardens, from flooring and window and kitchen displays to
patio furniture, swimming pools, and new landscaping ideas.
They had been together all day, just the two of them. Now
they were having an early evening meal. "I thoroughly enjoyed
the day."

"Felicia. . . ?"

She lifted her eyebrows in response.

"I enjoyed it, too. Immensely."

She averted her eyes, a warmness seeping over her. They'd
had three dates in the last week. Each one had been more
romantic than the last, if that was possible. Though they hadn't
even held hands, Jake had given her special attention and made
her feel cherished. *That's what romance means. And that's what
my heart craves.*

"It wasn't *just* because I was with you. I actually liked seeing the new home products." He stopped abruptly. "I'm sorry. I didn't mean it that way. It came out wrong—"

"It's okay, Jake." *If you only knew how much that statement means to me.* He was taking an interest in the things she liked, and she knew it was genuine and not pretend. She could read Jake Higgins like a book. He was really trying.

The waitress brought their food, then left.

"Shall we pray?" He reached across the table and took her hand. "Lord, we thank You for this food. . . ."

Felicia squelched a shiver. The moment Jake touched her hand, she felt a spark, like electricity flowing between them. Though they'd eaten together at the family buffet in Florida Springs, he hadn't taken her hand during the blessing, their custom for the past twenty-four years.

"Amen." He released her hand and looked surprised. "I'm sorry. I didn't mean to show disrespect. I grabbed your hand out of force of habit, not for any romantic overture." He reddened slightly. "That came out wrong. It *did* feel romantic—but that's not why I did it. Oh, I'm making a mess of this. I'm sorry."

"Jake, it's okay."

He smiled. "I remember hearing those words a few minutes ago. I seem to be saying 'I'm sorry' a lot this evening—sorry for saying I enjoyed going with you today and sorry for holding your hand. . . ."

"Then don't say you're sorry anymore, at least for things like that, especially that second 'I'm sorry.'"

"You mean"—he leaned closer—"I shouldn't have said, 'I'm sorry for holding your hand'?"

"Right." Her answer came out on a breathy sigh, and a little thrill surged through her.

❋

Felicia shifted positions on the blanket. For this date, Jake had suggested a sunset picnic on the beach. Looking like a scoop of orange sherbet, the sun had dropped into the Gulf of Mexico amid a sky brilliant with corals, pinks, blues, grays, and whites. Now, nearly dark, their deli bags in the nearby trash can, they sat peacefully on the blanket, enjoying the ocean breezes and pleasant conversation.

"Felicia, I've learned a lot of things these past weeks."

"I have, too."

"I've been reading books on marriage."

"Ditto."

"You have?" He scooped up a handful of sand and let it slide through his fingers. "I guess we should've been doing that all along."

She nodded. "I think it was my conversation with Charlotte that got me to thinking about it. At Chalet Renee."

"What'd she say?"

"Oh, it wasn't anything about marriage. But in a way it was. We were talking about gardening, and I told her my hobby started when I was a teenager. She complimented my garden and said that I must know everything there was to know about flowers. I told her that through the years, I'd read as many books as I could on gardening."

He smiled. "You could start a library."

She smiled back, shifted again, brushed up against him

accidentally, then righted herself. She repressed a shiver, and it wasn't from the wind. "I told her when something's important to you, you invest as much time and energy into it as you can. Late that night, it hit me that it's the same way with marriage. That's when I started reading books about marriage. Like I said, I'm learning a lot. And I'm glad to hear that you are, too."

"One thing I've learned is that women need time, tenderness, and talk. I've tried to give you those things lately."

"I noticed." A gust of wind caught strands of her hair and blew them into her face.

He reached over and tucked the strands behind her ear, then dropped his hand as if he'd been touched by a hot coal. "Felicia, I—I can't afford to touch you." His voice grew husky. "You know what I mean?"

She nodded, knowing full well what he meant as her heart nearly beat out of her chest. She was falling in love with Jake, just as she'd done twenty-four years ago. The man was like a giant magnet, drawing her to him.

Neither said anything for long moments.

He broke the silence. "I have a lot more to learn."

"Me, too."

"So tell me. What are some things you've learned from the marriage books?"

"I've learned that it's entirely possible for husbands and wives to be opposites and yet happy, that in fact, many married couples are that way. I thought husbands and wives had to spend all their free time together in order to have a good marriage. I thought they had to see eye to eye on everything. That's where a lot of my unhappiness stemmed from—"

"I'm going to be as tender as all get-out when we get. . ." He stopped abruptly. "I shouldn't be presuming that we're going to. . .get back together. I'm sorry."

"There you go again. Saying you're sorry."

"I could say it throughout eternity, and it wouldn't make up for my—my lack in our marriage." He trailed his finger down her arm, from shoulder to wrist. Then he scooted away from her, leaving at least two feet between them. "I promised myself I won't touch you. If I let myself, I would—oh, never mind."

Her heart fluttered. *Oh, Jake.* She was falling in love with the Jake she had first fallen in love with. And she knew this could only lead to one thing—coming back together as husband and wife.

Things were looking good between them. Check.

They were enjoying each other's company. Check.

The sparks between them were bonfire-bright. Check. Check. Check.

But was she ready for this?

He leaned back on one arm, his long legs stretched out in front of him. "I love how we laugh together, Felicia. I love spending time with you. I love our conversations." He let out a long sigh. "I missed out on a lot when we were married—I mean, when we were living together. We're still man and wife."

Man and wife? She felt her face grow warm at the thought. *I'm missing out on a lot right now.*

"Like I said, I love what's happening between us. And there's something else I love, Felicia. You."

159

In one fell swoop, she slid over to him and wrapped her arms around him. She gave him a long, slow, heart-palpitating kiss.

"Wow!" He kissed her forever, it seemed, then drew back sharply. "Felicia, we can't do that." He was breathing hard, his chest heaving.

Her chest heaved, too, and she wished he would continue kissing her.

Suddenly he chuckled.

"What are you laughing about?" She certainly didn't feel like laughing. She felt like loving—him.

"Can't help it. A memory kicked in. I feel like I did when we were dating. Remember? It was so hard, trying to refrain from—"

"Physical relations. But we made it all the way to our wedding day."

"And then along came the Holiday Inn, thank You, Jesus." He laughed again, and she joined in with his laughter.

He hugged her, and they kept laughing, and they fell back on the blanket, the two of them giddy teenagers again. They lay there, staring up at the black velvet sky that was studded with stars, still laughing and talking about laughing together, rehearsing the time he had asked her if she liked him as much as she liked her begonias, and the time they saw the sign in front of the restaurant about broken teeth.

He turned toward her, their bodies stretched out and parallel. He traced her jawline with his finger.

She was alive to him—wanted him—and a shudder started

at her toes and worked up to her heart.

"Felicia. I said a minute ago how hard it was to refrain from. . .relations when we were dating. It's harder now, after a lifetime of loving you." He touched her ear, then the other one, trailed his finger down her neck, touched the tendrils of hair hanging on her shoulder. "Much more difficult."

She nodded, too breathless for words at this moment.

He kissed her, slowly and sensuously.

Jake, Jake, Jake. Surely the breath was being sucked out of her body.

He jumped to his feet, towering over her. "I made a promise to God that from now on, no matter what happens to our marriage, I'll try and put you and your feelings ahead of my own."

She sat up, brushing sand off her knit shirt, then her jeans.

"Tonight, I'm making a promise to you, too. I promise not to touch you again until you ask me to. I don't know how I'll manage to do that, but somehow I'll find a way."

She got to her feet. She was ready to ask now, at this moment. After all, they were married. They could drive straight to their house, to their bedroom—but wisdom said to wait. But wait on what? What more had to transpire before they could come together as man and wife?

"It's getting late. Are you ready?" His voice dripped with tender feelings.

You don't know how ready I am, Jake.

"Felicia?"

"I—I guess I need to be getting home, too. I told Curtis I'd jog with him. I told him we'd jog at least a few times around the circle."

❋

"I'm beat," Jake said to himself as he pulled down the bedspread in his motel room. "I guess that's what happens to you when you live alone. You start talking to yourself." He laughed. "I'll have to tell Felicia about this. She'll get a laugh, too."

His heart warmed. Felicia, his wife, the mother of his children, his sweetheart since his teenage years, was back in his life. Life couldn't be any better.

He smiled. "Oh yes it can." Visions of them wrapped in each other's arms appeared before his eyes. "Felicia, my darling, just say the word. Oh, please say the word."

❋

As Felicia jogged with Curtis, she contemplated her and Jake's future. If this was the Lord's doings for them to get back together—and she was sure it was, because God desired marriages to stay intact—then He would work everything out.

Lord, she silently prayed, *I'm willing to reenter the race of marriage that You have set before us. Now lead and guide us both. In Jesus' name. Amen.*

Chapter 14

Felicia checked herself in the full-length mirror. New jeans—a perfect fit. Red knit top—just right. Open-toe, backless heels—a nice showcase for her French pedicure.

She scanned upward. Hair: silky and voluminous from her shampoo and new conditioner. Makeup: becoming. Jewelry: simple earrings, necklace, and bracelet, plus her watch and rings. Rings?

She twisted her wedding rings on the third finger of her left hand. What did her and Jake's future hold? *I know in my heart what's supposed to happen. But how? When?*

R—r—r—ring.

She flipped off the bedroom light and headed for the front door. It must be Jake.

She opened the door.

"Hi." His arms laden with grocery sacks, he beamed a bright smile at her. "Wow, do you look gorgeous." His gaze roamed her figure.

"Thank you." She felt her face growing warm as she stood back and gestured for him to come inside. "Curtis is outside firing up the grill."

"Great. I'm starved." He stepped into the foyer. "I'm as hungry as can be."

"Curtis is, too." She touched her stomach. "And I'm famished myself."

He held up the grocery sacks. "Where do you want me to put this stuff?"

"The kitchen." She walked toward the back of the house. "But I told you, you didn't have to bring the food—"

"I wanted to." He followed along behind her. "Steaks. And I got the baked potatoes, salad, and bread from Outback. I didn't want you to have to do a thing. Except make sweet iced tea. And how I've missed your tea. Nobody makes it like you do. You *did* make some, didn't you?"

"I sure did."

"The two things you fix that I've missed the most are your sweet iced tea and your chocolate chip cookies."

"I made those, too."

"You did?"

Immediately she felt sheepish. "Well, I. . .know how much you like them."

Their gazes locked. In a million years, she couldn't describe his look. She only knew it sent tingles racing down her spine.

"Felicia—"

"Mom, the coals are ready."

She forced herself to break their intense stare, glanced at

the French doors, and saw Curtis standing there.

After dinner, Jake helped Felicia in the kitchen. He could count on one hand the times he'd done that in their marriage. He regretted it sorely.

He followed her into the family room at her invitation. He wanted to be careful about where he sat, wanting to respect her feelings. The recliner? No, she might think he was being forward—brash and brawny was how she referred to it, like he was taking over the place. He chose the sofa. Much safer.

She sat in her chair—a Lawson chair, she called it—and put her feet up on the matching ottoman. "The steaks were delicious."

"So was the sweet iced tea."

For thirty minutes they sat there, pleasantly conversing.

Why didn't you do this before, you big oaf? Why'd you always have that stupid TV blaring?

"Are you ready for your cookies now?"

"And how! Can we have some decaf with them?"

"Sure." She stood up.

"I'll make it." He followed her into the kitchen. "I can make coffee now. Believe that? I do it every morning. In my motel room. It has a kitchenette." At her lack of response, he knew he sounded like the spoiled husband he'd been, a husband who suffered with the malady of For-granted-itis. He groaned inwardly.

"The decaf's in the freezer. In the door. I keep it there because it stays fresher."

In minutes, the aroma of fresh-perked coffee filled the kitchen.

"Umm," he said.

"I love the smell of coffee, too."

"You're the only person I know who stands in front of the coffeepot and watches it drip."

She smiled. "Now don't start that."

He smiled back. It was an old family joke about her. His brother had noticed her doing that—on a visit here years ago—and had teased her relentlessly through the years.

"I only did that one time, and you know it." She stuck out her tongue at him, her eyes dancing.

"Yeah, right," he bantered back. He remembered her explanation. Curtis was a baby and had kept her up half the night with an ear infection. At daylight, he got her up again, and she decided she needed some caffeine to keep her awake. She'd stood and watched the coffeepot drip, and his brother had found her there.

"It smells so good." She breathed in the aroma as she placed cookies on a small silver tray. She pulled down two mugs.

"Can we eat outside?"

"Sure." She reached down to a bottom cabinet and pulled out a thermal carafe. "Coffee ready?"

"Done. Here. I'll pour it in the carafe. Hand it here."

Soon they were seated in the gazebo, eating her delicious cookies, a full moon above them and the scent of Confederate jasmine so thick you could cut it with a butter knife.

Jake breathed in deeply, surveying the surroundings. *I didn't know I'd have this kind of ambience to pop the question. Hurray for me.*

He finished off one more cookie, then turned toward her where she sat on the other end of the bench. A six-inch gap separated them. Good. There would be no temptation for her to base her decision on the physical realm. It would be cerebral only. And heartfelt, of course.

He dropped to his knees in front of her. "Felicia, will you. . ." He was stumped. Marry him? No. They were married. Remarry him? No. They weren't divorced. He hadn't expected this.

It was then that she got the giggles.

He laughed, too. But he didn't see anything humorous. This was a serious moment.

She finally quit laughing. "I'm sorry. Everything struck me funny. You on your knees—a middle-aged man. And us married but not married, and me wondering how you're going to word this. . ."

A tender look passed between them.

He rose to his feet and sat on his end of the bench. He wouldn't take her in his arms—as he longed to do—because he promised he wouldn't touch her until she said the word. But he *would* ask her to become man and wife again. Somehow.

"What *are* you going to say?" She giggled again.

"I—I'm going to tell you how deeply I love you—as deep as the ocean and as high as the heavens. I'm going to tell you how much I adore you, how I want to please you and make you happy. I'm going to ask you to be my wife—again."

"I accept."

"You do?"

"Yes."

"She said yes!" He grinned so widely he thought his face would crack in half. "Felicia, this makes me want to leap for joy."

"I feel the same way," she said in her characteristic quiet manner.

"I thought I'd have to try to convince you. I didn't know it would be this easy. Thank you—my darling." He paused. "The marriage books tell you to call your mate endearing terms. That's not like me. You know it. But things are going to be different from here on out."

She told him about the scripture that had become so real to her, the one in Hebrews about not becoming weary and giving up. She said the Lord had made it come alive for her as she sat here in the gazebo. "This will always be our special place, Jake. I found hope for our marriage, and I found"—she smiled at him—"you."

"Maybe we can come out here every evening before bedtime and talk awhile." He glanced up at the cupola in the cone-shaped roof, looked around the gazebo, and wiggled his eyebrows. "Maybe we can install a hot tub out here."

Another tender look passed between them.

He cleared his throat. "Like I said a minute ago, things are going to be different for us this time. I've learned a lot."

She nodded. "I hope to put some new things into practice, too. We need to go into this armed with tools to help us so we can succeed this go-round."

"I couldn't agree more." He longed to kiss her, to hold her, to caress her. But that would come. In its own time.

"There's one tool I feel we need before we retie the knot."

"What's that?"

"An in-depth marriage retreat. It's called 'Hope and Healing for Hurting Couples.' I read about it in the new issue of *Christian Woman Today*."

"But we don't need that. We're on sure footing. I've changed. And you said you have, too. We're going to make it this time."

"There won't be a *this* time if you don't go with me to this retreat." Steel was in her voice. "I've thought it through, and this is what I'm going to require."

He felt like he'd been hit by a fullback. This was a matter of trust. And if she didn't trust him now, what hope was there for their relationship?

"The retreat's in Colorado. It lasts for three days."

"It's not necessary for us to go to a retreat. Things are great between us. We laugh together, we spend time together, we—"

"It takes more than that, Jake. We've got to get to the underlying issues—"

"What underlying issues?"

She rolled her eyes. "That proves my point." She stacked their dessert plates and mugs with a loud *clank* and stood up.

"All right, already. I'll go."

"Dragging your heels." She stood there staring down at him, and this time there were no tender looks or romantic sparks passing between them. "I wanted you to embrace this idea."

"I—I'll try." He slowly rose to his feet.

"I guess that's all I can ask for." She turned and headed toward the house.

❋

Early the next morning, Felicia grabbed her Bible and slipped outside in her bathrobe. Her backyard was the place to reflect. And to recant?

She sat on a lawn chair in her English garden. She'd designed it to look like a garden she'd seen outside of London, on the only trip she'd taken without Jake, several years ago. She'd fallen in love with England and had always wanted to go back.

She remembered Jake reciting an old nursery rhyme on their first night together after she returned from Great Britain.

"Pussycat, pussycat, where have you been?"

"I've been to London, to see the queen."

She pushed the thought away. Weightier matters pressed, heavier than a truckload of mulch. She held her Bible, trying hard to trust. In the Lord. In Jake. In their relationship.

"If he's not willing to do this small thing for me," she whispered, "how can I commit to him? It'll be the same old, same old."

She glanced at the tangerine-colored daylilies she'd planted this week. A scripture came to mind, one she learned as a child but hadn't quoted in a long time.

"Consider the lilies of the field. . .they toil not, neither do

170

they spin." That was all she could remember by heart, but she knew the verse had something to do with the Lord caring for His own.

She scanned her concordance for *lilies*, found the passage in Matthew 6, and read portions of it.

> *"Even Solomon in all his glory was not arrayed like one of these. Wherefore, if God so clothe the grass of the field, which today is, and to morrow is cast into the oven, shall he not much more clothe you, O ye of little faith? . . . But seek ye first the kingdom of God, and his righteousness; and all these things shall be added unto you. Take therefore no thought for the morrow."*

She closed her Bible, her finger marking the page, and held the Holy Book heavenward. "Okay, Lord. If You can clothe my lilies, You can take care of me. And Jake."

Chapter 15

The leader of the three-day marriage retreat stood behind the podium in the auditorium, staring out at the seventy-five couples. "Yesterday it was in-depth teaching. Today it'll be knee-to-knee time."

That's the best part of this whole retreat. Jake smiled to himself. *I still haven't touched her. Even on the long flight out here.*

"You're going to put into practice some of the things you learned yesterday." The leader gave instructions about what they were to do in the knee-to-knee time and which rooms they were to go to.

"Pick up your discussion starters and rules as you leave. You're dismissed to go to your assigned rooms." The leader glanced at his watch. "We'll meet back here at eleven thirty for a short session, and then we'll go to lunch."

Twenty minutes later, Jake was seated across from Felicia in a metal folding chair, their knees almost touching. They were surrounded by couples in the same position. Advisors roamed the room. "They'll give pointers," the leader had said.

"You want me to start this?" Jake held the small green card in his hand, signifying he had the floor—how they'd been trained for this exercise.

She nodded but didn't say a word.

"I know. You can't talk while I have the card."

She nodded again.

"I'm supposed to talk several minutes, and then I'm to give you the card and you're to repeat what I said to you. You going to take this card home with us and whip it out every time we turn around?" He smiled.

She smiled back, then scribbled on her workbook and pointed to it, indicating for him to read it.

"As often as I need to," he read aloud. "Maybe even during Monday night football."

He laughed, then grew serious. "The directions say this exercise is supposed to train us to clearly communicate and also to listen and clearly understand what our mates are saying to us."

She nodded.

He glanced down at the directions. "Approximately every ten minutes," he read from the instructions, "hand the other partner the card and let him or her take the lead in the discussion, choosing whatever subject he or she would like."

He scanned a long list on one of the pages, chose a subject, and began.

Felicia couldn't believe how fast the time had flown. The morning session was history. So was lunch. Now they were in the afternoon knee-to-knee session.

"Each partner is to pour out your heart to your mate," Jake had read to her at the start of the sessions this morning. "Tell him or her exactly how you're feeling. Touch on areas in which you need to improve. State the steps you are going to take to achieve this. Then let the other partner do the same thing."

Felicia couldn't believe her eyes. *Jake is crying.* Never had she seen him do this. He was weeping as he admitted his failings to her, and it made her cry.

She glanced around covertly, saw other couples reacting the same way, and didn't feel as uncomfortable as she thought she would. In fact, she heard distinct sobs coming from all over the room.

Hope and healing. That's what's happening right here. Right now. For us. Hurting couples. Just like the name of the retreat promised.

On and on Jake went, doing what the instructions said. He poured out his heart to her. He told her how proud he was of her. She was so smart in so many ways, he said, and he'd always been proud of her. But he'd failed to tell her so. He'd also failed to compliment her. He talked about his lack of tenderness. He mentioned his failure to show the interest in her that she needed him to. He confessed his pride.

"I was full of pride." He unashamedly dabbed at his tears, the whites of his eyes showing little red lines from weeping. "I didn't want to go to marriage counseling, even though you begged me to, because of pride. I didn't want to see the pastor after you asked me to move out because of pride. But the biggest evidence of my pride was not wanting to come to this retreat. Felicia, this is the best thing that's ever happened to me, to us. Thank you for insisting that we come. It's opened my eyes."

"I've failed, too," Felicia said when it was her turn. She talked about her misconceptions about marriage and her unreasonable and unhealthy expectations. "I thought we had to be identical twins in marriage, you know, doing everything together, thinking alike, being alike. I thought that's what made a good marriage. I guess I thought that way because I know a few couples like that. Stacy, my teacher friend, brags about her relationship with her second husband. She says that's exactly how they are. But I read lots of books on marriage, and they said sometimes that *does* occur in a marriage, but lots of times it doesn't. I was misinformed and mistaken. I didn't leave any room in my thinking for our individual personalities and interests."

Jake looked contemplative. "And the real truth of the matter is that we have the most important things in common. Those are the things we need to focus on, right? Isn't that what we learned at this retreat?"

She nodded. "Our faith, our career goals, and our values."

"The most important areas of commonalities."

She nodded again, then continued on, confessing her faults. She told him she'd made him carry the burden of providing her happiness, which wasn't right. "As the teacher said yesterday, no person, place, or thing can make anyone happy. Only Jesus can give us deep-down, genuine happiness. I was putting that burden on you, and that was wrong."

"But I'm going to try to make you happy—darling. I'm going to pay more attention to you. I'm going to go more places with you. I'm going to free you to go to places you like, too. And I'm going to—"

Tenderly she touched his lips. "I love you, Jake."

"I love you, Felicia."

She talked at length about more of her shortcomings. She readily admitted her fault in their temporary separation. "I got my eyes off the Lord. I don't ever want to do that again. I had so much going for me in our marriage. I just didn't realize it. I was concentrating on the things I *didn't* have rather than the things I did. Oh, Jake, will you forgive me?"

"A millions times over. When we get back, I'd like us to get some marriage counseling. We need to reinforce what we've learned here."

"You really mean that?" She laughed and cried at the same time, so hard and so long she got the hiccups. He ran and got her some water, and they finally subsided.

They spent the rest of the session—thirty minutes—just looking at one another, drinking each other in.

She felt like reaching over and kissing him. But as she sat there looking at him, a plan formulated in her mind. . . .

Chapter 16

Felicia slipped on her wedding gown in the bride's room at Chalet Renee. Even after all these years, it was a perfect fit. Little shivers of excitement ran down her spine. Tonight she and Jake were celebrating their twenty-fifth wedding anniversary at a formal dinner. The kids had insisted on it, and Jake had asked her to wear her wedding gown.

"To signify a new start," he'd said with liquid eyes.

Six weeks ago, she and Jake had returned from the marriage retreat, and they'd gone to twice-weekly marriage counseling sessions ever since. Now they both felt they were on sure footing and ready to come together as man and wife.

Thank You, Lord, for healing my marriage. Tears misted her eyes as Cara buttoned up the back of her gown. *I give You praise and glory for all You've done for Jake and me.*

"Mom, you look fantastic." Cara backhanded a tear running down her cheek. "I'm so glad you and Dad are. . ." She laughed through her tears. "What *are* you doing tonight? You aren't getting married. And you aren't getting *remarried.*"

"We're getting reunited." It flew out of her mouth. And her heart. "Yes, that's it. Reunited. Coming together again. Rejoining."

Cara touched Felicia's sleeve where it ended in a point at her wrist. "Just think, Mom. You'll be buttoning up my wedding gown in a few short months."

"Look to Jesus for your happiness, Cara, not Justin. That's important in a marriage, for each partner. That's the key."

Cara nodded.

The door opened, and Felicia's mother walked in. "The emcee is ready for you. All set to go out there tonight and wow the crowd?"

Felicia smiled. "The only thing I want to do tonight is tell them how the Lord used a scripture to help me through this. 'Let us run with endurance the race that God has set before us. Don't become weary and give up.' Hebrews 12, verses 1 and 3." She paused. "And the other thing I want to do tonight is become Jake's wife again." *I'm ready. So ready.*

Later that night, after an evening of rejoicing with family and friends at Chalet Renee, Jake sat in the hotel suite, showered and changed into casual clothes. Felicia was in the shower now. He could hear the water running.

Tomorrow they were leaving for England, a favorite place of Felicia's. They would visit English gardens, shops, and historical sites. He didn't mind. As long as he was with Felicia. In fact, while looking into their travel plans, he'd discovered some interesting facts about his family, the Higginses. They hailed from England, and he was looking forward to doing some genealogical research.

He propped his feet on the ottoman and settled back into the comfortable chair. His mind meandered back to his and Felicia's dating days. He remembered when he first told her he loved her, and he thought about their first kiss. He recalled the night he asked her to marry him. He thought about their wedding and their honeymoon.

Honeymoon? He thumped on his chin. What had he recently read about honeymoons in one of those books about marriage?

Honey for a month? He smiled at the thought.

Felicia breezed out of the bathroom in a cloud of steam, wearing a pink satin robe.

He sat forward, his heart beating hard. He was about to begin a lifelong honeymoon with Felicia. He breathed in her flowery scent and took in her slim figure. Her blond hair had lost its slight curl on the ends from the steam, and it hung long and lanky on her shoulders, perfect for his fingers to run through. His breath came in short spurts envisioning it.

She stopped at her opened suitcase on the far side of the room and placed some items inside it.

Should he go to her? Say something to her? He wanted to do this the right way.

She walked toward him, stopped in front of him, then gestured for him to stand up.

He rose to his feet, feeling as nervous as a brand-new bridegroom. He wanted to show restraint, what he felt would convey his respect for her.

She came to him, then put her hands on his waist.

He didn't move, just probed her pale blue eyes where she stood at arm's length away from him. He remembered his promise to her. *"I won't touch you until you say the word."*

She brushed her lips across his in fine, feathery strokes, then drew back, love flowing from her eyes.

He thought his heart would burst from happiness.

"Come," she said.

The Beginning

KRISTY DYKES

A native Floridian, Kristy is an award-winning author, speaker, and former newspaper columnist. Her novel, *The Tender Heart* (Heartsong Presents), was a finalist in the Romance Writers of America Golden Quill Awards, and it won third place in the Barclay Gold Contest. "Shirley, Goodness, and Mercy," Kristy's novella in *Church in the Wildwood*, won third place in American Christian Fiction Writers 2004 Book of the Year contest (novella category). Her novellas have been on the CBA best-seller list and the top 20 list at christianbook.com. Kristy was voted as a favorite new author by readers in **Heartsong Presents** awards of 2004. She's written six hundred published articles, worked for two New York Times subsidiaries, and taught at many conferences and two colleges. She and her husband, Milton, a pastor, live in Florida. Kristy loves hearing from her readers. Write her at kristydykes@aol.com or c/o Author Relations—Barbour Publishing, P.O. Box 719, Uhrichsville, OH 44683.

love is a choice

by Sally Laity

Dedication

To all empty nesters who made it through the gloom and came out into the sunshine of God's love. May the joy of His presence be with you always.

"This is My commandment,
that you love one another as I have loved you."
JOHN 15:12 NKJV

Chapter 1

The house had never known such silence. Bess Wright shrugged off the somber thought as she approached the front door, one arm toting leftover refreshments from her youngest daughter's wedding. She turned her key in the lock of the L-shaped family home built in typical California contemporary style. October had come to an end, and as November took its place, multihued leaves clung to the huge fruitless mulberry and liquidambar trees that shaded the dwelling every summer, cooling the spacious haven that had always teemed with life.

Until today.

While her husband retrieved the remaining food from the car's trunk, memories of the day's festivities replayed in Bess's mind, along with some of her friends' remarks:

"Beautiful wedding. Just beautiful."

"Faith made such a lovely bride. She looked like a fairy princess."

"You outdid yourself, Bess. Four daughters married now. You and Art finally have the whole house to yourselves."

Yes, she commiserated. *The entire empty house to ourselves.*

The soft click of her heels echoed hollowly against the entry walls in the unnatural quiet. Such a contrast to the chaos of the past several months and the unbelievable jumble of plans and fittings involved in arranging a perfect event. Now that it was over and Bess could finally relax and take a deep breath, a whole new problem stared her in the face—one she'd refused to acknowledge before. How would she fill the endless hours yawning before her? She sighed as she placed her burdens on the tile counter and flicked on the oak kitchen's indirect lighting.

Arthur's sturdy footfalls grew louder as he approached the front door and came inside. "Free at last, Mother," he called cheerily, coming through the dining room and setting down the remains from the wedding reception. Tall and resplendent in his rented dove gray tux, he beamed and crossed his arms. The hair of his temples only recently had begun to silver, adding dignity to his already engaging appearance as unadulterated pleasure illuminated his patrician features.

Unable to manufacture even the most polite smile, Bess cringed. It was one thing to have him refer to her in a motherly capacity when four giggly little girls were underfoot, creating their particular kind of havoc. But here, now, when it no longer felt like she was anyone's mother—least of all *his*—the endearment irritated her.

Oblivious to the fragile state of her emotions, Arthur chuckled. "We did it. Palmed the last of the lot off on poor, unsuspecting Chad. The kid's so crazy in love, he doesn't have a clue what he's gotten himself into."

"I just hope they have nice weather for their honeymoon," Bess replied.

"Well, I for one have looked forward to this day for a long time." He loosened the violet satin bow tie he wore. "Now that there won't be any more young people conducting worship team practice out in the garage a couple times every week, I can take down the soundproofing that kept the neighbors mollified. Can't wait to have the place back for its intended purpose. Maybe I'll even get to use my workshop again."

"Right," she sniped, stacking Styrofoam containers on the refrigerator shelves. "But you'd better leave the soundproofing up. Power tools are just as irritating."

"Huh?" He turned a puzzled frown on her, a furrowed brow marring his otherwise happy expression.

Bess knew she'd spoken a touch harshly and felt her face warm as she gazed up into his blue eyes. Obviously he had no idea how much she'd dreaded this day that had arrived far too quickly. "Sorry. I know that's been your dream for months. It's just been a long afternoon."

He nodded. "Well, it's still early. Maybe I can catch the end of the Eagles game after I get out of this monkey suit," he announced, heading for the hall. "Sure could go for some coffee, when you have a minute."

Right. Business as usual. Bess squelched her annoyance and unpinned the corsage of white roses and violet carnations, placing the flowers in the fridge. It would be a relief to change out of her elegant dress into something more comfortable, too.

But before she'd taken her first step toward the bedroom, the phone rang, startling her in the stillness. Odd how the sound jarred her nerves.

Bess plucked the receiver from its cradle. "Hello?"

"Hi, dearie," came her mother's voice. "How'd everything go? Did we get our little Faithy all married right and proper?"

"Hi, Mom." She let out a pent-up breath. "Yes, the ceremony was just beautiful. You know what a stickler Faith is, always wanting everything perfect. Christina made sure Adam and Bethy carried out their duties as ring bearer and flower girl without a fuss. They really did look sweet. There was hardly a dry eye in the church. We all wished you could have been here." She paused. "How's your leg?"

"So-so. Still hurts like crazy. If there was any way I could have hobbled onto a plane with this ungainly cast from my toes to midthigh, believe me, I'd have been the first one at the church, I promise."

"We know that. Well, everyone took tons of pictures, as always, and Faith insisted on a video. We'll send you copies of everything so you'll be able to compare today's wedding to those of the other girls'. Maybe it'll make you feel like you were here for this one."

"I hope so. By the way, I'm not interrupting anything, am I? With the family, I mean. I thought maybe the others would come back with you and visit for a while."

"No. They were anxious to get home to their children—or in Christina's case, take the kids home after all the excitement. We're here by ourselves now."

"I suppose that's lucky for me, since you can let me know all the details while they're still fresh in your mind. It does make me feel old, though, having all my sweet granddaughters married now."

"I know what you mean. Seems only yesterday the doctor was putting my little twin babies in my arms and congratulating me on being a first-time mom. I couldn't wait to count Chrissy's and Dawn's fingers and toes. Where have the years gone?"

A moment of silence passed.

Bess cleared her throat. "Mom, can I ask you something?"

"What is it?"

"I don't know if I can put it into words. Did you feel—*strange*—when the last of us married? Did the house seem too quiet and neat when you came home? And did you feel. . . well. . .*useless*. . .all of a sudden? I mean, When Chrissy got married, I missed having her around, but I still had three other lively girls who needed me. Then when Dawn was a bride, I still had Eden and Faith. Now. . ." She sighed. "Do you know what I'm saying?"

Her mom gave a soft laugh. "You're not telling me anything I don't know about. We mothers spend so much time preparing our children to leave home and live in the real world, and when the day finally arrives, we want them to come back, have everything the way it was before, without change. I think it hurts most when the last of the lot is finally out of the nest."

Bess tried to turn her mental clock backward to the day of her own wedding, to picture her mother the way she'd been then, imagining her enduring a similar emotional seesaw. It was comforting, somehow, knowing someone before her had survived. "But how did you get through it all?" she had to ask.

"A day at a time. Years ago, there weren't so many opportunities for women in their middle years. Once a housewife, always a housewife. Nowadays, it seems gals have more freedom to delve into favorite hobbies or find new careers."

"New careers." Bess grimaced. "Even in this day and age, a person has to have qualifications, Mom. Can you picture me trying to compete with girls right out of business school who can take dictation at 120 words a minute and execute all types of computer programs with ease? Even if I did remember my high school shorthand, I could never keep up with a person speaking at a normal rate of speech—to say nothing of coping with the latest technological advancements. It's all I can do to operate a cell phone. Marrying right out of high school, I've only ever been a wife and mother. Never even went to college, unless you count that handful of night classes I took here and there. What kind of career could I hope to find now?"

"Well, you still are a wife, you know," came her mother's gentle reminder. "You still have Arthur to look after. Now that the girls are off living lives of their own, you two are free to do some of that traveling you never had time for before."

"On his three weeks' vacation?"

"And on weekends. I'm sure you'll find occasions to go off together."

Beth let out a huff. "He's tied down teaching our adult Sunday school class every week. Besides, he's already concocting grandiose plans to resurrect his workshop out in the garage and start a couple dozen projects. Of course," she added on a sarcastic note, "most of those will never see completion. They'll just join the pile of stuff he'll 'really have to break down and finish someday.' I don't know if I can stand it. You should see him— almost gleeful at the thought of this new freedom. It makes me want to scream. Right now he's so cheerful I can hardly abide being in the same room with him."

"Oh, don't say that, dear," her mom chided. "Not when you have so many blessings to count. Remember what a fine provider Arthur has always been. He's worked hard to make sure you had that lovely house you wanted, and he gave the girls the life he felt they deserved. None of you lacked for anything. I always appreciated the way he looked after you all."

As Bess listened, she glanced idly about the elegant rooms within her view. All were decorated with top-of-the-line furnishings in her own Victorian taste, which Arthur paid for without grumbling and put up with. Even though his preference leaned toward tailored, less fussy things, he'd never challenged her on anything.

"He's done his very best," her mother went on, "been a faithful husband and father, and I couldn't have asked for a more considerate son-in-law. And don't forget the woman or two in your circle of friends who've been left high and dry while the man they thought loved them ran off with a chick half his age. I think perhaps you should pray for an attitude adjustment."

Bess did know several "suddenly-singles" at church. Still, the last statement stung. Her mother didn't really fathom the depth of emptiness that threatened to suck the very breath out of her. "Maybe I should," she said without enthusiasm, knowing she couldn't even face turning to her Bible for comfort yet. No doubt she'd find the same unwelcome advice in its pages. "Well, I have to go change out of my dress. I'll call you tomorrow, okay?"

"Sure, dear. Bye for now."

"Bye, Mom."

A twinge of guilt niggled through Bess as she hung up the phone. Yeah, this was a lovely house, all right. Lovely and empty and oh so quiet. Maybe this hollow abode was paradise to Arthur, whose happiness at having this sudden freedom all but shouted off the walls. To her, it was more like a beautiful tomb she'd have to exist in for the next who-knew-how-many decades.

After starting some fresh decaf in the coffeemaker, she went along the carpeted hall to the master bedroom to change out of her mother-of-the-bride finery.

She averted her gaze on the way past Faith's now-deserted room. In her daughter's frenzy of packing for the honeymoon trip and leaving for the beauty parlor, the bed remained unmade, and an assortment of cast-off girlish treasures lay strewn about. The once every-pin-in-place little girl had evolved into a careless free spirit, who more than reveled in her exalted position as the pampered baby of the family. Would she make a good wife? Bess would have to take a day to sort through the belongings left behind and decide what needed to be saved. She'd deal with that soon enough.

In the master bedroom, she slipped out of her ecru lace and satin ensemble and hung it on a padded hanger in the walk-in closet. She saw that Art's tux had already been reassembled inside the plastic cover, awaiting its return to the rental shop. Despite his minor shortcomings that needled her, at least he'd never been a slob. That was one blessing she did appreciate.

After donning sapphire velour sweats and comfy house slippers, she checked her image in the bathroom mirror, leaning close to eye the fine lines the years had etched into her once-flawless skin. No doubt she could look worse, considering she was already the grandmother of four. She ran a comb through her short, stylish brunette bob and returned to the kitchen.

Moments later, she poured coffee into two mugs and carried them to the paneled den, where the halftime production blared from the big-screen TV.

Arthur rose from the leather recliner as she entered the room, a huge grin lighting his handsome features and a conspiratorial gleam in his eyes. He took the mugs from Bess and set them down, then swept her into his arms, swirling her around. "Ah, my beauty. I sure was proud of all my gorgeous girls today. Especially you. And I saved the last waltz for us—or should I call it our first? As they say, sweetheart, 'the best is yet to be.'"

Chapter 2

The next morning, dressed in her slip, hose, and a housecoat, Bess opened the kitchen blinds. The neighborhood lay shrouded in November fog, typical for this time of year. No doubt it would burn off before the church service ended, but for now the damp gloom added to her melancholy. She wished she'd have gotten up with a headache so she could stay home for once, rather than have to deal with crowds of well-intentioned, cheerful people at church and the Sunday school class Arthur taught.

Heaving a sigh, she filled the coffeemaker, then went to the fridge to gather the ingredients for a quiche. She could still hear the shower running and Arthur belting out a hymn, as always. Despite herself, she could not squelch a knowing smile at his ever-present optimism. Oh well, maybe church was what she needed after all. It certainly couldn't hurt.

When the pie finished baking in the wall oven, she set two places at the breakfast counter and poured their orange juice. With everything ready, she moved to the window and stared out at the day.

"Good morning, love." Her husband, in Sunday shirt and slacks, came up behind Bess and slid his arms around her. "Mmm. You smell as good as whatever's in the oven."

"It's quiche," she said, leaning her head against his solid chest. "And there are warm croissants."

He gave her a quick hug. "What a gal." Smiling, he poured decaf into their mugs and carried them to the counter, then took his place while Bess filled their plates and brought them over.

"I wonder where the newlyweds will go today," she mused, setting down the the food. "They had quite a list of sights to take in along the coast. I wonder if it's foggy there."

"This is the season for it—not that they'll notice." He gave a sly wink.

"I suppose you're right. I just miss having Faith at home. Right about now she'd be frantically trying on everything in her closet, looking for the one item she tossed into the hamper yesterday."

"Yeah, she was a real presence, all right. But she'll be okay; you'll see. You were a good mom. A great example for our girls to emulate." He reached for her hand, bowed his head, and offered a brief prayer of blessing on their grown daughters and the food.

❀

When Bess and Arthur arrived at Faith Community Church, the typical number of regular worshipers milled about the large sanctuary, their voices muffled by the burgundy carpet and quiet organ music. The first-service atmosphere was always more subdued than that of the second, more contemporary one. Bess felt a tap on her shoulder and turned.

"Hi, you guys." Her best friend, Madge Vincent, leaned close to give her a hug, while her charming golf-pro husband, Steve, shook hands with Arthur. "Glad to see you survived yesterday. I thought you'd be so worn out you'd sleep a week."

"I thought about it," Bess confessed, admiring Madge's chic suit. With that trim figure, everything looked great on her. "But it was our turn to bring donuts for Sunday school."

With a toss of her layered honey-blond hair, Madge laughed softly. "Let it never be said that the Wrights didn't meet their commitments. Uh-oh, sounds like the opening prelude. We'd better find a place to sit." Latching on to Steve's hand, she motioned for Bess and Arthur to tag along as they found a vacant pew.

As the foursome took seats, Bess's gaze settled on the matching flower arrangements from yesterday's ceremony flanking the platform, and her mind drifted to memories of the event. It took most of the song service and all of the announcements before she managed to harness her concentration. While the collection plate made the rounds, she gave herself a mental lecture and focused her attention on the soloist, then unzipped her Bible in readiness for the sermon.

"Good morning," Pastor Cliff Monahan said, stepping to the pulpit in his navy pinstripe suit. Eyes the same gray as his neatly groomed hair warmed with his smile. "Quite a goodly crowd, considering this pea soup of a Lord's Day."

A muted chuckle filtered through the congregation.

"I hope you brought your Bibles along today for a message I've entitled 'Recapturing Truth,'" he went on. "More and more lately, one cannot help taking sad notice of the downward drift of our once-proud nation. It's hard to believe that a country founded upon such a sure, strong foundation could so easily forget its roots and turn its back on our Creator. There are some segments of today's society that would excuse this gradual slide toward secularism, but we as Christians should have the courage to take a stand for faith and values and stem the tide. This morning we'll be looking at some instances in God's Word where people boldly stood for their convictions. Let's begin with the story of Stephen, in Acts, chapters 6 and 7."

More than glad she'd come to church, Bess quickly found the passage and anticipated another strong sermon from the minister she and Arthur considered a personal friend. His messages, always inspiring, rarely failed to meet her current need.

A short time later, having made it through not only the morning service but also the Sunday school session that followed, she breathed a sigh of relief. Only a few well-wishers had gravitated to her side with the expected comments about the loveliness of the wedding, and she responded with what she hoped were appreciative replies. Hoping to slip out quickly, she gathered her belongings and started for the door, where Arthur chatted with Steve and Madge. She caught her friend's eye and started toward her.

Just then, Naomi Fellows, this month's volunteer for putting away the coffee and condiments, stopped her in her tracks.

"Oh, Bess!" she gushed, her plump cheeks every bit as rosy as the cabbage roses on her floral polyester dress. "Faith's wedding had to be the prettiest thing I ever saw!"

"Thank you," Bess said politely. "I'm so glad you enjoyed it."

"Oh, I did, I did. And while I sat there, all I could think of was how much I needed your help in planning our little Tori's ceremony—she and her fiancé are getting married this spring, you know. In May, she says."

Bess's heart sank with dread.

Naomi, unaware, plunged onward with barely a breath. "She's our only daughter, you know. And the only girl in the whole family, to boot. I don't have the faintest notion about where to start in making all the arrangements, but after marrying off four girls already, you must have everything there is to know down pat. I hope it wouldn't be asking too much for the two of us to get together sometime so you could give me the scoop. Could you help me out?" she pleaded.

Hesitant to commit herself, Bess shrugged a shoulder. "Well, I'm kind of busy, you know, with—with things. But if there's some way I might be of help, of course I'll see what I can do."

"Oh, thank you, thank you! I'm sure Virginia Hastings could use some advice, too. Her daughter's getting married in a month or so." Naomi leaned in with a cushiony hug and beamed like a lighthouse. "I'll give you a call soon." She patted her limp, overprocessed hair and returned to rinsing out the coffee urn.

"Fine. See you next Sunday." Was this how her whole life

would wind down? Assisting other women who still had daughters at home? Bess let out a whoosh of exasperation and went to join her husband and their friends.

Arthur slipped his arm around her. "Steve and Madge are gonna eat at Mauricio's. Shall we join them?"

"Their new facility is much nicer than their old digs," Steven added, waggling his straight brows.

"Sure. Fine. Whatever." She met her best friend's questioning gaze and shook her head with an I'll-tell-you-later grimace.

A short while later, the foursome munched on warm tortilla chips and salsa in a booth in the newly opened Mexican restaurant. Bess noted the ever-cheerful mariachi music playing over the sound system as she squeezed the lemon slice in her glass, then took a sip of water.

"So what was that all about?" Madge asked, her blue eyes sparkling. "You and Naomi, I mean."

Bess suppressed a moan. "What else? Her daughter's going to be married, and she needs someone to coordinate the plans."

Arthur raised his brows and gave a half grin. "And I suppose you're it?"

"So it would appear. She also suggested I should give Virginia Hastings a hand while I'm at it."

"Well," Steven piped up, his mouth quirking into a smile, "you can't say you're not good at those things. This could be a whole new career for you, now that you've got all this extra time."

Madge, however, swallowed the bite of tortilla chip she'd

been chewing and tucked her chin. "Wait just a minute here. Why do I sense the thought of this sudden 'new career' might not exactly be Bess's dream come true? Is this what you want for your future, gal?" She met her gaze straight on.

Bess squirmed in her seat. "I don't know. I haven't had a chance to think about what I want to do now that our girls are out on their own. I do know I'll have lots of spare time—maybe too much. But I seriously doubt I want to spend it planning an endless stream of weddings for other people's kids."

"Then don't start letting anyone—even well-meaning friends—talk you into it," Madge urged. "Maybe you need to learn to say no for once. Give yourself time to decide how you want to fill your days."

"Sure," Arthur agreed. "There's probably tons of stuff you've never had time for before. Whatever you decide, I'll back you up any way I can."

"That's good to know," Bess managed, grateful that their orders arrived. She shifted her attention to the waiter as he placed the heated plates of food before them.

"I always did love their chicken chimichanga," Madge breathed, eyeing Bess's dish. "I shouldn't have ordered this combination plate."

Having drawn such limited comfort from her companions' comments, Bess had a strong suspicion she'd end up carting out most of her meal in a take-home box.

Art glanced into the family room on his way past. For days now, he'd arrived home from work to find Bess staring blankly at the TV. Had she heard even one sentence of dialogue in those afternoon movies she'd rarely had time for before? He couldn't help feeling concerned. Used to seeing her bustling about and up to her elbows in some project or other, it seemed uncharacteristic for her to be so listless now.

He stood unnoticed in the doorway, admiring his slender wife. Still young enough looking that she could almost pass for their daughters' older sister rather than their mother, only the finest of lines marred her delicate features, and very few silver strands peeked out through her shiny chestnut brown hair. Since the wedding, she'd been careful as ever with her appearance, and the house was immaculate. A delicious supper always awaited him when he came home, and he didn't lack for clean shirts. Still, Bess just wasn't the perky gal he'd married.

Not knowing what else to do, he tossed a packet of popcorn into the microwave. When it finished popping, he poured it into a bowl and went to join her.

She looked up and smiled as he handed her a can of diet soda and sat beside her with the popcorn. "Thanks. This smells so good," she commented, reaching for a handful of the salty snack.

"What are we watching?"

She shrugged. "I just have it on for noise. Haven't you noticed the quiet? I can't get used to it."

"Isn't there supposed to be some skating on tonight?" He picked up the remote and punched in the sports channel.

Bess slanted him a grin. "You hate figure skating."

"Ah, but I have you for company." He sat back, observing the energetic couple attired in frills and sparkles as they circled the ice rink with an intricate pattern of footwork and lifts. "Remember when we were first married and didn't have two nickels to rub together?"

She nodded, smiling slightly as she sampled another puffy kernel.

"Funny how happy we were, as long as we were together. We had our whole lives before us and could do whatever we wanted."

"Uh-huh. It was nice being young, being free."

Art took the bowl and set it on the coffee table in front of them. "Well, it's kind of like that again, sweetheart. We may not be young, but we still have our health. Besides that, we do have our share of nickels in the bank, and Lord willing, decades ahead to make a dent in them. Isn't there some dream you've had inside—something you might have tried if you hadn't always been busy looking after a family?"

Bess's finely arched brows dipped in puzzlement as she watched the current pair execute their ice routine. "I never had time for secret dreams. At least, none I can recall."

This was getting him nowhere. Might as well go flip channels in the den, Art decided. Standing, he picked up the bowl of popcorn, offering some to Bess before taking his leave.

She shook her head but seemed absorbed in the product being advertised during the commercial break. "Now that's something I wish I could do." She pointed to the display of oil paintings being offered in a weekend art blowout at a local hotel. "It must be wonderful to be able to create such beautiful scenes."

"Why don't you take some lessons?"

She frowned. "I couldn't do that. I can't even draw a straight line with a ruler."

"How do you know?" he challenged. "I'm sure it's not as difficult as it looks. In fact, I noticed in the paper the other day that a new gallery just opened across town. They're probably offering lessons. Why don't you check into it?"

Bess met his gaze then—fully, as if the TV screen suddenly lost its appeal. "I couldn't. What if I discover I don't possess a lick of talent? What if everyone else is tottering about in walkers and has white hair and there's no one my age to relate to?"

"Then they'll just be envious of your youth," he teased, "while they watch you paint circles around them, 'cause I seriously doubt you'll lack any talent." As he watched the first glimmer of hope light her serene hazel eyes, Arthur finally took heart.

Chapter 3

Jacaranda Art Gallery, an inviting new stucco building flanked by tall palms and jacaranda trees, crowned the knoll of a rise in northeast Bakersfield, its red tile roof gleaming beneath cloudless skies. Below, like a multicolored blanket, lay the East Hills Mall and an impressive view of Bakersfield, bedecked in autumn's glory.

Bess's heart pounded as she pulled into a parking space and exited her Camry. She'd come without so much as a charcoal pencil or a paint box, but the girl on the phone assured her the gallery had a goodly stock of supplies, and Arthur encouraged her to get whatever she needed. Never having been one to join things on her own, she looped the strap of her purse over her shoulder and stood for a moment debating whether to leave or see this whole scheme through.

Well, I'm here. It's now or never. Taking a deep breath for courage, Bess counted to ten before going inside, where a mixture of unfamiliar scents met her nostrils. She assessed the somewhat cluttered, yet efficient-looking room lined with shelves and cabinets all but bursting with an array of art materials. Several appealing finished paintings with price tags hung about the walls.

A thin, burgundy-haired girl with a crescent of studs and hoops in her ears looked up from behind a glass counter displaying painting and sketching paraphernalia. She appeared about the same age as Bess's youngest daughter. "Hi. I'm Tasha. May I help you?"

"Yes. I'm Bess Wright. I phoned yesterday about taking painting lessons."

"Oh yes. We've been expecting you. Class is already in progress, but there's always a couple of latecomers trickling in. It's right through that doorway." With the pen in her hand, she indicated the opening across the room.

"But I need to buy whatever I'll be using for the lessons. I didn't have any materials of my own to bring."

"No problem," Tasha announced cheerily. "I'll go check with Jeff, the instructor, and we'll get you all set up."

"Thank you." As the jeans-clad girl grabbed a scratch pad and took her leave, Bess glanced around at the shelves, cabinets, and cubbyholes sporting more items than any one artist could possibly use in a lifetime. She wondered how much of it she'd be carting home herself. Maybe she was biting off more than she could chew.

"Okay," Tasha said, breezing back into the room. "Here we go." She moved to the rack displaying different-sized canvases and drew one of them out. Then, checking the list, she chose a wooden paint box, several tubes of oil paints, some brushes, odorless paint thinner and linseed oil, a tablet of palette paper with a sealed palette holder, paper towels, and even a stretchy cord.

Bess felt her eyes widen as she observed Tasha adding still more items to the pile. Amazed at the amount of equipment required just to paint, she envisioned the wheelbarrow she'd need to lug it all back and forth.

"I think this is about it," Tasha said with a toss of her chin-length hair as she gathered an armful of the stuff. "I'll help you set up. We provide the easels."

Thankful for that small favor, Bess picked up the remainder and followed the clerk into an open room encircled by about a dozen easels, where other adults—mostly women—were already hard at work on what appeared to be the same scene. The mellow tones from an electronic sax floated from wall speakers mounted in each corner, providing background music from Bakersfield's slow jazz station.

Tasha organized the supplies on a folding worktable beside one of the two remaining easels in the place. Bess felt a little awkward about being right up front near the teacher. But a tall man with a head of thick, curly sable hair strode toward her, his hand outstretched.

"Welcome. You must be Bess Wright. I'm Jeff Bloomington, instructor of this fine-looking mob." His wide-set, chocolate brown eyes crinkled at the corners as he gazed deeply into hers and smiled, his hand outstretched. "Just call me Jeff. We go by first names around here."

"How do you do," Bess returned, extracting her fingers from his warm grip. A few inches taller than Arthur, he was easily as attractive as a Hollywood actor she admired, though she couldn't place him immediately.

"Hey, everyone," he called out, resting a friendly hand atop her shoulder. "We have a new member today. This is Bess Wright. Be sure to come by during our coffee break and introduce yourselves; make her welcome."

A little uneasy at his gesture of familiarity, Bess started to acknowledge all the smiles and nods. She breathed more easily when he removed his hand.

"As you can see, we're doing the landscape on display." Jeff indicated a finished painting on an elevated stand at the front of the room. Beside it stood another easel holding a partially finished identical scene, obviously used to demonstrate the various steps involved. "This class is for recreational painters, so I'm not as hard on you guys as I am on my students at Cal State. No one's gonna be graded. You have the option to do the basic sketch freehand, or you can use the projector in the corner to trace the outline. That's the first decision you'll need to make. After that, I'll show you how to mix the colors you'll be needing and help you get started."

Bess's head was swimming by the time she finished her preliminary tracing and got to work on her painting. The scene looked simple enough—a weathered barn on a hill with a large old tree in the foreground. Even the procedure Jeff used to demonstrate how to apply the sky didn't appear difficult. But she soon discovered that getting accustomed to the unfamiliar feel of the brushes and techniques so foreign to her presented no small challenge. She felt all thumbs as she listened to Jeff's pleasant voice taking the students through the various steps. Surely her feeble attempts at being an artist would fall way below everyone else's.

"Have you taken lessons before?" the slight, silver-haired lady with a cherubic face asked from the next easel, interrupting her musings. "I'm Priscilla."

"No, this is the first class I've ever taken," Bess admitted. "I'm not sure I'll ever get the hang of it."

"Sure you will," Priscilla said with a dimpled smile. "Jeff is a teddy bear. You'll love him; wait and see. And you'll catch on pretty quick."

"I hope so." Struggling to make the off-white smear in her sky resemble an actual cloud, Bess paused and glanced over her shoulder. Jeff was showing one of the other students, a plump, frizzy-haired matron in stretch pants and smock, how to do some type of brushstroke. Even his bearing exuded good-natured patience, and his laugh in response to something the lady said had a pleasing ring. He did seem to possess an exceptional personality—and he was so easy on the eye.

During the break, she had an opportunity to meet her fellow art students, all of whom seemed friendly and personable. She looked forward to getting to know them better in the coming weeks.

At the end of the three-hour class, Bess settled the considerable bill she'd acquired and stowed her painting along with others in the back room of the gallery where a shelf filled with rows of vertical dowels provided a drying rack. She waved good-bye to Priscilla and a few of the other ladies as she made her way to her car. "See you next Tuesday." Opening the trunk, she deposited the newly purchased oversize tote bag filled with her supplies. With one last check of her not quite paint-free hands, she smiled and climbed into her car. Maybe she wasn't exactly Renoir, but already she looked forward to next week's class.

❋

"So you enjoyed your venture," Art commented as he watched Bess take her place across from him at the supper table. "I hoped you would. It should make a great hobby."

"It was much more fun than I ever thought it would be. Harder, too."

Maybe it was his imagination, but Bess hadn't stopped smiling since he'd walked through the doorway after work. He watched her ladle some beef stew onto her plate and pluck a hot roll from the warming basket. "There were about eight other ladies—mostly my age or older, one disabled teenage girl, and two widowers. We're working on a landscape."

"How'd you do on yours?"

She smirked. "I'm pretty pathetic yet, trying to make those brushes do what I want them to. But I think I'll catch on eventually. You have no idea how much stuff I had to buy just to get started! Of course, I'm a little behind everybody else, since I started late. But the scene's fairly simple. Hopefully I'll catch up to the others pretty quick."

"I'll be anxious to see your painting when it's finished."

He saw a touch of surprise in her eyes. "That won't be for a few more weeks."

"I see." Art took a gulp of coffee, then set down his mug. "Who's the instructor?"

Her face came to life again. "A college professor from Cal State named Jeff Bloomington. He's incredibly patient. Says he's going easy on us since we're 'recreational' painters. He's not making us learn all the technical properties of the various types of paints—whatever that means—which ones are opaque or clear, and so forth. He's just showing us how to paint for fun. He has a great personality, and he's very nice. He doesn't seem to mind working with beginners. I was really worried about that and almost didn't go in at all. Now I'm glad I did."

"Me, too, sweetheart. It's good to see you smile again."

Her cheeks flushed, and she grinned sheepishly. "I've been pretty miserable lately, I know. I'm sorry about that."

"Hey, no problem. There's been a major change in our lives, now that our last little princess has left the kingdom. I figured we'd both be making adjustments." He paused. "Speaking of that, now that Faith won't be needing that bedroom, I've been thinking about converting it into an exercise gym. We finally have a place to set up the treadmill, stationary bike, rowing machine, and other things that have done nothing but gather dust for ages. What do you think? It would help us both keep from going to flab now that the colder weather and fog season are upon us."

That radiant smile flattened. "But I thought. . ."

"What?"

"I don't know. That we'd keep it as is. For a while, at least."

"You mean like a shrine?" He snorted.

Obviously not appreciating his attempt at humor, Bess stiffened. "Do what you want." And she abruptly vacated the table, leaving him to finish his meal alone.

❈

In the laundry room, Bess seethed as she folded Faith's freshly dried lavender quilt before adding it to the pile of other laundered bedding to be shelved. The smell of new paint drifted from the hallway, almost overpowering the fragrant scent of the dryer sheets. She pressed her lips together. Arthur and his projects. He couldn't wait to eradicate the last trace of their youngest daughter from the house. All that pretty furniture now sat disassembled in the garage, and tailored curtains hung in place of the ruffled priscillas that once graced the windows in that ultrafeminine room. A room now occupied by big, clunky, black exercise monstrosities.

Not that Faith would have had occasion to use that bedroom anytime soon, Bess conceded. Her and Chad's honeymoon was over, but the pair had scarcely had a chance to set up housekeeping before leaving to go on the road again, on tour with Chad's musical group. Things appeared to be going very well for the newlyweds as they followed the Lord's leading in their lives. Faith sounded enthusiastic and happy whenever she phoned home to keep her parents posted on the whereabouts of each upcoming church concert. Bess was thankful for that.

Still, redecorating her daughter's bedroom made everything seem so. . .final. And she couldn't help holding that against Arthur.

The kitchen phone trilled. Stepping around the brimming basket, Bess hurried to answer. "Hello?"

"Hi, gal," her best friend, Madge, said. "Did I catch you in the middle of something?"

"Not really. Just some laundry. Why?"

"Too busy to meet me for lunch?"

"Not at all. Sounds like fun. Where shall we eat?"

"Fresh Choice? I love their salads."

"Sure. A little before noon? We'll beat the rush that way."

"Sounds fine to me. See you there."

With Madge being an office administrator for a large insurance firm, her seniority provided a flexible schedule. Bess enjoyed the frequent lunch breaks the two of them had together. She dashed to the master bedroom and changed into slacks and a blouse with a coordinating blazer.

A short time later, she pulled into the vacant space beside her friend's silver Lexus. They waved at one another and exited their vehicles.

"So glad you could come," Madge said as they walked to the entrance. "I missed seeing you on Sunday. I really don't like skipping church, but Steve had a golf tournament in Palm Springs."

"I don't care to miss, either." Inside, Bess took a tray and silverware from the beginning of the salad bar and proceeded down the line, deciding which items looked tempting.

"So how's everything?" her friend asked. "You said you were starting art classes soon."

"Actually, I've already had my first one." Bess dished out

some of her favorite pasta salad and moved on to the hard-boiled eggs and multigrain muffins.

"Really." Madge finished making her own selections and followed Bess to the cash register and beverages, where they both chose ice water with lemon.

"So when are you going to come clean with the details?" Madge teased after they'd found seats and said grace.

Bess shook her head in wonder. "It's fun. I truly enjoy it. Of course, I'm not very good yet, but it's ever so relaxing—when I'm not struggling to master a certain brushstroke, that is."

"Where are the classes?" Madge poked her fork into her Caesar salad.

"Jacaranda Art Gallery. It's a new place up near the East Hills Mall."

"Really. I never heard of it. What's it like?"

"I don't have anything to compare it with. There are two good-sized rooms and a smaller one in back for storage, where we put our pictures to dry. There are about eleven other students in my class—all beginners, like me, so nobody's very far beyond my own level. And the instructor is a neat guy—a professor from Cal State, when he's not teaching us. Seems to enjoy his sideline." She bit into her muffin as pleasant memories of her first lesson came to mind.

"And I suppose the man is tall and thin with perpetual nasal drip and an artist's tam hiding his balding head," Madge teased.

Bess couldn't help laughing. "Far from it. He *is* tall and thin but has dark, thick, curly hair and a nice face. Think Ben

213

Cross in that *First Knight* movie you like so much."

"Do tell." Her friend nodded in contemplation as she sliced a chunk from a deviled egg. "A teacher that handsome would make an art class bearable even for someone like me, who's more than challenged artistically." She shook her head. "And what do we hear from the newlyweds?"

Bess felt an unexpected wave of relief at the change of subject. "They're fine. Faith calls quite often to let us know where the band will be playing next. They're happy as larks but don't have much time to spend feathering their nest."

"Cute." Madge winced. "I'm glad to hear they're doing okay. How about the other girls?"

Bess gave a negative shake of her head. "Same old, same old. Christina's still helping out at the Christian day care center, Dawn is repainting her new baby's nursery and trying to catch up on her sleep, and Eden's working part-time at a bookstore while Caleb's in preschool. They phone home whenever anything exciting happens."

"Funny how none of them stayed in Bakersfield," Madge commented.

"I guess they took the Lord's instructions a tad too literally," Bess said wryly. "That bit about leaving their father and mother. At least they're all within a few hours' drive, so we get to see them on special occasions—like Thanksgiving, which is coming up pretty quick."

"You're right. It is. Oh well, sounds like you're adjusting. You really are okay, though? You look more—I don't know. Settled or something."

"I'm getting used to it. I had no other choice. Kids grow up and move on. First we learn to live *with* them, then we have to learn to live *without* them."

"Yeah, well—at least you had children. Some of us had to fill our lives with other things, like travel, or overdecorating our houses with electronic gadgets. None of which phone home in the wee hours to disturb our rest."

Bess studied her friend. This was the first mention Madge had ever made that hinted at regret. "I guess we all play the hand we're dealt," she finally said.

"That we do." Madge checked her watch. "Uh-oh. I have a meeting in twenty minutes. I gotta rush off. See you on Sunday, right? And maybe we can have lunch again soon." She stood and brushed crumbs from her plaid wool skirt.

Bess got up, as well, and took her shoulder bag from the seat she'd vacated. "Sure. Whenever you're available. After all, I'm footloose and fancy-free these days—except for Tuesdays, when I have art class."

"Good. Well, have a great day, gal. Catch ya later."

In the parking lot, Bess waited for Madge to pull away first, then she drove across the lot to the drugstore to look for a witty card to send her friend just for fun. Up until now, she'd thought only she and Arthur had a house that felt too empty.

Chapter 4

Eagerly anticipating her second painting class the following Tuesday, Bess dressed quickly and went to the refrigerator to take out her sealed palette box. Tasha had told her the cool temperature would help keep the colors she'd mixed the previous week from drying out. Bess would wait until she got to the gallery to see if that theory proved true. She slid the chilled container into her tote bag with the other materials she'd be taking with her.

Several of the other students were in various stages of arrival and setup when Bess entered the building. As she approached her easel, she found her painting buddy, Priscilla, arranging her own supplies.

"Good morning," the older woman said. "Have a good week?" A charming smile dimpled her cheeks, the blue of her eyes heightened by the sky blue smock she wore over her street clothes.

"I sure did. How about you?"

"Same as always. This is the high point for me, leaving my

empty house and coming here to visit for a while and paint a pretty picture."

At the pensive tone of Priscilla's voice, Bess stopped her preparations and met the woman's wistful expression.

"I'm a widow," she explained. "Four years now, my Bruce has been gone."

"Oh, I'm so sorry. Do you have any other family?"

Her mouth pursed. "Two daughters and a son. But they're busy with their own lives. You know how it is. Do you have kids?"

Bess smiled. "Four daughters. The youngest just got married and moved away. She was the last one, so I'm in the same empty boat as you, except I still have my husband. The girls do call me every week. It's not quite the same as when they were at home, though. That's why I signed up for painting lessons; I was driving Arthur nuts, and vice versa." At the mention of his name, resentment rose to the fore.

Priscilla leaned over and squeezed Bess's arm. "At least you still have somebody. Be glad he's there for you. I'd give anything to have Bruce around again. Nothing like the good, sturdy sound of a man's footsteps in the house."

Recalling the new exercise room at home, Bess smirked. Men always had to spoil everything.

Her neighbor pointed at Bess's easel. "Oh, you need to go get your canvas, dearie. Class is about to start."

"Right. Thanks." She hurried to the storage room and retrieved her partially finished picture, which she discovered was dry to the touch. The sky looked better than she expected—as did the cloud that had given her untold grief—and the sight encouraged her as she returned to her place.

"Morning, everybody," their teacher, Jeff, said with a nod of his dark head. His gaze centered on Bess's and lingered. Standing at the front of the room in tan Dockers and a brown plaid shirt, he seemed taller than she remembered, but his smile was amiable as ever. "Since most of you are still working on background, I'll let you take up where you left off. Hopefully we'll start on the barn later this morning. Give a holler if you need help."

Bess hesitated, then raised a tentative hand.

"Yes. Bess, isn't it?" he said, coming to her side.

She nodded. "I'm not sure what to do next."

"No problem." A quick appraisal of her painting, and he grinned. "You need to start on the grass. With this." He squeezed a bit of sage green from her unused tubes of paint and divided it up, adding a touch of pale yellow to one part, white to another, and a smidgen of umber to yet another. "I'll show you how to get going."

Watching his skilled movements as he put down a thin base coat, then dabbed on different shades of grass with a fan brush to show her how to add shading and highlights, Bess envied the ease with which he worked. But did he have to stand so near? She inhaled the woodsy scent of his aftershave.

"Here you go," he said, his sable eyes twinkling as he handed her the brush. "You give it a try."

Bess took the fan brush and did her best to emulate the technique he'd demonstrated while he stepped back a little to observe. Having her instructor watching her every move set her nerves on edge, and she attributed any new awkwardness to his presence. He was so charming—so friendly.

"I knew it," he said with a grin. "You're a natural."

Comparing her efforts to the portion he'd done, Bess had serious doubts about that last remark, but his approval did much to bolster her spirits. Something about him made her envy girls who were young and unattached. But she quickly chided herself for such foolishness and simply returned his smile. "Thanks for the help."

He nodded and moved off to answer someone else's summons.

"Did I lie to you?" Priscilla teased, peering over the reading glasses she wore halfway down her nose. "He's a teddy bear. He makes us all feel talented. Makes me wish I were still a spring chicken."

Bess suppressed a flush at having similar thoughts and glanced after Jeff, who was now helping the disabled teen several easels away. She appreciated his infinite patience, the way he never gave the impression of being weary of offering personal attention. Bess realized she knew nothing whatsoever about the man but judged him to be a few years younger than herself. Someone that handsome most certainly had an equally attractive wife—not that it was any concern of hers. She returned her concentration to completing the grassy field in her scene. Still, it was difficult to dismiss that dazzling smile of his from her thoughts.

The three-hour session whizzed by at an unbelievable

speed, and suddenly it was time to clean up. That chore completed, Bess took her canvas to the storage room, then returned to gather her belongings. "See you next time, Priscilla," she told her new friend. Both exhilarated and relaxed as she unlocked her car and got in, she realized next Tuesday couldn't come soon enough. Painting class was quickly becoming the high point of *her* week, too.

After she'd eaten lunch, the quiet afternoon she'd chosen to use to go through Faith's belongings was shattered by the ringing of the phone. Kneeling before the partially filled cartons of her daughter's things, Bess brushed her hands down her pant legs and rose to answer.

"Hello? Bess?" an unfamiliar voice said. "I'm so glad I caught you at home. This is Naomi. You know, from church? Remember you offered to help me with my daughter's wedding plans?"

"Oh yes." *I wish I'd have had more sense,* her wayward thoughts added, *but you caught me off guard.* "What was it exactly that you needed?"

"Well, somebody mentioned that you sewed some of those lovely dresses your girls wore. I thought I'd try that, too, to save some money. I have the bridal gown partly cut out, but I've never used such pricey material, and I'm afraid I'll mess up. Do you think if I came over, you could help me get the rest cut? I see from the church directory that you only live a couple miles from me."

Bess looked at the wall clock. Still a few hours before Arthur would be home from work. She let out a silent sigh.

"Sure. Come on over. I'll see what I can do."

"Oh, thank you! You're an absolute angel. I knew the minute I asked you that you were the right person to see. I'll be there in about half an hour. Bye."

Well. That ought to teach you to keep your big mouth shut, Bess admonished herself.

Just as Naomi had forewarned, half an hour later the doorbell announced her arrival.

Bess plastered on a smile and opened the door. "Naomi. Hello." Then she caught sight of the oversized bundle in the woman's arms. "Do you need help with that?"

"I can manage." Her short, stout frame eased through the opening without dislodging her burden. She stopped just inside to cast a glance around. "Oh, what a gorgeous home you have! I could tell from the classy clothes you and your girls always wore that you must live in a house like this." She wagged her frizzy head in awe.

"Thank you. I'm glad you like it. Right through that archway to your left is the dining table. We'll probably need to work there."

"Whatever you say." Following Bess's bidding, the overweight matron dumped the contents unceremoniously on the tabletop Bess had cleared in anticipation.

Bess eyed the heaping rainbow of satin and tulle lengths. "All this is for the bridal gown?"

Naomi had the grace to blush as her pudgy fingers brushed a few strands of crimped salt-and-pepper hair out of her eyes. "Well, the white is, for sure. But I thought, hey, it's no more trouble to make two dresses than one, right? So I promised to do the maid of honor's gown, too. And then there's the little flower girl's. Course, I'm not as accomplished as you, but how hard can it be?" As she spoke, she extracted three patterns from the pile and began removing the contents from the envelopes.

Bess closed her eyes and breathed a silent plea for strength and patience. Lots and lots of patience.

Art sensed an odd tension in the house when he got home. Normally Bess had nice music playing when she was by herself—soft instrumentals or maybe an album by some popular Christian artist. Today the place was silent except for an uncharacteristic clanging of pots and pans reverberating from the kitchen. "Hello," he called out.

"I'll have supper ready in a little while," Bess groused through clenched teeth. "Sorry it's late. I've been otherwise occupied."

He moved up behind her and massaged the back of her neck, feeling no end of knots. "No hurry. If you're just getting to it, we could go out to eat. How 'bout that?"

She turned then, the barest hint of a smile curving her lips. "That is the best offer I've had all day. Just let me go change, okay?"

"Sure. Take your time."

A short while later they arrived at the Marketplace shopping center. Art rather liked the atmosphere at Tahoe Joe's Famous Steakhouse. Besides a light haze of tantalizing smoke from grilling steak, the place had energetic college-age servers bustling about in medium blue shirts and black slacks, and the food was consistently delicious. Being early on a Tuesday evening, they walked right in and were seated without a wait. He glanced around at the hunting theme decor enhanced by a huge moose head, a hanging canoe, and assorted related nature and trapper articles.

"What looks good, sweetheart?" he asked as he and Bess scanned their menus.

She tipped her head back and forth in thought. "I think I'll have a petite filet."

"Good choice. For me, only a New York steak will do. How about potatoes? Do you want mashed or baked?"

"Baked, and a side salad. I'm famished."

"Well, this'll help, then." He removed a warm roll from the basket the waitress had brought with their menus, then handed it to Bess, along with the soft butter.

She smiled then, the first real smile of the evening, as she visibly relaxed and bit into the cloudlike sustenance.

Art gave their orders to the attendant, then took out another roll for himself. Surprisingly, their meals arrived quickly, a bonus he attributed to the early hour's light crowd. "So how was painting today?" he ventured to ask, not knowing what had put her in her formerly testy mood.

As before, when asked about her new hobby, Bess's features softened, and her hazel eyes glowed. "Great, actually. I got quite a lot done on my scene—in fact, I've caught up to the rest of the group already. We're now working on the old barn in the picture."

He nodded, enjoying the dreamy expression on her face, the lilt of her voice.

"You know," she went on, "it's really strange. Even though we're all doing the same picture, no two paintings look alike. Everyone has a different style, a unique touch. And our instructor, Jeff, is so patient with us beginners. He never seems to mind when we ask for help with some new or complicated stroke. The man's a true gem. He has the patience of Job. He even complimented my work and said I'm a natural. I have to admit, he's had to give me quite a bit of individual help, but I'm starting to catch on."

"So you enjoyed the day, then."

"Well, that part of it, anyway." Her lips compressed into a hard line. "My day was going perfectly well until Naomi Fellows, from church, decided to come over to the house for a dressmaking lesson. Honestly! The nerve of that woman!" She jabbed at the air with her empty fork as she went on. "Would you believe it? She expected me to help her cut out not just a bridal gown but the maid of honor's and the flower girl's! Next thing you know, she'll be wanting help sewing the silly things, too. As if I have nothing else to do."

Art somehow managed to suppress his mirth. It wasn't Bess's story that seemed funny but her animation while relating it. At times she seemed her old self again. Then again, other times. . . He cleared his throat. "Well, as Madge said, you don't have to let her walk all over you. Stand up for yourself. If she's taking unfair advantage, tell her you're too busy to help her. Simple as that."

A sheepish smile flickered across her lips, and her tone softened. "Yes, but then I'd hurt her feelings, and I really don't want to do that. I just want her to go away. Find somebody else to take charge of that wedding. I don't want to be everyone's expert. Is that wrong?"

"Not at all. I'm sure it'll all work out. You'll see." All he knew was the painting class was bringing his wife back to life again. Things were definitely looking up. At least he hoped so.

But reflecting on the way her face lit up at the mention of the instructor, a small part of Art wondered if the same thing happened when Bess talked to other people about *him*. . . .

"Hi, Mom."

Bess's heart contracted with bittersweet joy at the sound of Faith's airy voice over the phone line. A vision of her youngest daughter with the ultrashort, almost boyish hairstyle flashed to mind. "Hi, honey. How are you? Where are you?"

"I'm fine. We're fine. I never imagined it was possible to feel this happy."

"I'm glad to hear that."

"We're home now, in our apartment. It's so nice here in San Diego. The weather's gorgeous, and we have two whole weeks before our next concert. It'll be in Ventura. That's not too far from Bakersfield, you know. Wish you and Daddy would come hear us sometime."

"I'd sure like that, honey. Problem is, you know Dad got talked into teaching one of the new Sunday school classes, so we've kind of been stuck here in town. I can't remember the last time we actually went anywhere. Maybe one of these Sundays we'll arrange for a sub. Then we can drive to wherever you're performing."

"I hope so. It would be cool to introduce you as honored guests."

"We'll see, I promise. Well, how do you like your little place? Does it feel like home yet?"

"Kind of. Everything's all new and pretty. We got so many beautiful wedding gifts. I have hardly anything here from my old life." A tiny pause. "I miss you."

Bess's eyes stung. She blinked quickly to keep her emotions in check. "Me, too. By the way, I've been going through the things you left behind. Is there anything in particular you want me to toss? Anything special you want to be sure I save?"

"Toss whatever old clothes are there, for sure. I left those on purpose. I'd like my yearbooks and journals and anything personal that I got from Grams. Use your judgment. Put stuff in boxes, and I'll go through them next time we visit."

"That'll be Thanksgiving, right? You could do it then."

"No, not really. Chad wants us to go to his mom's. She's got stuff all planned for us and everything. Hope you don't mind. A bunch of his relatives will be there."

Bess fought a wave of disappointment. She'd known inside that she'd now be sharing her youngest girl with the in-laws on some holidays, the way she did with her other daughters. But she'd harbored the hope that it wouldn't start quite so soon. "It's fine, hon. Whatever you decide."

"Whew! I'm glad you're not mad. Anything else new back

home? Daddy okay and all?"

Bess nodded, then remembered her daughter couldn't see her reaction. "We're both fine. I've started taking art classes— painting. That's new."

"That's so cool, Mom! I always thought you had a gift for artsy things."

"You did?"

"Are you kidding? With all those neat costumes you were forever creating for us? Those original invitations you designed for our parties? All our friends were so jealous."

"Guess I never thought much about it."

"Well, you should. I know you'll do some fantastic pictures. And as it happens, we have lots of bare white walls here—hint, hint."

Bess had to laugh. "I'll do my best. I'm not sure when my work will be worthy of such eminence, but I'll see what I can do."

"Great, Mom. Well, I gotta go. Chad'll be in any second. We're supposed to go meet somebody about hosting a concert. Tell Daddy I send my love."

"Will do. Take care. Tell Chad hi."

"Sure. Catch ya later. Bye-bye."

"Bye, love."

Nothing like a call from one of the girls to brighten a mother's day, Bess mused. She looked forward to them nearly as much as she did her art classes. Funny, such a short time ago she'd thought her life was over. Yet in some strange way, it seemed like it was just beginning.

Chapter 5

There was no painting class scheduled for the week of Thanksgiving. Bess felt the loss, because for the first time in ever so long, she was an individual. No one at the gallery thought of her as Arthur's wife or Christina, Dawn, Eden, or Faith's mother. She was just Bess—and she reveled in the heady experience.

But there was another reason, too—one she couldn't quite admit to herself. The occasional admiring glance or compliment from her instructor made her feel. . .special. . .desirable. . .young again. Whenever he came to her easel to help her through some difficulty, he stood so near her hands trembled. No doubt she was letting her imagination get the best of her. Besides, it was downright disloyal to Arthur for her to be entertaining such ridiculous daydreams. In all likelihood, the man was married anyway.

Still, Bess couldn't quite dismiss the joy of anticipating every upcoming class and being around her personable instructor again—and Arthur did seem to be going out of his way to give her space lately. She would just have to get her head back on straight, corral her reckless thoughts, and concentrate on nothing but painting.

To occupy the free Tuesday, Bess threw her energy into baking pies, sugar cookies, and fudge for the family get-together two days away. Only half of her family would be driving to Bakersfield for Thanksgiving, since their oldest daughter would be celebrating the occasion with her husband's relatives, and Faith would be with Chad's. But Bess consoled herself with the fact that at least the two middle girls would be coming with their husbands and children. Surely there'd be enough family present to ensure lively conversation and a fun-filled day—even if it would pass too quickly and they'd all be returning to their homes that evening.

When the holiday finally arrived, Bess strived to make everything perfect. As she flicked the lace tablecloth into place and set it with the good china and silverware, the delicious aroma of roast turkey wafted through the house—Arthur's specialty. He always took charge of the bird, leaving her with the other fixings. She placed the autumn-colored floral centerpiece on an oval mirror in the middle of the table and added tall candles on each side, then went to the kitchen to cut veggies for the relish tray. The delicious-looking pies and cookies she'd baked lined the counter. A glance at the clock assured her the girls should be arriving soon.

The doorbell chimed just then, and Dawn breezed in. "Hi, Mom, Dad. We're here."

Bess dried her hands on a kitchen towel and hurried to the entry to greet the willowy twin, who held a pink bundle in her arms, her porcelain doll face aglow with motherly pride. "Hi, honey. Oh, I can't wait to hold that precious angel. Where's Jordan?"

Dawn gave a soft laugh. "He's coming. He's the one who gets to lug Emily's gear in from the car." As she spoke, she placed her two-month-old daughter in Bess's arms. "I'll go see if he needs any help."

Bess inhaled a whiff of delicate baby powder and gazed down at her sleeping granddaughter's soft cheeks and rosebud mouth. "Hi, Grama's little love. Aren't you the pretty one," she crooned, inclining her head to kiss Emily's chubby face. She loosened the crocheted shawl enough to get a look at the tiny dress the baby wore, all ruffles and ribbons, as expected. Her mommy had been the one who loved frilly, fussy things more than the others. A stretchy lace headband circled the infant's downy head. "And don't you look like a fairy princess."

Sable-haired Dawn returned just then, the strap of a diaper bag hooked over her shoulder and a rocking infant seat under her arm. She headed straight up the hall to the guest room that once had been her boudoir. A moment behind, her husband, Jordan, entered toting a folding travel bed and an armful of fuzzy toys. Ruggedly handsome, with almost-black eyes as dark as his wavy hair, he retained a boyish charm Bess had always found captivating.

"Hi, Mom." Setting down his burdens inside the door, he came to plant a kiss on Bess's cheek. "Isn't she something?" He beamed a new-father smile in his baby's direction, his eyes twinkling.

"She sure is. She's just as pretty as her mama was at this age. Are you two getting any sleep yet?"

He grinned, displaying a row of even pearly whites. "Now and then."

"Dawn took the baby's things to the guest room," Bess told him. "That must be where she wants those you brought in, too."

He nodded. "Whatever Mama wants, Mama gets." Still smiling, he retrieved the infant's belongings and went after his wife.

Bess drew Emily close to her heart. "I think I'll just hide you somewhere when your mommy and daddy aren't looking," she whispered. "Maybe they won't notice."

The electronic chime rang again, and a four-year-old live wire barreled through as his mom opened the door. "Grama! Grama!" Caleb nearly knocked Bess off balance as he reached up and threw his arms around her middle. "Is Pop-Pop here?"

"Yes, love. He's outside in the backyard, setting up the croquet hoops for later. Go tell him you're here." She watched after the tot as he charged off to comply.

"Hi, Mom," Eden said. With the fair coloring and blond hair she and Faith had acquired from Arthur's side of the family, she tipped her head to get a closer look at baby Emily. "Oh, how sweet. May I hold her?"

"I knew I'd have to relinquish my dolly sooner or later," Bess teased, handing her over. "Her parents are stowing her things in the guest room."

Eden cooed at her tiny niece and kissed her cheek, then swept an appreciative glance around. "The table looks beautiful, Mom. You always make everything so pretty."

"Thanks. I like things to be special when my girls come home."

Eden's sandy-haired husband, Zach, closed the door after himself and came to offer a hug. "Hi, Mom. Smells incredible in here."

"Thanks. Everything's about ready to be put on the table, too, once we round everybody up."

"Faith and Chrissy aren't coming?" Eden asked, her slender brows forming a V in disappointment.

"I'm afraid not. Their 'other mothers' requested their presence this time."

"Oh. Rats. I wanted to see them. They said they were going to try to be here." She sighed. "What can I do to help?"

Before Bess could answer, the back door opened, and Arthur came in from the yard with Caleb's small hand dwarfed in his much larger one. "Us menfolk are powerful hungry," he drawled, then bent down to his grandson's level. "You go to the crick an' wash your hands for chow time, cowboy, while I go rustle up some grub for us. I believe there's a big ol' prairie chicken in the oven that's wearin' our brand." He tousled the towhead's hair.

"You're funny, Pop-Pop," Caleb said. Letting go, he made an obedient beeline for the bathroom.

"Well, well. I see a couple of my precious gals have graced our house," Art stated, giving Eden a cautious embrace that would not disturb the slumbering little one in her arms. "Such a treat to have lots of pretty faces around here." After a tender look at his granddaughter, he gave a collective wave toward the

232

pair returning from the guest room and Zach. "Hi, everybody. Find a place at the table. Dinner'll be on in a jiffy."

"Oh no you don't," Dawn announced, coming right to him. "First I get a hug. Then I'll take a seat. Unless Mom needs any help, that is."

An imitation frown creased his forehead. "It's a trial, but I guess we dads must do our duty every now and then." He put his arms around her and kissed her cheek. "Glad you came, sweetheart."

A short while later, after Emily was settled in her travel bed in the quiet of the guest room, the girls helped Bess bring the food to the table. Arthur offered his usual elaborate blessing over the meal, extending the prayer to include the missing family members and their celebrations. While the platter of turkey made the rounds, Bess gazed at her dear ones and breathed her own prayer of thanks.

"I see you guys converted Faith's old room into a gym," Jordan commented, reaching for the bowl of glazed carrots.

Aggravated by her husband's satisfied grin, Bess held her sentiments in check.

Arthur nodded. "Us old fogies gotta keep in shape, you know."

"Mind if I try out that Nautilus machine later?"

"Not at all. Have at it."

Bess eyed their son-in-law. Muscular and in great condition, anyone could see he lifted weights on a regular basis. He'd have a grand time working out in their new "gym."

"So, Mom," Eden said, dishing some mashed potatoes

onto her son's plate and then taking some for herself, "how's that art class of yours?"

"Let me tell you." Bess smiled. "I'm having the time of my life."

"Who's teaching it?" Dawn chose a slice of turkey breast and passed the platter on.

"A professor from Cal State, actually. Jeff Bloomington's his name."

"You're kidding!" Eden gushed. "That hunk is handsome enough to be a movie star! He used to date my friend Paula's mother when the two of us were in high school. We'd drool just looking at him and fantasize that we were the ones he was really interested in. Did those two ever get married?"

"I have no idea." Bess took a sip of water from her goblet. For some unaccountable reason, the thought of Jeff being romantically involved put a damper on her enthusiasm. "All I know is he's very nice."

"Guess what, Grama," Caleb chimed in, interrupting her contemplation. "I know all my ABCs."

"You do?"

"Uh-huh. A-B-C-D-E-F-G...," he singsonged at the top of his lungs, while everyone around the table stifled smiles.

"Why, that's really good," Bess said when he reached the end. "I'm proud of you."

"I can count to twenty, too," he went on, his chest puffing out with pride.

Eden touched his arm. "Right now, I'd rather you eat, pumpkin. You can show everybody all your tricks later, okay?"

234

" 'Kay," he murmured, visibly deflating.

"Gonna watch the game today, Dad?" Zach asked, taking second helpings of mashed potatoes and dressing. "Dallas is gonna tromp all over Green Bay."

"You bet. But I wouldn't count the Packers out so quick."

"What a bore," Dawn said with a toss of her shiny dark hair. "We girls will do something much more fun—like play a rousing game of croquet."

"Just don't break any windows," Art teased. "I know how wild you gals can get when you're together."

"Oh, Daddy," they moaned in unison. "You and Mom act just as nutty sometimes, and look how old you guys are. You're coming up on your twenty-fifth anniversary next month."

"And may you all be as happy as we are," he returned. "Old or not."

Happy! Bess thought, recalling the way the emptiness of the house still continued to eat at her. *If this is happy, what is miserable like?*

Finally it was time for dessert, which led to the usual round of planned activities. The hours passed quickly, and all too soon the family day came to an end. It seemed to Bess that her family had barely arrived. Now, suddenly, the dishes were done, the football game was over, and the croquet match was a mere memory. Caleb had grown whiny from missing his nap, and the young mommies were eager to get their little charges home to bed. Bess and Arthur followed the little troop out to their cars and stood arm in arm in the driveway, waving as their loved ones drove away.

"That was nice," he remarked.

"Only it wasn't long enough," Bess added. "Sure wish they lived in town."

Art kept his arm around Bess as they went back inside. His wife always seemed subdued whenever one of the girls would leave after a visit—but today he sensed that she'd been in a downer long before the day reached its conclusion. In fact, the sparkle, disappeared from her eyes while the family was in the middle of their feast. He tried to think back on the conversation that had transpired at the time. It was about that teacher, wasn't it? That Jeff guy. So he was good-looking, huh? Well, for his own sake, the professor had better have scruples, as well, or Art would drive up to that place and—and what? He had no reason not to trust Bess.

As she eased out of his grasp, Art watched her fuss about, picking up stray crumbs, straightening things that were already neat. She'd always been easy on the eye, and even after all these years, he couldn't help staring at the fetching picture she made as she brushed a tendril of light brown hair from her forehead. Did the professor find her foxy, too?

She met his gaze. "Would you like some decaf?"

Yep, he trusted Bess implicitly. As always. He kept his tone light. "Sounds good. And some pie, if those guys didn't eat it all."

"Actually, there's one in the fridge they didn't know about. I planned ahead."

"That's my girl." He thought he detected a slight wilting

quality in her smile, a drifting of her attention as she turned toward the kitchen. But he wasn't positive. "Shall we have it in the den? Might be a decent movie on tonight, being a holiday. We could watch it on the big TV."

She looked back at him in surprise. "Sure, whatever. Maybe I should give Mom a callback while it brews. There was so much confusion when she phoned earlier that we could barely hear one another. I'll bring a tray when the coffee's done."

"Do that, sweetheart. I'll set up the TV trays."

On his way up the hall, Art wondered where Bess's thoughts had wandered when she looked so far away—and how he might bring her back home.

To stay.

Chapter 6

The Wednesday after Thanksgiving, Bess met Madge for lunch at the China Palace, another restaurant within close proximity to her friend's work. A small-boned Asian girl ushered them to a red vinyl booth in the ornately decorated eatery, and they went immediately to the buffet line to choose their entrées.

Taking their seats, they assessed one another's choices. Madge offered a brief prayer over their food before sampling her sweet-and-sour chicken. "So how's everything?" she asked between bites. "With painting. At home. With the girls. We haven't had a chance to talk lately. Have you finished your Christmas shopping?"

Bess groaned. "Don't even mention Christmas; I've hardly given it a thought. Anyway, it's still a couple of weeks off. As for my family, everything's fine. And at home—well, that's something else." She gave a weary sigh.

"Is Naomi Fellows still bugging you about her daughter's wedding?"

"No, thankfully," Bess said with relief. "I haven't heard another word about that. Not yet, anyway. This is more. . . personal."

Her friend glanced up from her food, and her mouth fell open. "Oh no. Not you and Art? Don't tell me you guys are having problems, with your silver anniversary right around the corner. Your marriage has been one of the ideal examples the rest of us have been trying to emulate."

"Right." Bess fought a twinge of exasperation. "A match made in heaven. We did have a marvelous Thanksgiving, though. Dawn and Eden were able to come with their families, and we had a wonderful day together. But since then, Arthur's been like a stranger. I don't know what's gotten into him. Or maybe it's me. Who knows?"

Madge frowned. "He seems okay at church when we see him, and Steve hasn't mentioned anything odd. You know how those two always have their heads together."

"Right. Well, things are *somewhat* normal, I suppose. Arthur and I still eat breakfast together before he leaves for work, and when he comes back home afterward, we have supper together. At least when he does come home. He's been working late quite often. After supper, though—and in all his spare time, for that matter—he's either shut up in the den supposedly studying for the next Sunday school lesson, or else he's out in his workshop. A few nights ago he spent an entire evening drawing up the most elaborate plans for who knows what, then dashed out first chance he got to buy a whole bunch of lumber and other stuff. Since then all I hear is sawing and hammering until all hours."

"What's he building?"

Bess shrugged a shoulder. "Your guess is as good as mine. I made some fresh coffee the other evening and took some out to him, and he barely acknowledged my presence. He did look up and thank me, then went right back to what he was doing, as if I wasn't even there."

"Didn't you ask him what he was making?"

She nodded. "I tried. His exact words were 'shelves and cabinets.' But where he's going to put them is the thing. The entire wall of that workshop is already lined with the ones he put in when we first moved into the house."

"Maybe he's planning to upgrade. Something like that."

"Why would he bother? Nobody sees them but us."

"Could it be for somebody else, perhaps? One of the girls, maybe?"

"Possibly." Bess toyed with her egg roll, dipping it into the tiny saucer of apricot sauce. "I'm starting to wonder if he's avoiding me. I know I haven't been the best company since Faith's wedding. The house was way too quiet, and it really got to me. For a while, Arthur would keep me company in the evening and watch movies on TV. But it didn't take long before he got bored. Everyone knows romantic stories can't begin to compete with football or the news."

"Yes, but wasn't he the one who suggested you start taking up painting," Madge cut in, "to occupy some of your empty days? Maybe he's just taking his own advice. By the way, how are your classes going?"

"Terrific." The mention of her new hobby perked Bess up. "My first picture is nearly finished." She paused to formulate her next thought, then met Madge's gaze. "You know, I sure enjoy going to the gallery. So much, in fact, I was beginning to feel guilty about it."

"Guilty! Why would you say that?"

"Because. . . I don't know. When I'm there, I can tune out everything else in my life. Know what I mean?"

Madge didn't respond, so Bess went on.

"It's a different world there. I'm an individual. Nobody knows Arthur or the girls, so I'm just myself. And it feels so. . . invigorating. I like it a lot. I almost hate to go home afterward. Especially now that Arthur's *otherwise occupied*." She blinked back the sting of tears and took a sip of water.

"Well, look, gal," Madge said, reaching across the table to pat Bess's hand. "I don't think there's anything to really worry about. I'm sure there's a logical explanation for why Art's been so busy. And you know how dense men can be. He's probably oblivious to the fact you're even concerned."

Bess looked askance at her.

"I'm serious. But if you'd like to get away for a little while, remember the church's annual women's retreat is coming up pretty quick. Maybe a chance to get away and clear your head would do you some good. And a few days without you might give Art pause for thought, too. As they say, absence makes the heart grow fonder. How about we sign up? We could room together, stay up all night talking, like when we were teenagers. What do you say? Sunday's the last day to register."

The thought of leaving town for a few days and basking in the clear air of the Tehachapi Mountains did sound particularly inviting. And Bess was uncomfortably aware she'd been neglecting her personal devotions for weeks, another thing that added to her guilt. Perhaps a chance to renew her spirit was just the ticket. "Sounds wonderful."

"Good. I'll get in touch with the church secretary and make our reservations."

When Bess arrived at the gallery the following Tuesday, Tasha was in the process of stringing Christmas garlands around the windows and doors. The decorations did much to brighten the neutral interior of the establishment.

Aware that she'd soon have to do the same thing at home, Bess smiled at her and strode through to the next room. The early arrivals were already setting up, chatting as they readied their spots and started right to work. She greeted them on her way to her easel and exchanged pleasantries with her silver-haired neighbor, Priscilla, as she arranged her own supplies. Then she went to retrieve her painting from the back room.

In this final stage of the picture, students worked independently, while the instructor quietly made the rounds to observe everyone's efforts and offer help wherever needed. Conscious of his ever-nearing presence, Bess curbed any improper fantasies and immersed herself in finishing her first "masterpiece." The soft jazz floating down from the wall speakers helped her tune out her problems and concentrate on adding a few last highlights and shadows to the tree in the foreground. Then she stepped back to assess it.

Jeff reached her easel at the same time. Tipping his curly head to one side, he crossed his arms and studied her scene. "Looking great."

"Really?" Though quite proud of her first effort, Bess was more than aware she was still a novice, so she retained some doubts regarding her ability.

"Sure," he affirmed. "No one will ever guess it's your first rendering—especially once it's put in the right frame."

His approval made her spirit soar. Still. . . "I don't know if I'd go quite that far." She turned a critical eye on it. "Considering all the help I needed, at least half the work must be yours."

He chuckled, sable eyes twinkling. "Hey, we all have to start somewhere. You've been a fast learner. My star pupil, in fact."

"That's exactly what I've been trying to tell her," Priscilla added, her slight form leaning nearer as she wagged an arthritic finger. "She's forever putting herself down."

Jeff slanted a gaze at Bess. "No need for that when you have such natural talent, Bess. Hold that beautiful head high. Have confidence in yourself. The next one'll go a lot easier, wait and see."

A flush heated her face at his compliment, and for an instant she couldn't think. "I'll try to remember that."

He gave a nod. "By the way, your canvas is dry around the edges. Soon as you sign your painting, try out some frames. I'm sure we have one or two that'll show off its best qualities." Clamping a warm hand on her shoulder, he administered a friendly squeeze and a wink. "Great job." He grinned and left to respond to someone else's summons.

Bess's pulse beat at an erratic rate. She shook her head to rein in her imaginings and turned to Priscilla. "Looks like your picture's about done, too. Let's go check out the frames, okay?"

A short while later, her now-framed landscape stowed in the trunk, she headed for home, smiling as Jeff's remarks echoed in her mind. She couldn't help wondering if Arthur would be so enthusiastic about her masterpiece.

Or, for that matter, if he'd even notice it.

When Bess got to the house, she didn't take chances. She propped the picture up in a prominent spot where he'd be sure to see it the minute he came home from the office.

That afternoon she cooked Art's favorite meal for supper and set the table with the good dishes, then freshened up and spritzed on the perfume he'd always liked. As a last special touch when the time neared for his arrival, she chose a favorite instrumental CD from their collection and started the stereo so there'd be nice music playing while they ate. Maybe it was overkill, but she didn't care. It wasn't every night that a budding artist got to exhibit her talent.

As she pushed the START button on the coffeemaker, the phone rang. Automatically, she dried her hands on a tea towel, then reached for the receiver. "Hello?"

"Hi, hon. It's me," Arthur said. "Something came up at the office, and it looks like I'm gonna be stuck here for a while."

"You're kidding."

" 'Fraid not. I've no idea when I'll be finished. I won't be needing any supper, okay? And don't wait up. I probably won't get home 'til late."

"Fine. Whatever." The line went dead. Replacing the receiver on its cradle, Bess looked at the crisp golden chicken she'd fried to perfection, the lovely fresh garden salad in its pretty crystal dish, the salt-crusted baked potatoes and glazed green beans—everything that would now be leftovers. In the twenty-odd years Arthur had worked as a CPA, he'd rarely ever stayed after hours. Until lately. That necessity hadn't been called for since he'd become a full partner in the business with his old school buddy, Fred Perkins. After all, it wasn't as if Arthur was some hireling who needed overtime. If she'd had any doubts before about her husband's attention being directed elsewhere, this little episode drove the point home.

Maybe she wasn't the only one who'd been entertaining fantasies about some charmer. Maybe the poor attitude her mother had spoken of had driven him away!

Her appetite fled. Woodenly, Bess packaged all the food in refrigerator containers and cleared the table, counter, and stove. Then she took her painting to the hall closet and turned the picture to the wall. It still had to dry anyway.

"Whew! What a night," Arthur exclaimed the next morning over coffee.

Buttering an English muffin at the counter, Bess didn't bother to look up at him. "Really." She rolled her eyes and grimaced.

"Yeah. Fred and I finally managed to land that account we've been trying to snag for the last couple months. Had to take the fellow out to wine and dine him—well, *dine* him, anyhow, since we don't drink. You know what I mean."

She only nodded.

"The guy's new in town. Relocating here from San Francisco," he went on, not picking up on her mood. "We're supposed to meet him again first thing this morning and finalize all the nitty-gritty." He finished the last of his muffin and egg, then took a gulp of coffee. "By the way, Fred says his wife's going to the women's retreat this Friday. I think you should go, too. Do you some good to get away."

Bess cut a glance to him. Now he was trying to get rid of her for a whole weekend. Could he be involved in something beyond mere daydreams? She chewed the inside corner of her lip to keep from blurting out something she'd regret.

"I should be home the usual time," he continued. "It's prayer meeting night. Wanna eat at the church? Sunday's bulletin says they're serving fried chicken. You know how I love that. Besides, I need to talk to Pastor Monahan about something after the service."

Chapter 7

B ess avoided Arthur as much as possible as the weekend approached. It really aggravated her to think he actually *wanted* her to leave town. Well, truth be told, she was just as eager to go. Let him have the whole house to himself, if that's what made him happy. Far be it from her to get in the way of his *fling*. She planned to put everything out of her mind and focus on the anticipated spiritual blessings a retreat always provided.

Adding another warm outfit to those she'd be taking with her, she tucked it around her cosmetics bag and zipped the suitcase closed.

The door chime announced Madge's arrival. Bess made a last check to be sure she hadn't forgotten anything, then took the rolling luggage to the door to greet her.

"Hi, gal." Her honey blond friend smiled and stepped inside. "All set?"

"Sure am," Bess said, feigning cheerfulness. She slipped her arms into her plaid wool jacket and picked up her purse.

"I can't wait to breathe some clean mountain air."

"Isn't that the truth. Hope it's not too much of a shock for our systems," she teased. "They predict clear weather for the next several days—and no fog, for once."

The forty-mile drive from the valley floor to the bustling mountain community of Tehachapi passed quickly in the luxurious comfort of Madge's Lexus. In no mood to talk, Bess was glad that after minimal chitchat, her friend inserted a classical CD into the player. She centered her attention on the winter-barren scenery, at the leftover snow from a recent storm, glistening beneath an incredibly blue sky. She was awed to see how built-up the town had gotten since her last visit.

Madge turned onto the road to Stallion Springs, where the retreat would be held, and within moments, they arrived at the Stallion Springs Resort. Several familiar vehicles already dotted the hotel parking lot as other women from the church retrieved their belongings and made their way inside the chalet-style building.

"This should be fun," Madge commented. She turned off the ignition and pulled the trunk release lever. "Hope they serve some memorable desserts."

The registration process, a reception, and a short devotional took up most of Friday evening. When the pair finally returned to the room they'd be sharing, they opened their information packets and sat opposite each other at the small table to choose the workshops they'd attend the next day.

"Hmm." Madge tapped her index finger against her lip in thought. " 'Ten Steps to Getting Organized: An Orderly Life

Is a Christ-Centered Life.' I could use that one."

Bess cocked an eyebrow. "How can you possibly need to get organized?"

"Are you kidding? With Steve on the go all the time? He buys stuff everywhere, and I get to figure out where to put it all. It's time for us to have a *major* garage sale." She paused. "Have you picked a morning workshop?"

"Not yet. I see 'Praying from the Heart' is scheduled at the same hour as 'How to Get the Most Out of Your Bible.' Same with the afternoon. 'Recapture Your Inner Beauty' runs concurrently with 'Helpmate or Hindrance: Becoming the Wife God Meant You to Be.' In my case, I'd better focus on courses relating to prayer and marriage. I have a lot of time invested in Arthur. I'm not quite ready to throw in the towel yet—even though things do appear to be worse now than I thought."

Obviously shocked by Bess's confession, Madge gave her an empathetic pat on the forearm. "Want to talk about it?"

Bess shook her head. "Right now I'd better keep this between the Lord and me. I need to listen to what He has to say. Truth be told, I have some guilt of my own to work through."

Her companion remained silent for several seconds. "Listen," she said gently, "I still believe things are not as they seem to be at the moment. Art's never done anything to make you doubt his love before, and I don't think he's purposely doing anything to hurt you now. Just relax and make the most of your time here. Open your heart to whatever the Lord has for you. When you get back home, keep on being yourself, the gal Art first fell in love with. Things'll work out. I know they will."

A smile teased Bess's lips. "For some reason, when you talk, things don't sound so hopeless."

"Just ride things out. As they say, 'This, too, shall pass.'" Madge eyed her momentarily, then spoke again. "You do realize that once this retreat is behind us, we need to figure out how to celebrate that milestone anniversary of yours. The week after Christmas, isn't it?"

Bess nodded. "We originally planned to get married on Valentine's Day, but we were hopelessly in love and didn't want to wait." A tender memory brought a bittersweet pang to her heart.

"I imagine your girls will probably want to throw a big shindig," her friend continued with a smile. "Invite the entire church, plus everyone you ever met. Rent a hall, hire an orchestra. . ."

She shook her head. "I don't think so. We've never been ones for big parties."

"Now see? That's a good sign," Madge said, her eyes sparkling.

"What is?"

"You saying 'we.'"

Whether it was her friend's optimism, the fresh mountain air, or simply putting some space between her uneasiness and herself, Bess felt some of the ice that had formed on her heart melting away. While Madge took a leisurely shower, Bess changed into her nightshirt, knelt beside her double bed, and poured out her pain to God.

Father, I don't know what's going on in Arthur's heart. I only know what's happening in mine. I've been so wrong, harboring silly daydreams about a man I don't even know, when You already gave me the best husband a woman could have. Please forgive me for being disloyal to You and to the man I love. Help me not to forget my blessings. And when I get home, please help me to be the best wife ever. Help me to win back Arthur's love.

She slept soundly that night and awoke early, eager for the day. Madge was still asleep, so Bess showered and dressed. Taking advantage of the morning quiet, she turned to the passage about the virtuous wife in the thirty-first chapter of Proverbs, rereading phrases that especially touched her heart:

> *Who can find a virtuous wife? For her worth is*
> *far above rubies. The heart of her husband safely trusts*
> *her. . . . She does him good and not evil all the days*
> *of her life. . . . Her children rise up and call her blessed;*
> *her husband also, and he praises her. . . . Charm is*
> *deceitful and beauty is passing, but a woman who fears*
> *the LORD, she shall be praised.*

Bess closed her Bible and bowed her head. *That's the kind of wife I want to be, Lord, one my husband and children can admire rather than be ashamed of. I pray that You will take control of this present situation and work it out to Your glory.* After a few more moments of reflection, Bess went to rouse her companion.

"Is it morning already?" Madge asked, her voice raspy from slumber.

"I'm afraid so. Up and at 'em, or we'll be late for breakfast."

✻

Bess basked in the atmosphere of the women's retreat, soaking up memorable Bible verses and quotes at each devotional and workshop. When she learned that the topic at the afternoon session she planned to attend would center on the last chapter of Proverbs, she smiled inwardly.

She arrived at the designated room early enough to grab some coffee from the back, then took a seat beside another lady she knew from Sunday school. When she glanced around at the mostly familiar faces of the other attendees, it came as no surprise that the majority were younger than she. But focusing on her own needs, she set her coffee on the empty seat next to her, opened her notebook and her Bible, and turned her attention to the front.

After a flattering introduction from Pastor Monahan's attractive wife, Helen, the guest speaker, known for her to-the-point talks on sensitive issues of the day, took the podium.

"I'm honored to be here," the fashionably coifed and dressed lady said, her smile encompassing the group. "Before we begin our study on the thirty-first chapter of Proverbs, let's open in prayer."

As the woman prayed, Bess closed her eyes and asked God for wisdom and guidance. Then, accepting the printed handout the workshop helper passed around, she turned to the passage announced.

"King Solomon set forth quite a lofty ideal to emulate in that chapter, didn't he?" the speaker began. "And sad to say, it's pointless for us to try to live up to these instructions and attempt to be godly wives when we have the wrong priorities. An individual who is starving and undernourished cannot offer a healthy, balanced diet to others. We must realize how imperative it is for each of us to nourish our own personal relationship with God on a daily basis. Only then can we give out what our husbands and other family members need."

Bess identified with the central point immediately. She'd been neglecting her private devotions since Faith's wedding. It's no wonder she'd started drifting away from Arthur and looking for faults in him rather than recognizing her own— not to mention entertaining desires the Bible commanded her to flee.

"So much emphasis," the lecturer continued, "is placed on the word *love* as a noun. We all need love, desire love. Some people even make extremely bad decisions in the name of love. But there's another facet of love that we shouldn't forget, and that is its more important side. *Love* is also a verb. It's something we're commanded to do. 'Love one another as I have loved you,' the Bible says. 'By this all will know that you are My disciples, if you have love for one another. Doing thoughtful things for our loved ones, being there for them, providing for their needs, being a listening ear, encouraging them—all demonstrate the love of Christ in our hearts. Let's face it. Marriage is not easy. Perhaps your mate isn't the easiest person to live with. Perhaps *you* aren't. But you can still build a strong marriage—by choosing to love your partner anyway. Love is, after all, a choice."

The lecture wasn't anything Bess hadn't heard before, but somehow, because of her present need, it spoke to her heart in a new, fresh way. She couldn't help noticing how the younger wives were enthralled as they listened to the speaker and took copious notes. She'd done the same thing in her early years; only lately she'd forgotten to follow those instructions. By taking her focus off the Lord, not only had she been less than loving to Arthur, and even critical of him, she had allowed herself to fantasize about a man she barely knew. All those things would change. She breathed a silent prayer for forgiveness, then renewed her determination to get her priorities straight again and to become the godly wife God intended her to be. It was no less than God commanded and Arthur deserved.

"So how were your workshops?" Bess asked Madge the following afternoon as they drove back to Bakersfield after the Sunday devotional.

Madge chuckled. "From all the great suggestions in the handouts the speakers passed around, by this time next month, I'll be the best organized gal you ever saw! Of course, I have to admit yesterday's session on inner beauty was also pretty inspiring."

"I'm glad you took the classes opposite mine so we could share all this new knowledge," Bess quipped. "I was reminded of a lot, too. I'm really glad we came."

"So am I. I think we both needed it."

"So tell me what transpired in the class about beauty. I'd have liked to have gone to that one myself, if I hadn't felt compelled to take the other one."

Her friend nodded. "Well, you're familiar with that passage in First Timothy, about how a godly woman should dress modestly—and isn't *that* a foreign term in today's world." She laughed lightly. "But all of us can stand the reminder that we should spend less time in front of our mirrors and more time reflecting Jesus. The speaker managed to get her points across without it sounding like a bunch of platitudes. Truth is, when a woman's relationship with the Lord is a close one, there really is a glow that shines from her being—a beauty that's intangible and lasting, no matter what her age is. I know several ladies I admire who display that glow of inner loveliness."

Enjoying the musical quality of Madge's voice, Bess relaxed deeper into the plush seat and listened to her friend relating the concepts that especially stood out in her mind. Then she passed along some of the gems from her own workshops.

Bess was more than aware there were tons of things to do once she got home. Christmas lurked right around the corner, and she had yet to write out a single card, let alone drag out the artificial tree and all the holiday decorations she normally put up the week after Thanksgiving. Still, with new hope in her heart as the miles ticked by, the passing landscape seemed prettier than before and the sky bluer.

But even more than that, she could hardly wait to get home to Arthur.

Chapter 8

I'll be praying for you, gal," Madge said. "Everything'll work out, I promise."

"Thanks. I appreciate that." Despite her renewed optimism and noble intentions, Bess's insides were on tenterhooks as she exited her friend's car and approached the house. Would Arthur even be home from church? Would he be glad to see her? And would he want to *celebrate* their silver anniversary at all?

Pulling her wheeled luggage behind her up the front walk, she breathed a prayer for courage and strength. Immediately an indescribable peace filled her heart. No matter what transpired, she had reestablished her relationship with the Lord, and she had confidence that somehow He would see her through.

Bess's pulse throbbed and the fragile hope in her heart rose to clog her throat as she tried the latch. The door opened easily. *He's home.*

Stepping inside, she heard the muted sounds of a football game coming from the den. *Just what I need—to interrupt some crucial play,* her thoughts taunted. She swallowed past the thickness in her throat. "I'm back," she called out tentatively, slipping off her warm jacket and hanging it on the coat tree.

A *thump* sounded as the recliner snapped into sitting position, and Arthur ambled down the hall, an incredibly joyous smile on his handsome face. "Hello, my love," he said, his voice husky. He opened his arms, and Bess melted into his embrace, enjoying the soothing feeling of his soft flannel shirt against her cheek.

"I—I. . ." She couldn't get words past her teeth, but it didn't matter, as Arthur lowered his head and captured her lips with his. This was *home*—having his strong heart thundering in tempo with hers.

"It's good to have you back," he said against her ear, hugging her tighter. "Feels like you've been gone a month."

"I missed you, too," she said, astonishment rendering her voice a notch higher.

"How was your time up in the mountains?" He eased his hold and moved away enough to gaze down at her.

"Wonderful. Perfect. Truly marvelous, physically and spiritually."

"Good. I was praying you'd enjoy it. The girls have been calling ever since I got home from church. They're all wanting you to phone them with news of the retreat."

"I will in a little while, after I unpack and catch my breath."

Arthur gave a nod, an evasive smile lighting his eyes. "There's fresh coffee."

"Thanks. Just let me get rid of this luggage, and I'll come have some with you."

Marveling over the enthusiastic welcome, Bess took her belongings to the bedroom. *He missed me. He actually missed me!* It was what she'd hoped for, what she'd prayed for, but the reality still amazed her. Especially considering the dour suspicions that had nagged her before she'd gone away.

One thing did niggle at her now, though. Arthur seemed. . . strange. As if he had something to tell her. She tried not to draw any conclusions as she deposited her suitcase on the bed, then returned to the kitchen.

She found her husband filling two mugs with the fragrant vanilla bean decaf she favored. He handed one to her with a lopsided grin.

"Thanks." While she added a dash of creamer, she felt him watching her but tried to remain nonchalant as she took a cautious sip of the hot brew. "Arthur, is something wrong?"

"Wrong, sweetheart?" An absurdly innocent look came over him.

Alarm bells went off in Bess's head. "Yes. You seem. . . mysterious."

He chuckled and set down his mug. "I guess I might as well come clean. I do have something to show you. I wanted to wait until later to let you in on my little surprise, but as always, you read me too well. No point in putting it off."

"What is it?" She felt a slow smile tugging at her lips.

A sheepish grin erased years from his face. "It's in the, uh, gym."

Bess couldn't begin to imagine what new piece of exercise equipment he'd gotten this time. Possibly a fad thing she'd seen on TV and made some remark about? That Gazelle Trainer, perhaps? Those did look interesting.

Arthur took her hand and led the way to Faith's old room. He opened the door and flicked on the light switch, then made a gallant bow to usher her in before him.

She gave him a sidelong glance and stepped past him, then stopped short. No new exercise machine met her incredulous gaze. In fact, there were no *old* ones, either. Newly finished cabinets and shelves now lined the room, along with work-tables and even a stool. In one corner he'd put an easel. He'd turned the whole place into an efficient artist's studio!

"I decided you'll make better use of this room than I ever would," he said simply, "seeing as how you enjoy painting so much. I saw an arrangement like this in one of your art magazines and tried to copy it best I could. And the window gets the north light; I hear that's supposed to be good for artists."

Bess was speechless. How could she have thought he'd been ignoring her? Or worse yet, involved with someone else? A sheen of tears blurred the incredible sight before her eyes, and she buried her face in her hands.

"Don't you like it?"

She lowered her arms. "Like it?" she choked out. "It's the most precious surprise you've ever given me. And so much more than I deserve, after being so miserable since Faith's wedding. Thank you so much, Arthur. I—"

"I know you'll probably still want to take lessons for a while," he cut in, "but now you can paint here, too, whenever you feel like it. And once you master all the techniques the professor is teaching and no longer need his guidance, then you can paint at home—to your heart's content."

Bess had to hug him. She nuzzled her nose into his chest, inhaling the masculine scent that had become so familiar during their lifetime together. Then she eased back slightly and raised her lashes to meet his gaze. "I love you, Arthur. I will always love you. You alone."

"And I love you, sweetheart—which brings me to the rest of my surprise."

"There's more? What more can there be? Don't tell me you built a gazebo out back!"

A laugh rumbled from deep inside him. "No, not yet. It's on my list, though. This has to do with our anniversary, once Christmas has been put away."

"The girls aren't planning to throw us a huge party, are they?"

"Nope. They did try to suggest that, but I talked them out of it."

"Thank you." She frowned. "Then that's the surprise? That there's no party?"

He shook his head. "Far from it. I have a different celebration planned for us. After all, it's not every day a couple has a silver anniversary, you know. I figured we'd take two or three weeks and drive up the coast, just you and me. Hit all the spots we did on our honeymoon." He traced her cheekbone with the backs of his fingers. "You're even more beautiful today than you were as my bride, do you know that? And I'm very proud to be seen with you. What d'ya say?"

"Sounds lovely. But what about our Sunday school class? We're not exactly free to just take off whenever we want to. And there's your job. . . ."

"Everything's under control. What do you think I've been doing since you went away?"

She blushed. "I didn't really know."

"Well," he said as he grinned, "as for work, a partner can take time off whenever something important comes up—and what's more important than our anniversary? And as for the class, Pastor Monahan approved Steve Vincent's stepping in as a sub. He doesn't have any golf tournaments until mid-February, so he's more than willing to take over. All I need now is for you to agree. So how about it? Will you come away with me on a second honeymoon, my love?"

It came to Bess then that the house she and Arthur had lived in all these years, where they'd raised their children, was far from being empty. Not with the lifetime of laughter and love that would forever remain within its beautiful walls.

Bess bracketed his face with her palms and stretched up on her toes to kiss him. "Dear, sweet Arthur Wright, I will go *anywhere* with you. *Anywhere.* As long as life shall last." *Thank You, Lord, for answering my prayers beyond even my wildest dreams. I love You, too.*

The phone rang just then. Bess knew it had to be one of their daughters calling for an update. Well, she did have a lot to talk about. But at the moment, gazing into her husband's smiling eyes, she could think of other things she'd rather do.

SALLY LAITY

Sally spent the first twenty years of her life in Dallas, Pennsylvania, and calls herself a small-town girl at heart. She and her husband, Don, have lived in New York, Pennsylvania, Illinois, and Alberta, Canada, and now reside in Bakersfield, California. They are active in a large Baptist church where Don teaches Sunday school and Sally sings in the choir. They have four children and fourteen grandchildren.

Sally always loved to write, and after her children were grown, she took college writing courses and attended Christian writing conferences. She has written both historical and contemporary romances and considers it a joy to know that the Lord can touch other hearts through her stories.

Having successfully written several novels, including a coauthored series for Tyndale, nine Barbour novellas, and nine **Heartsong Presents**, this author's favorite thing these days is trying to organize a lifetime of photographs into memory pages.

wherever love takes us

by Carrie Turansky

Dedication

To my husband, Scott, who shows me every day what it means to truly love and serve one another. Thanks for twenty-seven wonderful years and for encouraging me to follow my dreams.

Where you go I will go, and where you stay I will stay.
Your people will be my people and your God my God.
RUTH 1:16 NIV

Chapter 1

"Mom! Watch out!"

Tessa Malone gasped and slammed on her brakes as an eighteen-wheeler slid in front of her van. The truck's rear lights flashed. She pumped her brakes, praying they would hold the van back from a collision.

"What a jerk!" Brianna, Tessa's sixteen-year-old daughter, scowled at the offending truck as it sprayed their van's windshield. "He ought to check his mirrors before he changes lanes."

The truck pulled ahead, widening the space between them. Tessa bit back a corrective comment. It would only increase the tension she and the children felt as they drove through the storm.

"This weather is crazy!" She strained to see through the foggy windshield and wiggled the useless temperature and defroster buttons. How many times had she told her husband, Matt, they needed to take the van in to have the defroster repaired? Why didn't he ever listen to her and follow through on things like that? Didn't he care about their safety? Did she have to do everything herself? She tried to put a lid on her resentment, but it bubbled like a pot on high.

Evan, her eleven-year-old son, tapped the back of her seat. "Mom, what time is Brie's orthodontist appointment?"

"Four thirty." Tessa glanced at the dashboard clock and blew out a frustrated huff. They were going to be at least fifteen minutes late.

"Mom, you know Dr. Fisher hates it when we're not on time. He'll probably make me wait forever."

"Well, there's nothing I can do about that now."

"But I told Ryan I'd be home by five fifteen so he could call."

"Brie, please, I'm doing the best I can." Tessa pulled in a deep breath, trying to calm her frazzled nerves. The wipers beat out a furious rhythm, but they couldn't keep up with the torrent flooding the windshield.

This wasn't the best time to be out driving, but what other choice did she have? They could only afford one car, so Matt expected her to pick up the kids from school, stop by the dry cleaner's, return the overdue library books, and then take Brie to the orthodontist—all before going home to prepare and serve dinner in time for her and Matt to make it to the parent-teacher conference at Evan's school tonight.

She loved her family, but working full-time and dealing with all their needs often left her feeling out of sorts and weary to the bone. But she couldn't imagine giving up her job. She loved Sweet Something, the cozy tea and gift shop she and her younger sister, Allison, had opened three years ago in Princeton, New Jersey. The shop was more than a moneymaking endeavor; it gave her a place to shine and use her baking and artistic talents.

"Mom?" Evan called from the backseat.

"What?"

"I think I've got a problem."

"What do you mean?"

"I forgot my science stuff at school."

"Well, you'll just have to call a friend and get the information from them."

"I can't. I need my papers tonight. The project's due tomorrow."

Tessa gripped the steering wheel. "Honestly, Evan, what do you expect me to do now? Turn around and drive all the way back?" Cornerstone Christian Academy was twenty minutes from their house on a good day with no extra traffic, and this was definitely not a good day!

"But, Mom, I really need those papers."

"I'll have to get them tonight when I go back to your school."

"Okay, but that means we'll have to stay up really late."

Tessa wearily massaged her forehead. Getting to bed before eleven wasn't happening tonight.

Tessa heard the front door open. She glanced at the clock and then continued stirring the simmering spaghetti sauce.

"Dad!" Evan thundered through the living room. That set

off Chaucer, their golden retriever. His excited barking added to the confusion.

"Hey, sport. How are you doing?"

From the sound of things, Tessa knew Matt was wrapping their son in a bear hug and squeezing him tight. For just a moment she wished that hug were for her. The sauce bubbled and splattered. She frowned and wiped the red spot off the stove top.

"I'm okay," Evan said. "Except I'm probably getting a D in science."

"Why? You love science."

"Mom won't take me back to school to get my stuff, and my project's due tomorrow."

"I see. Well, maybe we can work something out. Come on, let's see what's cooking." Matt's briefcase thumped to the floor, and he walked into the kitchen. Lifting the lid of the largest pot, he sniffed and smiled at her. "Mmm, smells good."

It was just plain pasta again. Tessa wiped her hands on a dish towel, ignoring his comment.

He replaced the lid and studied her for a moment, his gray eyes soft and welcoming.

"Did anyone get the mail?" Brie trotted into the kitchen, her dark brown ponytail swinging.

"I didn't have time." Tessa turned away from Matt's gaze and walked over to the refrigerator. Matt followed her and slipped his arms around her waist. She stiffened.

"What's wrong?" He rubbed his rough chin against her cheek. "Have you had a tough day?"

How about a tough three years? Tessa pressed her lips tighter. She would not say it in front of the children.

When she didn't soften or return his hug, he sighed, dropped his arms, and walked out of the kitchen.

Tessa shook off the wave of guilt. What did he expect? She had run around like a madwoman all afternoon taking care of everything their family needed, and now he was looking for a little romance in the kitchen. No thanks!

She had to get dinner on the table and then get them back out the door by six thirty. She jerked open the refrigerator and snatched the salad and Italian dressing from the top shelf.

"How long 'til dinner, Mom?" Evan picked up his basketball from the corner by the garage door.

"Five minutes. There's no time for basketball right now."

"Aw, Mom, please?"

"Evan, stop. Dad and I have to leave in a few minutes." Tessa deposited the salad on the table with a *thump*. "How about helping?"

He mumbled something under his breath and shuffled across the kitchen. "How many people?"

"Just four. Justin has a late class at the college."

Scowling, he rummaged around in the silverware drawer.

Why did she always come out looking like the bad guy? Evan adored his dad and gladly followed any instruction he gave. But when she asked for a little help, he considered it torture.

Brie returned with a stack of mail and tossed it onto the counter. "Why don't I ever get any mail?"

Tessa lifted her brows. "You have to send a letter to get one back." She picked up the pile and sorted through the bills and junk mail.

A thick white envelope caught her attention. She lifted it from the pile and studied the return address. Why would a lawyer in Oregon be writing to Matt? A chill raced down her back. Was this another legal problem from Matt's business failure? She'd warned him not to take on Patrick Stokes as a partner, but he hadn't listened. They'd ended up losing their home and been forced to move into this small condo. All the money from the sale of their house and their savings had been used to repay the disgruntled investors and prevent any lawsuits. What more did those people want?

Tessa's hand trembled as she recalled the terrible storm that had blown into their lives three years ago, nearly shipwrecking their marriage.

Matt walked back into the kitchen. He slowed when their gazes connected. "What's wrong?"

"I don't know. Why don't you tell me?" She tossed the envelope onto the counter.

A perplexed frown settled over his face. "What is it?"

"A very heavy letter from a lawyer in Oregon." She bit out each syllable and sent them flying at her husband like poison-tipped arrows.

Matt ripped open the envelope and pulled out the thick sheets of stationery. His gaze darted over the words as Evan and Brie gathered around.

"What is it, Dad?" Evan asked. "Are you in trouble?"

"No, I'm sure it's not. . ." Matt sank onto the stool. "I don't believe it."

Tessa gripped the counter, bracing herself for the terrible news.

Matt burst out laughing. "This is incredible! Unbelievable!"

"Dad! What does it say?" Brie leaned over his shoulder.

"It's the answer to our prayers. I knew the Lord would come through. I just didn't expect Him to work things out like this." He scanned the page, then looked up at Tessa. "Remember my uncle Don in Oregon?"

"The one who died last January?"

"Yes. I hadn't seen him since our family moved out here when I was a teenager."

"What about him?" Tessa wanted to grab Matt and shake him. Why couldn't he hurry up and explain?

Matt smiled and waved the letter in the air. "It seems I'm in line to inherit my uncle's property on Lost Lake."

Tessa stared at him in stunned surprise.

"Where's that?" Brie asked.

"In the Cascade Mountains in Oregon."

"Wow, that sounds cool," Evan added. "A house on a lake!"

"Not just a house," Matt continued. "It's twelve acres of virgin forest with a large lodge and seven guest cabins."

Brie settled on the stool next to her dad. "So it's like a camping place or. . .a motel?"

"Well, I haven't been back there in years, but I'd say it's sort of a mountain resort. Uncle Don lived in the lodge and rented out the cabins to vacationers. It's a great place for fishing and

271

hiking in the summer, and in the winter there's skiing nearby."

"Why would he leave it to you?" Tessa asked.

Matt glanced at the letter again. "He originally left it to his son, Charles, but he passed away before his dad, and the will was never changed. I'm the next closest relative."

Excitement tingled through Tessa. "That property must be worth a lot of money. How many acres did you say?"

"Twelve. And it's beautiful. Tall fir trees, cedar, vine maple. . ." Matt sprang from the stool. "Where's the atlas? Let's take a look at the map of Oregon."

"I'll get it." Evan ran from the kitchen.

Tessa hugged herself. "This is wonderful! I'm sure it will be enough."

Matt turned to her, confusion in his eyes. "Enough?"

"Yes! We can buy a house and another car. And we can pay for Justin's college expenses and Brie's orthodontic bills." The thought of lifting the burden of debt off their shoulders made Tessa feel almost dizzy with joy.

Matt frowned. "What are you talking about?"

"Selling it, of course!"

"Tessa, you don't understand. This is like a miracle. I've been praying for a way to get out of this dead-end job and change careers."

"What?" Heat flooded her face, and her mind spun. "Matt, how could you possibly manage a resort in Oregon when we live here in New Jersey?"

"We'd have to move there." Matt rubbed his hands together, the excitement of a new challenge glowing on his face. "If we lived in the lodge and rented out the cabins, all the money we'd make would be free and clear." He stepped closer and took both of her hands in his. "Just think of it, this is our chance to start over, fresh."

She pulled her hands away. "Start over?" Panic nearly choked off her voice.

"Yes, it would be a great opportunity for all of us."

"How can you even think of moving? Our family is here. Our life is here." Tessa shook her head. "No! We've got to sell the property and use that money to get back on our feet financially."

Matt pulled in a deep breath and pressed his lips together. "Tessa, we can't throw away a great opportunity like this."

Fury built inside Tessa like a volcano about to erupt. "How could you even consider dragging us all the way across the country for another one of your harebrained business schemes?" Once she opened the vent on her anger, she couldn't stop the flow. "You've been praying! Well, I've been praying, too. We're barely scraping by on less than half the money we made before. And now you have the perfect opportunity to pay off all our debts and start rebuilding our lives, and you want to toss it all away on some silly childhood memory!"

"Tessa, come on." Matt's voice remained controlled, but she could see the color rising in his face and a muscle twitching in his jaw. "Look, I know this is a surprise, but I think—"

"Surprise! Oh no. What surprises me is that you care so little about what I want or what's best for this family!"

Anger and hurt flashed across Matt's face. He spun away

273

and strode out of the kitchen.

Her bitter words had hit their mark. Brie and Evan stared at her in frightened silence.

Guilt poured over her like hot wax dripping from a candle. It burned and coated her heart like a heavy weight. She tightened her fists and turned back toward the stove.

Why should she feel guilty? Everything she said was true. This proved he didn't love her or the children. All he cared about was running after some foolish dream. Well, she wouldn't stand by and let it happen again. She had put up with more than enough from Matt Malone!

Chapter 2

M att pushed open the door of the bagel shop. The jovial bell did little to lift his spirits. He scanned the small tables and soon spotted his friend Keith Stevenson.

"Morning, Matt." Keith pushed a steaming cup of black coffee and a cinnamon raisin bagel toward him.

Matt settled into the chair on the opposite side of the table, thankful his friend knew what he always ordered. "I got some great news."

"Really? You'd never know it by looking at you."

"Thanks."

Keith chuckled. "So what's going on? Were you up late with the kids?"

"No, Tessa and I had a fight last night." Matt took a quick sip of the hot brew. "Couldn't sleep much after that."

Keith's smile slipped away. "Sorry. I take it she's not responding to your plan to be more affectionate?"

Matt scoffed. "No, I'd say our relationship has gone from

cool to below freezing."

"Well, hang in there. You've got a lot to overcome. We're not talking about a little sheet of ice that built up overnight. It's more like an iceberg. And it's taken three years to freeze that deep. It's going to take awhile to melt."

"You're just full of encouragement today, aren't you?"

"I want to give it to you straight." Keith munched on his blueberry bagel and then looked back at his friend. "So what's the good news?"

He told Keith about the letter he had received from the lawyer in Oregon. "I'm now the proud owner of Lost Lake Lodge." Matt smiled in spite of his tired condition and the memory of his wife's hurtful response.

"That sounds great."

"Yeah. I want to move there. That's why Tessa's so upset. She doesn't even want to consider it."

Keith nodded. "Most women don't like moving. And with everything that's happened, I can see why she's not too enthusiastic about the idea."

"You should have heard her." Matt shook his head, recalling the stinging words Tessa had flung at him last night. There was no way he would repeat them to his friend. They were too humiliating.

"So what are you going to do?"

Matt blew out a deep breath. "I don't know. I want to win back Tessa's trust and love, but that seems just about impossible with the way things are going."

"Hey, come on. This is no time to give up. God's on your

side. He wants your marriage healed, and He gave you this land for a reason. You just have to figure out how it all fits together."

Matt nodded and tore off a bite of his bagel. He and Keith had been praying together for the past few months and looking for practical ways for Matt to renew his relationship with Tessa. So far his efforts seemed useless. Tessa hadn't softened at all. But maybe this was all part of God's answer—he just didn't see it yet.

"Let's do our Bible study, and then we'll spend some time praying this through."

"Sounds good to me." Matt reached into his briefcase and retrieved his Bible. He might not know what to do about the Oregon property or how to convince his wife to believe in him again, but he knew this much—the answers he needed were in his hand between the pages of this book.

Tessa pulled the tray of apple walnut muffins from the large commercial oven. Their sweet, spicy fragrance filled the tea shop kitchen. They were the fastest-selling muffins at Sweet Something, but she wasn't even tempted to taste one this afternoon. Last night's argument with Matt still tumbled around in her mind, setting her nerves on edge and stealing away her appetite.

Tessa's sister, Allison, walked into the kitchen wearing a white apron over her long black skirt and white ruffled blouse. She had pulled her golden brown hair into a low ponytail and tied it with a bright red ribbon. They hardly looked like sisters.

Tessa's olive skin and dark brown hair were like their father's. She wore her hair in a short, carefree style with fringy bangs that framed her face and fit her petite stature. Allison was taller and blue-eyed like their mother, and her movements always reminded Tessa of a graceful ballet dancer.

Allison reached for a tray of delicate teacups and saucers. "What time is that group of ladies from the historical society coming in?"

"I think they said three o'clock." Tessa absently laid the hot pads on the counter.

Allison studied her a moment. "What's wrong?"

"Nothing. Why?" Tessa picked up a knife and began tilting each muffin so they would cool without getting soggy on the bottom.

"Come on, I know something is bothering you. You've been distracted and moody all morning." Allison stepped over and plucked a hot muffin from the tin. Peeling off the paper, she gave her sister a steady look.

Tessa blew out a slow, deep breath. She didn't want to tell her sister she might be moving, but how could she avoid it?

"I'm waiting." Allison took a bite of her muffin and leaned back against the counter.

"All right." Tessa huffed and set aside her knife. "Matt inherited some property in Oregon, and he has this crazy idea we should move there."

Allison's eyebrows lifted. "You mean live there permanently?"

"That's what he said. Can you believe it?" Tessa closed her eyes and shuddered. "I'm just sick about the whole thing. We had a terrible fight last night right in front of the kids. You should have heard him. He was going on and on about wanting to change careers and moving out there like it was nothing more than a two-week vacation."

"Maybe he'll change his mind when he thinks about it a little more."

"I doubt it." Tessa thrust her hands into her apron pockets. "That man is so stubborn!"

"Funny, I never would've described Matt like that. He's always seemed like a pretty reasonable guy to me."

"Allison! How can you defend him? You know all the trouble his business failure caused us. Justin had to go to community college, the kids had to stop all their music lessons and sports, we lost the house and our savings. We almost lost everything!"

"Tessa. You had to move into a condo and get used to one car again. I wouldn't exactly call that losing everything."

"We lost a lot more than our house and savings. We lost our sense of security, and that's hard to restore."

"At least you have a family," Allison said softly.

Immediately Tessa regretted her hasty words. Allison and her husband, Tyler, had recently learned they might not be able to have children. "I'm sorry, Allie. I know you're going through a lot, too."

Allison wrapped Tessa in a comforting hug. "It's okay." Then she stepped back and looked at Tessa with a sad smile. "I know this seems like a huge issue right now, but let's not let it rock our boat. Our anchor is firm. The Lord's in control."

But Tessa felt like a little boat tossed on a stormy sea. "Moving would be terrible. I don't even want to think about leaving Princeton."

"No one is moving today. This whole thing may just blow over. Let's trust the Lord and see what happens." Allison picked up her tray and headed into the dining room. "I'll go set those tables."

"Thanks." Tessa chewed her lip as she considered her sister's words. Sometimes Allison's spiritual strength amazed her. How could she hold on when her prayers went unanswered? Her faith seemed like a rock, strong and unshakable.

Tessa shook her head sadly. *I used to be like that.* But the last three years had left her feeling weak and beaten down.

But whose fault was that? She was the one who had slipped away from midweek Bible study, and she rarely took time to pray or read the Bible on her own. Sunday mornings were no better. She struggled to get herself out of bed in time for church and only made it to services two or three times a month. Matt and the kids went every Sunday, with or without her.

Allison returned to the kitchen. "Tessa?"

"Hmm?"

"Don't worry. This is all going to work out for the best."

Tessa forced a small smile for her sister's sake. But she couldn't shake the turbulent feelings swirling through her stomach.

✵

The phone rang in Matt's office. He looked up from his computer screen and rubbed his eyes, thankful for the break.

Though he had a degree in accounting and was a CPA, he hated working with numbers all day long. But as a supervisor for Ampler, Madden, and Politzer in the auditing and accounting department, he had no choice. They serviced small to midsized companies in the pension, not-for-profit, and manufacturing industries. The job held little interest or challenge for him, but it paid the bills and provided for his family. So he kept at it, day in and day out.

Matt picked up the phone on the second ring.

"Matt, it's Keith. You got a minute?"

"Sure. What's up?"

"I've been praying for you and Tessa all morning, and I think I've got an idea."

"Okay, shoot."

"I know you've been looking for extra things to do around the house to make it easier for Tessa, right?"

"Yeah, I spent all last Saturday cleaning out the garage." Matt turned his chair away from his desk. Outside his third-story office window, the first traces of golden-green leaves sprouted from the oak tree.

"What did she say?"

"Nothing. She's been bugging me to do it for weeks, but she didn't even notice."

"Wow, she didn't say anything?"

"No. She's too busy with the kids and the tea shop to notice anything I do, unless it's a mistake, like forgetting to give her a phone message or taking the car when she needs it."

"I think it's time to bring out the big guns."

"What do you mean?" Matt spun back toward his desk and picked up a pencil.

"Plan something big, something she can't miss."

"Like?"

"Like a really romantic date. What does she like? French food, Broadway plays, classical concerts?"

Matt scratched his chin. "It's been awhile since we did anything like that. Money's been tight. We usually just rent a video or grab some pizza."

"See, that's what I mean. If you plan a really special date, that's bound to get her attention. She'll have to warm up a little."

"You think that'll work?"

"Yeah, women love romance. Trust me."

"Okay, I hope you're right, 'cause I'm in the doghouse and fresh out of ideas."

Chapter 3

Matt hopped out of the van and hustled to open Tessa's door.

She looked up at him with a perplexed expression, her dark eyes serious.

He smiled, glad she seemed to notice his gallant efforts. She looked great tonight. She wore a red and black flowered dress made of soft, gauzy material. It wasn't a new outfit, but he hadn't seen her dressed up like that in quite a while. Black beaded earrings dangled from her ears, and her lips were painted an inviting warm red. He had done a double take when she walked down the stairs at home, and he'd told her how great she looked. But she'd waved away his compliments as though she didn't believe him. Regret hit his heart. He hadn't complimented her often enough.

He let his gaze drift over her again, and it made him wish that she didn't hold herself so aloof every night. It had been too long since they had enjoyed each other as husband and wife.

Maybe tonight would help melt the ice. That was all he

hoped for, just a little hint that she might be willing to rebuild the closeness they'd once shared. Of course he wanted more than that, but he was a patient man. He could wait.

Tessa glanced around as they stepped through the restaurant door and smiled. "I've always wondered what this place was like."

Matt held back a grin, thankful he had chosen the Lawrenceville Inn. A friend at work had recommended it, telling him the atmosphere was romantic and the food was excellent. He checked out the room and nodded. Tessa would like this. The owners had converted a historic home into a cozy restaurant complete with antique furniture, vintage lighting, glowing candles, and original paintings on the walls. The delicious smell of roasting meat and hot bread floated out from the kitchen, making his mouth water.

A smiling hostess seated them at a linen-covered table in the renovated parlor and handed them each menus.

Tessa smiled as she glanced around the room. "This is very nice." Suddenly her smile faded. She lifted her gaze to his. "Matt, can we afford this?"

"Don't worry." He reached across the table and took her hand. Her cool fingers didn't move, and he wished with everything in him that he could change the choices he had made—they had cost them much more than their savings and home. They had stolen away the trust that had characterized their relationship for almost twenty-five years.

"It's okay. Tonight's special." He forced a small smile. "Let's relax and enjoy it."

Slight lines of worry still creased her forehead, and unspoken questions shadowed her large brown eyes. "All right," she said softly, then focused on the menu.

Tessa's silence shook Matt. Thankfully the waitress came and took their order. Tessa seemed to relax a bit when he asked her about the plans for her sister's upcoming art show at Sweet Something.

Matt looked up and smiled as the young waitress returned with their salads and bread. He led in a brief prayer, then dove into his meal. Focusing on the delicious seared rib eye, he ate with only a few brief comments directed toward his quiet wife. About halfway through his meal, an associate from Matt's office walked up to their table.

"Hey, Matt, enjoying your dinner?" Ryan Fisher's eyes lingered too long on Tessa. "And who is this lovely lady?"

Irritation flooded Matt. Who did Ryan think he would be having dinner with? "This is my wife, Tessa. Tessa, this is Ryan Fisher from work."

She smiled and nodded, then lowered her gaze.

Ryan chuckled. "Well, aren't you a lucky man to have such a lovely wife."

Matt glanced across the table and read the discomfort on Tessa's face.

"Say, I heard about that land you inherited out in Oregon. What an opportunity. When are you moving?"

Matt clamped his mouth shut and glared at Ryan. This was the one subject he had promised himself they would not discuss tonight.

Ryan leaned closer, grinning like some stupid Cheshire cat. "So when do you think I should apply for your position?"

"I haven't made a decision yet," Matt said, barely hiding his irritation. Ryan had worked under Matt for only about eight months. There was no way he had the skills necessary to step into Matt's job.

Tessa stared back at Matt with wide, pain-filled eyes, her face flushed.

"Come on, let me in on your plans," Ryan continued. "You *are* leaving, aren't you? I mean, that's what I heard from Ben Stackwell."

Tessa's chair scraped on the hardwood floor as she pushed back from the table. "Excuse me." She snatched her purse and hurried off toward the restrooms.

Matt turned to Ryan. "I don't want to discuss this with you right now."

"Sorry, I didn't know it was a secret. Everyone's talking about it at work. You did tell your wife, right?"

"This isn't the time or place for this discussion. Now if you'll excuse me, I'd like to finish my dinner."

"You don't have to get huffy. I get the point." Ryan walked away, looking offended.

Good! He had a lot of nerve, bringing that subject up here in a restaurant in front of his wife. What would he say to Tessa now? Could he salvage the evening? He closed his eyes and shot off a quick prayer.

❁

Tessa took one last glance in the restroom mirror. No matter how much makeup she used, it didn't help. Her reflection seemed to shout: "You've been crying." Tessa sighed and pushed open the restroom door. She needed to get back to their table. There was no use pretending they didn't have a huge problem to work through.

As she reached the bottom of the stairs, a tall man stepped into her path.

"Tessa! This is a wonderful surprise." Bill Hancock's gaze traveled over her with a look of slow-warming delight. The recently divorced, forty-something owner of Hancock's Flowers made a habit of complimenting Tessa's creativity and baking every time he came into her shop for coffee. He seemed to notice each time she got her hair cut or wore a new outfit, things Matt never noticed or bothered to mention.

Heat filled her face. "Hello, Bill. It's nice to see you." Her glance darted across the room to the table where her husband sat.

"This is a nice place. I guess we read the same restaurant review." His blue eyes danced, and the dimple beside his mouth deepened.

"My husband picked it." Tessa nodded toward Matt.

Bill's smile faded as he looked toward their table.

"Why don't you come over and I'll introduce you?"

"That's all right. I don't want to interrupt. I'm in the middle of dinner myself."

"You wouldn't be interrupting."

"No, I'll see you at work tomorrow."

His meaningful look sent a shiver up her back, and then

he turned and walked upstairs. Watching Bill go, she felt torn. This was crazy! What was she thinking? Bill was a friend, and her husband of almost twenty-five years sat across the room waiting for her.

She turned and wove her way through the tables to rejoin Matt and face the discussion she dreaded.

"Everything okay?" he asked.

She nodded and sat down.

"Who was that you were talking to?"

"Bill Hancock. He owns Hancock's Flowers across the street from Sweet Something."

Matt frowned toward the stairs.

Tessa could almost see the wheels turning in his mind. Did he suspect the way Bill flirted with her? Was he jealous? A little thrill ran through her at that thought.

Matt reached for her hand again. "I'm sorry Ryan interrupted our dinner. He's. . ." He shook his head. "I can't think of a nice thing to say about him."

"It doesn't matter." Tessa slid her napkin onto her lap. She'd lost her appetite, but focusing on her food was the only way to avoid the probing look in Matt's eyes.

"Yes, it does matter. I wanted tonight to be special. Just you and me with plenty of time to enjoy each other."

Tessa felt a little smile tugging at her lips. That was such a sweet thought. Not at all like the things Matt usually said.

"I didn't want to talk about the Oregon property tonight."

Tessa's smile faded. "Did you tell someone at work that you were leaving?"

"No, but I did ask Marlene how much vacation time I have coming. She wanted to know where I was going, so I told her I was flying out to Oregon to check out some property I inherited."

Tessa's stomach churned. "What about our plans to go to the Jersey shore with my family in August? We've been saving for that since last summer."

"I didn't say we couldn't go to the shore. I have three weeks coming since I only took one last year."

"And you want to spend that extra week in Oregon?"

"Yes." Matt looked at her like she was being very thick-headed. "How can we make a decision unless we take a look at the property?"

"We? You mean you expect me to go along?"

"Of course I want you to come. I think the whole family should see it. I'd like us to make this decision together."

Tessa laid her napkin on the table. "And how are we supposed to afford this trip?"

"We can work it out. I'll go on the Internet and find the lowest fares. I'm sure I can get a good deal."

"When did you intend to go? We can't pull the kids out of school whenever the whim strikes us."

"I thought spring break would be a good time. Come on, how long has it been since we've had a fun family vacation?"

"Exactly three years and five months." The wounded look on Matt's face sent a guilty stab through her heart.

"Tessa, I can't change what happened in the past. All we have is the future. Please don't be afraid to grab hold of this

289

gift and enjoy it with me."

"Enjoy it? Matt, do you hear yourself? How could I enjoy uprooting our family and traipsing off into some forest fantasyland?"

Matt grimaced at her caustic words. "God gave us this property, and I think it's a great opportunity for our family to start over in a new place."

"Matt, I don't think this is a good idea." Tears filled her eyes as she laid her trembling hand over her heart. "It's just like last time. I have this feeling in here that it's all wrong."

Matt pressed his lips together, and a stern, stony look filled his face. "Tessa, I'm the leader in this family. I want you and the kids to come with me to Oregon to see this property."

Anger flashed through her, and she blinked away her tears. So that was what it came down to. He was pulling the old I-am-the-leader-so-you-better-submit trick.

Tessa shuddered and glared at her husband. He didn't care what she thought. He had backed her into a corner. She had no choice at all.

Chapter 4

Tessa gripped the door handle of their rental car as they hit another pothole on the rutted pathway Matt had the nerve to call a road. She glanced at his white-knuckled grip on the steering wheel and his intense expression and could almost read his thoughts. *I will conquer this road if it's the last thing I do!*

They had landed in Portland two and a half hours ago, claimed their bags, picked up the rental car, and set off for the wilds of the Cascades and Uncle Don's mountain lodge on Lost Lake.

Tessa sighed and shifted her focus to the sparkling forest outside her car window. Snatches of clear azure sky peeked through the tall firs and cedars, still dripping from a recent shower. Lush patches of sword fern and leafy rhododendrons waved in the breeze as the car passed. Maybe a week in the mountains wouldn't be so bad. She might even enjoy it as long as Matt didn't pressure her too much about moving here.

"How much longer 'til we get there?" Evan called from the backseat.

Brie groaned. "Cut it out, Evan. You just asked that five minutes ago."

"Both of you pipe down," their older son, Justin, added in a disgusted tone. "We'll get there when we get there."

Tessa glanced back at her children sitting shoulder to shoulder in the rear seat. Justin's head almost touched the roof of the compact car. Cramming the kids in like sardines had already led to petty arguments and bruised feelings. Why hadn't Matt reserved a van or a larger car? *Probably trying to save money.* She closed her eyes and sighed again.

They hit another pothole. Tessa opened her eyes and gasped. Mount Hood rose before them like a mammoth, snow-covered pyramid, its jagged features reflected in the deep blue waters of Lost Lake.

"Check out that mountain!" Justin said.

"Let me see!" Evan squeaked, pulling on his brother's arm.

Brie strained to get a better view. "Wow, it looks so close."

"The base is only a few miles away." Matt smiled and slowed the car. "It's really something, isn't it?"

Tessa nodded, stunned out of her disgruntled mood. She had spent all of her life on the East Coast and never imagined the rugged beauty of the Oregon Cascades. Matt slowed and turned into a private drive.

Tessa glanced to the right as Matt rolled to a stop in front of a run-down structure built of large rocks and rough timbers stained almost black with age. Tangled vines and tall bushes hid a good portion of the old building. Wild blackberry brambles obscured the front walkway. Holes gaped in several broken windows, and a gutter pipe swung in the wind, screeching a foreboding welcome.

Matt peered out the rain-spattered windshield. "Well, here we are."

Tessa stared at the startling scene. *This* was the lovely mountain lodge Matt had described to her and the kids? Had he purposely lied, or was he unaware of the toll the years had taken on his uncle's property?

"This is it?" Brie asked, a shudder in her voice.

"Hey, it's not so bad," Justin added. "It sort of reminds me of a big log cabin or Swiss chalet. Look at those two stone chimneys. It must have a couple of nice big fireplaces."

"I think it looks cool!" Evan unhooked his seat belt. "Maybe it's even haunted!" He scrambled over his sister and out the door. Justin piled out on his side and followed his younger brother toward the lodge.

"Wait for your father," Tessa called, but the boys only slowed a little.

Matt climbed out, then paused to stretch before he looked back at Tessa and Brie. "Let's see if we can find the key the lawyer said she'd leave for us."

Brie settled back in the seat. "I think I'll wait out here."

Tessa crossed her arms. *My sentiments exactly!*

Matt leaned back inside the car. "I'm sure it's safe; come on."

Tessa stared past her husband's shoulder and tried to swallow the panic rising in her throat. How could he look so happy? She knew the old place was probably full of spiders and snakes—maybe something worse.

Matt offered Tessa his hand.

She couldn't sit in the car all day, looking like a scaredy-cat, so she braced herself and climbed out. Brie followed, mumbling something about bats and the ghost of Bigfoot.

Justin whistled. "Hey, Dad, check out those wheels."

Tessa followed Justin's gaze and spotted a sleek black BMW partially hidden by the bushes at the side of the house.

The front door squeaked open, and a blond woman in a long navy raincoat stepped out on the porch. "Hello there, you must be the Malones."

The woman had a flawless complexion and stunning violet eyes. She was at least ten years younger than Tessa and gorgeous by anyone's standards. Little vines of envy wove around Tessa's heart, making her feel like a dowdy pigmy.

Matt leaped up on the porch and reached to shake the woman's hand. "Yes, I'm Matt Malone, and this is my wife, Tessa, and our children, Justin, Brie, and Evan." The woman sent him a slow, seductive smile.

Tessa's stomach clenched.

"I'm Mallory Willard, your late uncle's lawyer." She released Matt's hand and flipped her long hair over her shoulder. "I got your message at the office, and I thought I'd drive out and meet you. How was your trip?"

"Great. Smooth flight. No problems."

"Wonderful." Mallory nodded and smiled.

Matt glanced around the porch and ran his hand over the sagging railing, looking as though he was assessing the repair work that needed to be done.

"Why don't we go inside, and I'll give you a tour." Mallory's voice sounded as smooth as warm honey.

Tessa shivered and pulled her navy wool jacket closer. She followed Matt and Mallory inside, and the kids trooped in behind. As she stepped into the living room, a damp, musty smell assaulted her nose, making her long to throw open a window and let in some fresh air.

"Your uncle was quite a recluse. He said he'd lived here by himself for the last thirty-two years."

Matt nodded. "He always said he didn't mind living on his own, but it sounds like a pretty lonely lifestyle to me."

Tessa's gaze traveled around the large rectangular room, taking in every depressing detail. Cobwebs clung to the light fixtures and stair railings. An overstuffed, red plaid couch and two mismatched chairs with sagging stuffing sat facing the hearth. Cluttered bookshelves and a sturdy rolltop desk occupied one corner near the large stone fireplace. A coffee mug and stacks of papers sat on the open desk as though someone had walked away and intended to return.

The thought that no one had lived here since Matt's uncle's death sent goose bumps racing up her arms. The sooner they finished this tour and were on their way, the better. But how would she convince her husband to abandon his plan of spending the entire week here?

Matt laid his hands on the back of the old sagging couch and stared into the cold fireplace, a wistful smile on his face. "I remember sitting right here and listening to my uncle tell stories about being on the Mount Hood Ski Patrol. Then there were all his hunting and fishing stories." He chuckled and shook his head.

Mallory smiled. "I'm glad you have such pleasant memories of your uncle. He loved this property. But his health declined the last few years. I suppose that's why he let the place go a little."

Shock waves rippled through Tessa. "A little?" Everyone turned toward her, and her face flamed, but she continued. "This place is falling apart. Just look at it." She waved her hand in a broad arch. "It would take thousands of dollars to make it livable." She glared at Mallory. "What do you expect us to do with it?"

"Well, that's entirely up to you and your husband." Mallory's gaze shifted to Matt. "It does need some cleanup and repairs, but I'm sure you can see the value and potential."

"Of course." Matt nodded and sent Tessa a sideways glance that seemed to question her sanity.

Tessa fought to keep her mouth closed. Mallory Willard didn't care how much effort and expense it would take to repair this lodge. She would have to be paid whether they sold the property or not.

"Shall we continue our tour?" Mallory led them through the dining room past a sturdy pine table and chairs and into the large kitchen. "I know your uncle was a widower. I suppose he didn't like to spend too much time in the kitchen."

Tessa stared at the grease-stained, rooster-patterned wallpaper and the chipped yellow cabinets. A small sink hung from the wall at an odd angle, surrounded by red Formica counters. An ancient refrigerator and a cast-iron woodstove filled the rest of the wall space. How could anyone cook any-thing edible under these conditions? She exchanged a heated glance with her husband.

"All the bedrooms are on the second floor," Mallory con-tinued, leaving the forlorn kitchen and leading them back into the living room and up the wide wooden stairs.

Evan ran ahead. Brie and Justin hurried after him.

"Hey, I want this room," Brie called. "It has a great view of the lake."

"This one has bunk beds!" Evan leaned out the second bedroom door and looked at her with pleading eyes. "Can I sleep on top, Mom? Please? I promise I won't fall off."

"We'll talk about that later." Matt gave Evan a look that said no argument allowed.

Justin disappeared into the next room, and Tessa heard him opening drawers and rummaging around.

"Here's the fourth bedroom." Mallory pushed open the door and stood back for Matt and Tessa to enter.

Tessa held her breath and peeked inside. To her surprise, it looked a little better than the other rooms they'd passed through. Three large windows on the south wall flooded the room with warm light. A cozy blue quilt covered a metal-framed double bed, and an old pine dresser sat in the corner. An oval braided rug covered a large portion of the hardwood floor, giving the room a welcoming appeal.

"This is nice." Matt turned to Tessa.

She knew he wanted her to say something positive. It was

the best room in the house. That wasn't saying much, but at least—

A little brown mouse dashed across the floor near Tessa's feet. She screamed and jumped back, bumping into Matt. He reached out to steady her.

Mallory gasped.

Matt lunged and stomped his foot, missing the mouse by several inches. The frightened little critter spun in a circle, skittered across the floor, and disappeared into a large crack by the baseboard in the corner.

Justin dashed into the room. "What's going on?"

"Mom, are you okay?" Brie hurried in behind Justin.

Evan slid in past his siblings. "What did I miss?"

"It's all right." Matt put his arm around Tessa's shoulders. "Your mom saw a mouse."

"Mom screamed 'cause of a mouse?" Evan cocked his head, looking puzzled. "Why'd you do that? You used to like my pet mice."

Tessa sighed. "I know. He surprised me, that's all."

"I'm sure you can get some traps from the hardware store in town," Mallory said.

"Traps?" Evan squeaked, looking horrified. "We don't want to kill them!"

Tessa knew their young son's sensitive spirit couldn't tolerate cruelty to any living creature, even stray field mice. She shot a quick look at Matt, sending a silent message.

Matt's gaze met Tessa's for a split second, then turned to Mallory. "We'll see if we can find traps that catch them alive, and then we can release them in the woods."

"Whew!" Evan pushed his straight brown hair off his forehead. "For a minute there, I thought our family was going to be guilty of mice murder."

Brie leaned closer to her father. "Good move, Dad." Adoration shone in her eyes. Then she placed her hands on her brother's shoulders. "Come on, Evan. I want to show you the view from my room."

Mallory turned to Matt. "I guess your children are real animal lovers."

"Yes, they are."

"They seem like great kids," Mallory added.

"Thanks. We think we're pretty blessed." Matt smiled and squeezed Tessa's shoulder. His eyes glowed, sending a private message that sent tingles through her.

For some silly reason her throat tightened, and she felt tears prick her eyes. What was the matter with her? Of course their kids were great. She knew that. And her husband was pretty special, too. Tessa returned a tremulous smile. Sure, Matt was a crazy dreamer, but sometimes she wished she believed in his dreams. Maybe then they could recapture some of what they'd lost.

Chapter 5

With a sleepy yawn, Tessa rolled over and pushed the blankets away from her face. Soft morning light filtered through unfamiliar windows. So it wasn't a dream. She really was in Oregon. A smile played at her lips as she remembered the special time she and Matt had shared the night before. If only he would give up this crazy idea of them moving to Oregon. Maybe things could settle down and they could focus on making their relationship a priority.

She squinted, searching the room for her husband. Why was it so hazy? She sniffed and sat up. Could that be smoke? "Matt?" She climbed out of bed, her senses coming fully awake when her bare feet hit the cold floor. "Matt!"

No answer. Her heart began to pound. Could the lodge be on fire? Her mind fought to grab hold of reality. She snatched her robe from the end of the bed and slipped it on. When she pushed open her bedroom door, a thin bluish haze hung in the air, heightening her fears.

"Justin, Brianna!" Tessa hurried down the hall. "Wake up!"

Her older son appeared at his bedroom door dressed in sweats and an old T-shirt.

"Put on your shoes and get your brother," Tessa ordered.

Brie opened her door. "What's going on?"

"I smell smoke. Put on a sweatshirt and get your sneakers." Tessa dashed back to her bedroom and slid on her shoes. She returned to the hall in time to see Justin ushering Evan toward the stairway. Brie trotted down the steps just ahead of her brothers.

"Where's the fire?" Evan asked, excitement lighting up his young face.

"We don't know. Just keep moving," Justin ordered, hustling his brother ahead.

Brie slowed halfway down the stairs and looked back. "Where's Daddy?" Her pale face and wide-eyed look made Tessa's heart lurch.

"I don't know, honey. Just keep going. We'll find him."

The hazy curtain thickened as they reached the living room. Tessa shot a glance toward the fireplace, hoping she would find it was the source of the smoke, but it sat cold and empty.

Justin shoved Evan toward her. "You take Evan and Brie out front. I'm going to find Dad." The determined look in his eyes sent a tremor through Tessa.

"No, I'll find him." Tessa steered Evan back toward his brother. "I want all three of you to go outside."

"Shouldn't we call 9-1-1?" Brie coughed and squinted against the smoke.

Tessa grabbed her cell phone from the table. "Here, Justin,

301

take my phone. Give me a couple minutes, and then make the call. Now go!"

Justin grabbed the phone and urged his younger siblings out the door. Tessa bent lower and headed toward the kitchen door where the smoke seemed thicker.

Oh, Lord, please help me find Matt. And I know I said I don't want to live here, but I didn't mean I wanted the place to burn down!

Tessa pushed open the swinging door to the kitchen, and her prayer came to an abrupt halt. Matt stood in the center of the smoky room waving an old dish towel, red-faced and coughing. Smoke poured from the cracks in the stovepipe of the woodstove.

"What are you doing?" Tessa stammered.

"I'm trying to cook breakfast. But this crazy stove is impossible." Matt reached for the cast-iron frying pan full of half-congealed eggs. "I don't understand it. The fire is roaring, but there's not much heat coming out on top."

"Did you open the vents?" Tessa blinked against the stinging smoke.

"What vents?"

"There must be dampers or something. You probably have to open them like a flue on a fireplace chimney." Tessa coughed as she walked closer to the belching black stove. "Here, let's try this thing." She turned a handle near the firebox and stood back. Immediately the smoke stopped flowing out of the pipe cracks.

"Oh. I never saw that." Matt strode to the back door and shoved it open.

"I'll open a window." Tessa struggled to raise the window over the sink. Looking outside, she saw her three children huddled together by their rental car, anxiously watching the lodge.

"It's okay," Tessa called through the dirty screen. "You can come back inside. It's just your father—cooking breakfast."

They groaned in unison and shuffled toward the lodge.

"What are they doing out there?"

"I smelled smoke upstairs and thought the lodge was on fire."

"Sorry. I didn't realize the smoke had drifted all the way upstairs. That must've been an awful way to wake up."

A smile tugged at her lips as she watched her husband stir the pan of half-cooked eggs, his apron stained with soot. "It looks like your breakfast plans backfired."

Matt tossed aside the pot holder with a mischievous grin. "Backfired. Ha! That's very funny."

Tessa covered her mouth to hide her snicker.

"Hey, I think I deserve a little appreciation since I've been slaving over a not-so-hot stove to make you this gourmet breakfast." His eyes glowed with warmth and humor as he walked toward her. "Come here."

She met him in the middle.

Matt wrapped his strong arms around her. He smelled deliciously like wood smoke and spicy aftershave. His embrace tightened. "I'm sorry, Tessa. I didn't mean to scare you or the kids." He sighed into her hair. "I never meant to hurt you. Never."

Was it the smoke or his tender words that brought tears to her eyes? She blinked them away and pulled in a shuddering breath. She could easily forgive him for this smoky breakfast, but how could she let go of the painful memories and trust him again after all his failures had cost them?

Matt pushed aside his empty plate and settled back to enjoy his coffee. Tessa had come to his rescue in the kitchen, and working together, they had managed to prepare an edible breakfast. The kids gobbled up their food like hungry lumberjacks. Matt smiled. He had always heard that mountain air made people feel hungrier. The old saying seemed to hold true for his crew.

"This jam is good." Evan licked his lips and popped the last bite of toast into his mouth.

Tessa smiled and reached over with her napkin to wipe a purple smear off Evan's cheek. "So you like boysenberry?"

Evan grinned. "Uh-huh."

"Want me to finish up these eggs?" Justin asked.

"Sure, go ahead." Tessa looked at her daughter. "Unless you want some more, Brie."

"No, thanks. I'm full." Brie drank the last of her orange juice. "That was pretty good. Thanks."

Matt nodded. This beat their normal cereal-and-milk routine by a mile. That was all they had time for most mornings, before they all rushed off to their separate lives.

Evan scooted back from the table. "When can we go down to the lake?"

Tessa frowned. "I don't want you going down there by yourself, Evan."

"I'll go with him." Brie wiped her hands on a napkin.

"I'm ready to do some exploring," Justin added.

Matt held back a surprised grin. Back in Princeton, Justin preferred spending time with his friends rather than his siblings. Here was another good reason for them to move to a quiet, rural setting where they could all spend more time together.

"Okay, but I want you to stick together, and don't go in the water." Tessa bit her lip, an anxious frown creasing her forehead.

Justin rolled his eyes. "Mom, that water is probably freezing. There's no way we'd go in."

"Not unless I push you." Brie grinned.

"Oh yeah? Just try it!" Justin gave her a playful shove as they headed toward the door.

"Wait, don't forget your jackets," Tessa called.

"I won't be cold," Evan insisted, plucking at his green sweatshirt. "I've got two layers."

"I know, but I don't want you—"

Matt laid his hand gently on her arm. "Let them go, honey. They'll be fine." Tessa's worried frown squelched everyone's joy. He wished he could help her relax and trust someone—anyone. Why was she always on guard like that? Of course he was thankful she was a caring, responsible mother, but Tessa's caring often slipped over the line into overprotective anxiety.

He sat back, watching the kids clatter across the porch and

305

disappear down the shady path leading to the lake.

"I hope they stay together. I can't imagine Justin slowing down when Evan wants to catch a frog or a turtle."

"They'll be okay. I'm glad they're occupied for a while. That'll give us time to talk."

Tessa shot him a wary glance. "About what?"

Matt clasped his hands and rested his elbows on the table. "We've known about this property for six weeks. It's time to make some decisions."

"What do you want me to say?"

"I want to hear what you're thinking." He smiled, hoping her responsiveness last night was also an indication she was softening toward him—and his desire to move.

Tessa looked at him with a guarded expression. "I know you love this place, but I think we should do some cleanup, find a good Realtor, and list it. I'm sure some developer or nature lover will snap it up."

As her words sunk in, his throat ached with defeat. "You still want to sell?"

"Of course I want to sell," she said with an irritated huff. "We'd have to totally renovate if we were going to live here. And that would take too much time and money." She sent him a pointed look. "Money we don't have."

His anger flared, and he shot off a prayer for patience. "I know we'd have to put a lot of sweat equity into this place to make it nice enough for our family, but look at the property. There's nothing like this in New Jersey. And we'd own it free and clear, unlike that dinky condo we're renting now.

Everything we put into this place would be ours, and with a little help from a few people, we could get the work done and open by midsummer."

"Open? What do you mean?"

Matt swallowed. Maybe he had made a mistake by waiting until they arrived here to spring this part of the idea on her, but she'd refused to discuss it at home. "I want to rent out the cabins as soon as possible and then build a meeting room and dining hall so we can accommodate groups by next summer. I've researched it and done a complete business proposal. I even have a few people in mind who might be willing to get involved as investors."

"You can't be serious. How could you even consider asking other people to get involved in this—this disaster? Look at this place!" She waved her hand toward the broken front window, sagging curtains, and peeling wallpaper. "We're talking about thousands of dollars for renovations, with no idea how or when we would be able to pay them back. No, Matt!" Tessa sprang from her chair and retreated to the living room.

Matt followed her but paused to pick up a folder from the coffee table. "Sit down with me and take a look at these plans."

Tessa silently stared into the cold fireplace.

"Tessa, please. Listen to me. Share my dream." His voice grew thick with emotion. "I know I've made some mistakes before, but I believe the Lord gave us this property for a reason."

She spun and faced him. "Yes, He did. He gave it to us so

we could pay off the van, get a decent home again, and be able to send our kids to college."

Matt growled and flopped down on the couch. "This isn't about Lost Lake Lodge, is it? It's about what happened before."

"No!" But her indignant scowl and quick answer confirmed he was right.

His pulse pounded in his temple. "When are you going to forgive me and let it go?"

"How can I, when you're ready to turn right around and do the same thing all over again?"

"How can you say that? You haven't even looked at the plans."

"Because I know you, Matt. You're a dreamer with your head in the clouds, while your family is down here scraping by, just trying to survive."

Angry words boiled up inside him, threatening to overflow at her painful exaggerations. Their lifestyle was a far cry from scraping by. They had both worked hard to overcome their financial problems, and they were making good progress.

"You don't trust me. That's the real problem. You don't believe I have enough common sense and business know-how to make this work." He clutched the folder holding the detailed plans he had created to provide protection for them and any investors who joined them in developing the property. But she wouldn't even look at them. Her heart was as hard as granite.

"You're wrong about me, Tessa. I may be a dreamer, but I

love you and the kids, and I want what's best for our family. I've slaved away for three years at a job I hate to provide for us and dig us out of this hole."

His hand shook as he pointed at her. "The real issue is you're afraid to take a risk. Even when God dumps a diamond in your lap, you run away screaming, 'The sky is falling!'"

Tessa gasped. "Oh, you're so—"

"No! Don't say anything else you'll regret." He got up and walked out the front door, slamming it behind him.

Chapter 6

The door banged shut. Tessa jumped, and fear prickled up her spine. Matt rarely got this angry. What would he do now? Take a walk to cool off or climb in the car and go for a long drive?

She paced to the front window and shoved aside the dusty curtain. Matt strode down the drive but slowed as a black BMW rolled to a stop beside him. The window lowered, and Mallory Willard looked out.

The sudden smile on Matt's face jolted Tessa. She gripped the curtain and stared at their animated expressions. *Oh, Matt, don't make a fool of yourself with that woman.* Tessa balled her fists. *Ooh! If only I could read their lips.*

Mallory parked her car and climbed out. Matt continued talking to her and politely shut her door. She flashed him a smile and tossed her blond hair over her shoulder. She looked more like a fashion model than a lawyer in her slim black pants, bright red blouse, and black leather jacket.

Tessa straightened her shoulders, preparing to confront

her. But rather than walking toward the lodge, they turned and headed down the secluded path toward the lake.

Tessa's eyes bulged and her heart began to pound. Why would Matt take a walk with that—that woman? The answer about slapped her in the face. Of course he wouldn't want to bring Mallory back to the lodge after the way Tessa had been acting.

Regret cooled her anger. Perhaps she should have at least looked at his business proposal. But how could she even consider moving here? His plan would plunge their family back into debt and destroy her sagging sense of security. She'd have to give up her business and move far away from her family and friends. She'd lose daily contact with her sister. And with what Allison was going through, she needed Tessa.

But what about Matt? Shouldn't her first commitment be to her husband?

Tessa sighed and closed her eyes as her confused thoughts tumbled through her mind. She didn't want to give up her life in Princeton for the frightening risks of Matt's far-fetched scheme. Why couldn't he settle down and be happy in New Jersey where everything was safe and predictable? Why couldn't he understand her needs and desires?

Matt pulled in a deep breath of cool mountain air. There was nothing like the refreshing scent of Douglas fir and the pungent aroma of the damp, mossy forest floor. Being here made him feel alive. These woods were nothing like the steel and glass cityscape he viewed from his third-floor office window.

"Matt?"

"Sorry." He glanced at Mallory. "Guess I was daydreaming."

"That's okay. This place inspires me to do a little dreaming myself." She gazed up at the huge fir trees along the path leading back to the lodge. "Do you know how lucky you are to inherit a piece of property like this?"

He nodded and then frowned slightly, realizing once again the awesome responsibility his uncle's gift had placed on his shoulders. Would he be able to develop the land in a way that preserved and protected the forest, or would he be forced to sell it to someone who wouldn't care about its natural beauty?

"I'm sorry I forgot that list of contractors," Mallory said. "Would you like me to give you a call when I get back to the office?" They stepped from the shade of the forest path and crunched across the gravel drive toward Mallory's car.

Matt glanced toward the lodge. "Sure. That would be fine." The memory of Tessa's angry words rose and squelched the delight he had felt only moments before. He was too embarrassed to tell Mallory that he and Tessa couldn't agree about the future of his uncle's property.

"Anything else you need, just give me a call." Her gaze lingered, and he noticed her eyes were the same deep blue as Lost Lake.

"Dad! Look what we found!" Evan rushed toward him, carrying a rusty coffee can. "Justin said it's a salad-mander."

Justin laughed and shook his head as he and Brie followed Evan out of the forest. "That's *salamander*, Ev."

Matt leaned down to take a look at the squiggly black

creature swimming in the slimy-looking lake water. "Well, look at that."

"Isn't he cool?" Evan grinned with delight. "I never saw one of these before except on the Nature Channel. His back is really smooth. You want to touch him?" Evan held the can out toward Matt and Mallory.

She shook her head and melted back against the car. "No, no thanks."

"He won't hurt you." Evan lifted the can a little higher.

Matt held back a chuckle. "I think that's close enough, Evan." Mallory might appreciate the beauty of the forest, but she obviously wasn't too fond of the creatures inhabiting the lake.

Brie sent her dad a knowing glance. "Come on, Evan. Let's take him back to the house and show Mom."

Evan's eyes lit up at this new possibility, and he streaked off toward the lodge, lake water sloshing out of his can.

Matt studied Mallory as she brushed a tiny drop of water from the sleeve of her leather jacket. In spite of the perturbed pucker of her lips, she was a very attractive woman. But her chin had a haughty tilt, and he'd noticed an edge in her voice when she spoke to the kids, hinting at another person behind the smile.

"You certainly have your hands full with these kids." She looked up and caught him watching her. She smiled. "But I like the way you handle them."

"They keep me on my toes." He watched his kids scale the front steps, each one unique and so special. He'd do just about anything to make them happy and be sure their future was secure.

Mallory climbed into her car and closed her door. Lowering the window, she smiled at him once more. "Call me. Anytime. I want to do whatever I can to help you. It's a wonderful plan, and I can tell you're just the man who can pull it off."

A warm rush of pleasure shot through him as he replayed Mallory's flattering words, but it faded away as he watched her drive off.

He turned and trudged back toward the lodge. He dreaded facing his wife. Why had he stormed off like that? He rarely walked out on an argument, and he never slammed doors. As he considered what to do next, he could almost hear what his friend Keith would say. *"You blew it, Matt. You need to go back in there and apologize. You'll never win Tessa over by bulldozing her."*

Matt rubbed his forehead. *Lord, I haven't been handling this very well. You know how much I want to make this move. I think it would be best for all of us. Please soften Tessa's heart, and help me trust You to work this out.*

Matt pulled open the screen door and walked into the living room.

"Evan, would you please put that salamander outside?" Tessa straightened up from tying twine around a large stack of old newspapers. "Then go up and change into a clean pair of jeans. You're all muddy." She shot a glance at Matt and then averted her eyes.

"Aw, Mom, can't I keep him in here?"

"Listen to your mother, Evan." Matt crossed the room

toward them. "He'll be fine on the porch for now. After lunch, I think we should take him back down to the lake and let him go."

"But, Dad, I want to keep him for a pet."

"Think about that, buddy. There's not much food for him in that can. You wouldn't want him to starve, would you?"

Evan's eyes widened. "No, I guess not."

"Take him outside, and then run up and change." Matt gave his son a playful swat on the seat of his pants. Evan scampered out to the porch. He shot back past them and dashed up the stairs.

Matt watched Tessa kneel down to tie another stack of newspapers. Her faded blue jeans and a loose red shirt couldn't hide her attractive, petite figure. Even at forty-seven she still looked great to him. She had replaced her usual dangly earrings with little gold posts, and she'd tucked her short dark brown hair behind her ears while she worked. It reminded him of the way she looked that first day they met.

His heart twisted. "Listen, Tessa. I shouldn't have walked out like that. I'm sorry."

She focused on tying the twine into a tight knot.

He squatted down next to her. "I know I haven't really heard what you have to say about moving here, so. . .I'm ready to listen."

Her hand froze, and she slowly lifted her gaze to meet his. The suspicion in her eyes cut him to the heart. Would he ever win back her trust?

"I don't want to move here, Matt. I want to stay in

Princeton." Her voice trembled.

He nodded and waited for her to say more, but she silently blinked back tears and looked away.

"Okay. I hear you, and I'm not going to force you into this. But I think we both need some more time and information before we make a final decision. How about I call a Realtor or two and have them come out and do a market analysis? We can ask some questions and find out what we would need to do to put it on the market."

Tessa sat back on her heels and looked at him doubtfully.

"I'd also like to have a contractor come out and look at the lodge and cabins and give us some estimates on renovations. Then I'd like us to sit down and talk things over. We don't have to make a decision this week, but I think we should look at all the possibilities while we're here, including my business proposal."

Tessa pressed her lips together. "Okay. I suppose that's fair."

"Then there's one more thing I'd like us to do."

"What?"

"I'd like us to pray about this—together."

A wary look returned to Tessa's eyes. She stood and folded her arms across her chest.

He knew his request surprised her. They didn't have a habit of praying together. The last time they had prayed as a couple was when his father faced a serious heart surgery more than two years ago.

She released a soft sigh. "All right."

Chapter 7

Tessa wrapped her hands around her teacup and let the warmth flow into her fingers. Settling back in the chair, she took a sip and stared out Sweet Something's rain-drizzled front windows. Cars buzzed down Princeton's historic Nassau Street, but the rain had kept all but a few hardy customers away.

She lowered her gaze to the wholesale grocery order form on the table in front of her and squinted at the tiny print. It would be impossible for her to fill it out without going back to the kitchen for her glasses.

Growing older could be such a pain. But it wasn't only blurred vision that bothered her. The decision hanging over her head left her feeling anxious and unsettled. They'd returned from Oregon three days ago, but she and Matt still couldn't agree on the future of Lost Lake Lodge. Oh, she'd looked over his business proposal. And they'd received bids from two contractors for renovations, but the money required to move ahead on either of those options had shocked her into angry silence.

Praying with Matt only made her feel more pressured. And now the kids were getting excited about the possibility of moving—even Brie! Tessa couldn't believe the way her daughter had turned traitor and sided with Matt as soon as her boyfriend, Ryan, began discussing attending Oregon State University.

Tessa rubbed her forehead. How would they ever be able to send any of their kids away to college if their finances became tangled up in that crazy lodge project?

The bell over the front door jingled. Bill Hancock stepped inside and glanced around. He smiled and waved when he saw her. He wore charcoal slacks and a soft-gray V-neck sweater over a light blue shirt that matched the color of his eyes. Threads of silver in his dark hair and deep creases created by his smile added to his good looks.

"Welcome back." He laid his hand on the back of the chair opposite hers, obviously waiting for an invitation to sit down.

"Can I get you something?" she asked, rising from her chair. "I just took some blueberry scones out of the oven a few minutes ago."

"Sounds great." He winked, and his smile deepened.

She blushed and silently scolded herself. Bill was just a friend—though his compliments and lingering looks suggested he might like to be more if circumstances were different. But he'd never done anything more than flirt, and she'd never done anything except enjoy his attention; still, a small cloud of guilt shadowed her heart.

"Would you like coffee?"

"Yes, thanks." He took a seat, and she felt his gaze follow her as she turned and walked away.

When she stepped into the kitchen, her sister Allison met her. "More customers?"

"Just Bill Hancock. I'll take care of him."

A fleeting frown crossed Allison's face. "Don't let him monopolize your afternoon."

Tessa heard the subtle warning behind her sister's words. She turned away and poured Bill's coffee into a mug. "I can't very well ignore him. He's a good customer and a fellow business owner." She chose the largest scone on the cooling rack and put it on a plate.

"I know, but I don't trust him."

"Why would you say that? He's always been friendly to me."

"That's exactly what I mean." Allison lifted her brows and sent Tessa a serious look. "Just be careful."

"Don't worry." She scooped up the tray and strolled out of the kitchen. Sometimes her sister could be such a wet blanket. There was nothing wrong with talking to Bill. His visits made her forget about her troubles. And for a little while each afternoon, he made her feel young and attractive again. What was wrong with that?

"Wow, that looks delicious." Bill smiled as she set the scone and coffee on the table in front of him.

Tessa glanced at her half-full teacup.

"I didn't mean to cut your break short," Bill said. "You've probably been on your feet all day. Please, sit down."

Something melted inside her at his thoughtfulness, and she

took a seat. "Thanks. I am feeling a little tired. Jet lag, I guess."

"How was your trip?" He poured cream into his coffee.

Conflicting emotions swirled through her. "Oregon is beautiful. I've never seen huge mountains and evergreen forests like that." She hesitated and looked into Bill's eyes. "My husband wants us to move there."

"You're kidding." Bill frowned and laid aside his spoon.

"My husband's uncle left him an old mountain lodge with seven guest cabins. Matt thinks we should renovate the property and rent out the cabins. But we'd have to take out a huge loan or find investors to pay for it." She clucked her tongue, and disgust crept into her voice. "I don't understand how he can even consider it. I'd have to pull the kids out of school, and we'd be all the way across the country from my family. And who knows how long it would be before we'd make an income from the cabins." She shivered at that frightening thought.

"What about Sweet Something?"

Her throat tightened. "I'd have to give it up." She glanced around the tea shop and remembered how she and Allison had hunted all over Pennsylvania and New Jersey to find just the right antiques to give Sweet Something a special look. They'd tested recipes and developed the menu, stocked the gift shop, and worked long hours to build their business. What would happen if she pulled out and left Allison to manage it on her own? The tea shop was important to her sister, but spending time with her husband and creating paintings for her limited-edition print collection took time, too.

"Is the decision final?"

"No, but Matt's pretty determined to go."

Bill's blue eyes took on a frosty glint. "Don't let him push you into doing something you'll regret."

"What choice do I have? If he says we're going, it's settled." She crossed her arms and tried to swallow the angry lump in her throat.

Bill pulled back and looked at her curiously. "Wait a minute. Why should he be the one to make that decision? What you want is important, too. You've worked hard to make your business successful." He pressed his lips together in a firm line. "Don't let him force you into giving up your shop."

An uncomfortable shiver passed through her. "Well, he's not really forcing me. He thinks it would be a good move for the whole family, and running his own business has been his dream for a long time."

"If that's what he wants, maybe you should let him go for it. But that doesn't mean you have to go, too."

Surprise rippled through her.

"People's goals and desires change. Sometimes everyone is happier if they follow their own path and pursue their own dreams."

She'd never considered the possibility of staying in Princeton while Matt worked in Oregon. Didn't some couples live in different cities and commute to see each other on weekends or vacations? But what kind of marriage would that be? How would an arrangement like that affect their children? Doubt swirled through her.

"This is an important decision, Tessa. There's a lot at stake."

Bill rested both arms on the table and leaned toward her. "Don't make the mistake of throwing away your dreams."

Matt stuffed his hands into his jacket pockets as he crossed the park toward the Little League baseball diamond. Birds sang in the maple trees, and the air had a fresh rain-washed scent. If only he had different news to tell Tessa. But maybe this was best. At least the decision was out of their hands.

He focused on the small crowd seated on the metal bleachers and soon spotted Tessa and Brie in the third row. Justin stood by the dugout, his black baseball cap pulled low over his eyes as he watched his little brother's game. Matt smiled as his gaze settled on Evan standing behind third base. His son leaned forward, ready for the next play.

Matt greeted a few parents and then climbed the bleachers. Tessa scooted over and made room for him. He settled on the bench next to her. "How's Evan doing?"

"He's played three of the five innings, walked once, and struck out twice."

Matt nodded, watching Tessa, trying to guess her mood. It had been a rocky week. His patience had been strained to the max as pressure increased at work and Tessa remained set against moving. If he hadn't had Keith's support, he didn't know how he would've made it. His friend's advice ran through his mind again. *Love her. Listen to her concerns. Wait for the Lord to bring her around. Don't push it.*

He blew out a deep breath. What would Keith say now? Today's events had changed everything. He cleared his throat.

"Brie, is the concession stand open?"

She leaned forward and looked around Tessa. "Yeah, why?"

"Would you get us some sodas?"

"You feeling okay, Dad?"

He grimaced and reached for his wallet. "I'm fine." She didn't need to remind him that one trip to the concession stand could wipe out their entertainment budget for the week. They usually brought drinks and snacks from home to save money. Well, those days were almost over. He handed his daughter a ten, and she climbed down the bleachers.

"What was that about?" Tessa watched him curiously.

"We need to talk, and I thought it would be better to do it without an audience."

Apprehension creased her forehead. "What is it?"

"Madden sold out. My job's been cut."

Tessa gasped. "They fired you?"

"No, they eliminated my position. But don't worry; they gave me a severance package."

"What are we going to do? The money I get from Sweet Something will barely cover our rent. How will we pay for utilities or food? And what about the car payments?"

He glanced around, hoping no one had overheard her frantic questions. "Calm down, Tessa. It's not like we're going to be homeless next week. The severance package should cover our expenses for at least three or four months. The kids can finish the school year, and then it will pay for our moving expenses and help us get started with the renovations."

His wife's face paled. "What are you saying?"

He took her hands. "We asked the Lord to show us if we should move. I'd say this makes it pretty clear."

She stiffened and pulled back. "Just because you lost your job, that doesn't mean we have to move. You can look for another job here in Princeton."

"Tessa, you know how tight the job market is here."

"But you have experience and connections. Surely you can find something."

"Why should I look here when we own Lost Lake Lodge? We can develop a great family business there and live the kind of life most people only dream about. I'm not talking so much about a big income. I think that's going to happen eventually, but I mean being a closer, stronger family."

Tessa's hands trembled in his, and fear darkened her eyes. If only he could infuse her heart with more faith—faith in him and in God. But she had to make that choice herself. All he could do was tell her the truth and pray she would understand.

"I believe God's leading us to move there. I think this will be good for all of us." He gripped her hand more tightly, feeling like he stood balanced on the edge of a huge cliff. "I need you, Tessa. Come with me, be my partner, help me make this plan work."

Tears pooled in her dark eyes. "It doesn't make sense to me, Matt. We'd be giving up so much. How can I say yes?" She pulled her icy hands away and lifted her chin. "You go ahead and chase your dream. The kids and I aren't going anywhere."

Her words slammed into him like a Mack truck doing seventy, and he felt himself fall over the edge of the cliff.

Chapter 8

Matt tucked a heavy green sweatshirt into his suitcase next to his hiking boots. Though it was almost Memorial Day, the temperatures would probably still be cool in the Cascades. He reached for his Bible on the nightstand, but his hand hesitated over the family photo taken last Christmas. The kids' smiling faces shone back at him, hope and mischief lighting their eyes.

He ran his finger along the top of the frame and lifted it for a closer look. A shard of pain twisted through him. He'd never been away from them for more than a week. How long would it be this time?

His gaze moved to his wife's pensive face. Even in this Christmas photo, apprehension clouded her expression. He'd tried everything he could think of to convince her to go to Oregon with him. But she wouldn't budge. She didn't believe he had what it took to make the lodge project successful. Bottom line: She didn't trust him.

Maybe his pride and self-sufficiency were leading him

toward a dead end. But what other choice did he have? He couldn't just sit here in New Jersey and do nothing. He needed to bring in an income, and getting the guest cabins ready to rent this summer was a start. He studied the photo a moment longer, then carefully wrapped it in a T-shirt and laid it in the suitcase along with his Bible.

"Hey, Dad." Justin leaned in the doorway. "What time is your plane tomorrow?"

Heaviness settled over Matt. "I'm leaving around five thirty in the morning."

Justin nodded and stuffed his hands into his jeans pockets. He glanced at the suitcase and back at his dad. "I want to come out there as soon as finals are over."

Matt's heart warmed. "I could use your help, but I thought you planned to work full-time for Pete this summer." Matt knew his son's hours at the construction company increased with warmer weather, and that would provide the money he needed for college classes next fall.

"If I give my notice now, I could come by mid-June."

Matt walked over and laid his hand on his son's shoulder. "It would be great to have you there with me, but I don't want to make you miss a semester."

"It's okay, Dad. I'm not talking about quitting college. I just want to take some time off to help you out."

Matt's throat tightened, and he squeezed Justin's shoulder. "I appreciate that, but your mom wants you to stay on track so you can transfer to a university in another year."

"It wouldn't hurt to take a semester off. Once we get the

cabins cleaned up and rented out, we'll make enough money to pay for school. And if I go with you this summer, I can establish residency and apply to schools in Oregon."

For a moment Matt could see it all happening. He and Justin would work together over the summer, building a closer relationship as they fixed up the cabins and restored the old lodge to its former beauty. Tessa, Brie, and Evan would join them after school was out, and the whole family would be together. But reality quickly washed over him. Tessa would never agree to it. She'd already signed Evan up for summer day camp. Brie had a part-time job lined up at the mall. Tessa wouldn't hear of Matt disrupting the children's summer plans. If he forced the issue, it would only hurt their relationship more. She left him no choice. He was going alone.

Sorrow shrouded Matt's heart as he looked into his son's eyes. "I'm sorry, Justin, I think you need to stay here, hold on to your job, and stick to the plan we made with Mom."

"But, Dad—"

Brie and Evan marched into the room. "We want to go, too," Brie insisted.

Evan stepped in front of his sister. "Yeah. Why should I have to go to day camp when I could be in the real woods with you?"

Matt suppressed a proud grin. "You two sound pretty serious about this."

"We are!" Brie's dark eyes flashed. "All of us staying here while you go to Oregon is a bad idea. Come on, Dad. This is never going to work."

How could he convince them to accept a plan he didn't feel

was best? But for Tessa's sake he had to squelch this mutiny. He motioned them all closer. "Look, this is a really tough time for all of us. Neither your mom nor I are happy about this decision, but it's the best we can come up with right now." His gaze moved around the semicircle of gloomy faces. "So while I'm gone, I want you guys to cooperate with Mom and help her out. She's going to need you." Matt's voice grew thick as he thought of leaving Tessa and the kids on their own.

Out of the corner of his eye, he caught a movement and looked up. Tessa hesitated in the doorway. A painful expression crossed her face.

Matt straightened and focused on the kids. "Why don't you guys head on out. I'll come around and say good night in a little while."

With tired sighs and sagging shoulders, the kids filed out the bedroom door.

Matt focused on his suitcase and rearranged a few pairs of rolled-up socks.

"They blame me for everything." Tessa's voice vibrated with emotion. "It's not fair. This is just as much your decision as it is mine."

Matt closed his eyes, reining in his temper. He would not argue with Tessa. This was their last night together for who knew how long.

"Did you pack some warm clothes?" Her voice softened.

"I'll be fine." Matt pulled another turtleneck from the drawer and folded it into the suitcase. He heard Tessa cross the room. His heart hammered. Did she finally realize how much her painful choices were costing their family?

"You don't have to do this, Matt. It's not too late to change your mind."

His hopes crashed, and his heart hardened. He slowly turned and faced her. "The door swings both ways, Tessa."

Her stony expression faltered, and tears glistened in her eyes, but she turned and walked away.

Tessa lay in bed, still as a stone, pretending to be asleep. She peeked out from under the comforter. Matt lugged his suitcase toward the bedroom door. He slowed for a moment, his bulky silhouette outlined in the soft glow from the night-light in the hall. She closed her eyes so he wouldn't guess she was awake. Saying good-bye again would only hurt more.

The door closed with a soft click. Darkness enveloped the room. Tessa heard the suitcase wheels roll down the hallway. Hot, silent tears coursed down her cheeks. She didn't think he'd really leave. But it was happening. And somehow she felt like the nightmare had only begun.

"Bring me more towels!" Panic rushed through Tessa as she tried to hold back the rising water with the pile of sopping towels.

She'd sent her daughter next door to get their elderly neighbor, Walter Cooper. Hopefully he would know how to stop the torrent gushing from the broken cold-water handle in the shower.

For the hundredth time, she moaned and berated herself for sending her husband off to Oregon. What kind of fool was she?

Handling life on her own had been nothing short of a disaster.

On Tuesday the dryer broke, and the repairman couldn't come until next week. On Wednesday her key jammed in the ignition, and she had to have the van towed to the dealer. Last night Justin had stayed out past his curfew—again. When she confronted him, he'd glared at her and insisted he shouldn't have to stick to the same schedule he'd kept, since his classes at the community college were finished. That same day, Brie broke up with her boyfriend, Ryan, and was inconsolable. Then just before dinner, Evan's teacher called and said she was concerned about his moodiness and poor performance over the last two weeks—exactly the length of time Matt had been gone. And now this plumbing catastrophe!

"Brie! Where are you?" Tessa gritted her teeth and tried to shove the sloppy wave back toward the shower stall, but it gushed over the top of her towel barrier and surged toward the door. Tears flooded her eyes like the mini tidal wave in her bathroom. If only Matt were here. He'd know what to do. He was so good with the kids, and he could fix anything.

The doorbell chimed. Tessa groaned, leaped over the towel barricade, and headed downstairs. Glancing in the mirror on the wall of the entryway, she skidded to a stop. Tears still shimmered in her eyes, mascara smudged her cheeks, and her wet clothes clung to her. *Well, there's nothing I can do about it now.* She pulled open the door and froze.

Bill Hancock stood on the porch holding a large arrangement of bright spring flowers. His eyes widened. "Tessa? What happened?"

Embarrassment zinged through her like an electric shock. "My—my daughter was taking a shower, and the handle broke off. I've got a flood upstairs, and I have no idea how to shut it off."

"Would you like me to come in and take a look?"

Relief washed over her. "Oh, would you?"

"Sure, show me the way." He set the flowers on a nearby table. "These are for you. You've been so down in the dumps, I was hoping they'd cheer you up."

She bit her lip, torn by his kindness and a feeling of guilt. "Thanks, Bill."

Within two minutes, Bill turned off the water to the entire house. Then he followed Tessa upstairs and insisted on helping her clean up the mess. Brie finally arrived with Mr. Cooper. She'd caught him napping in front of the TV and waited for him to put on his shoes and collect his tools before they came to help. Tessa thanked her neighbor and sent him home. She introduced Brie and Bill and then gave her daughter a pile of wet towels to tote to the laundry room. When Brie returned, she stood in the doorway and glared suspiciously at Bill.

Tessa forced a smile. "Thanks, Brie. I think we're about finished here."

Her daughter lifted her eyebrows, silently asking, *Who is this guy, and what's he doing here?*

Ignoring her daughter's look, she turned to Bill. "Good thing you stopped by. We'd have drowned without your help."

He grinned. "Glad I decided to deliver those flowers myself."

"Flowers?" Brie's gaze darted from Bill to Tessa.

"Yes, Bill brought us a lovely bouquet to cheer us up. He had no idea we needed a plumber."

He chuckled. "Well, it doesn't take too much talent to push a mop around."

Brie rolled her eyes and flounced off down the hall.

Tessa swallowed her embarrassment and turned to Bill. "I do appreciate your help. And thanks again for the flowers. You didn't have to do that."

"Well, I admit I have another motive for my visit." He grinned and leaned against the doorjamb. "I have two tickets for the Princeton Medical Center gala dinner next Saturday, and I wondered if you'd like to go."

Tessa's breath caught in her throat. "I don't know, Bill."

"It would be a great way to make connections for Sweet Something. You'd be networking with Princeton's finest." When she hesitated, he sent her an understanding look. "You don't have to decide right now. Check your schedule. See if you can work it out."

She struggled to focus her spinning thoughts. Was he trying to help her business, or was he asking her out on a date? She looked into Bill's eyes, and something there hinted this invitation was more than a friendly business offer.

"No pressure. Just think about it, okay?"

She couldn't decide tonight. She needed more time. "Okay," she said softly. But as soon as she answered, doubt tossed her emotions back and forth like a choppy sea.

Chapter 9

Matt strapped his leather tool belt around his waist and leaned the extension ladder against the side of cabin number four. Once he fixed the roof, this cabin would be ready for rental. A warm sense of satisfaction flowed through him as he climbed to the top and glanced at the other three classic 1920s log cabins he had repaired over the last two weeks. They each slept six and had a river rock fireplace and full-length plank porch. He still had three more cabins to refurbish, but he could begin taking reservations anytime.

He pulled in a deep breath of fresh, evergreen-scented air and listened to the wind in the fir trees. The quiet had been hard to get used to at first, especially after living in a busy family of five. Though he'd grown accustomed to his peaceful surroundings, he missed his family and the comfort of the relationships and routines they shared every day.

His only contact with home was his nightly phone call. Sometimes that hurt so much he could hardly force himself to dial the number. The kids poured out their stories, making him ache to be there, but Tessa always kept her conversation brief and businesslike. She never even hinted at missing him or changing her mind about coming to Oregon. His heart hurt every time he thought of all that separated them—not just physical distance, but broken dreams and shattered trust.

He heard a car approaching and leaned to the left to check it out. A black BMW pulled in and parked. The car door opened, and Mallory Willard stepped out. Matt's stomach tensed. This was her fourth visit since he'd returned to work on renovations. He was beginning to think she had more than legal work on her mind.

Long blond hair shimmered in the sunlight as it fell over her shoulders, and her black pants and blue sweater showed off her great figure. Heat seeped up his neck, and he shifted his focus. Maybe if he didn't say anything, she'd think he wasn't home and leave. He huffed out a disgusted breath. What kind of coward was he? He could handle Mallory Willard.

"Hey, Mallory, I'm up here." He waved.

She looked up and sent him a dazzling smile. "Well aren't you the brave one. What are you doing way up there?"

"Just working on the roof." He climbed down and walked over to meet her.

"Everything looks wonderful. I can't believe all you've accomplished in just two weeks."

"Thanks." He let his gaze travel around the property. She was right. It looked like a different place. Earlier this week, he'd hired a couple men to clear out the weeds, trim the bushes, and begin some basic landscaping.

"I hope you're hungry." She reached back into her car and pulled out a large wicker basket.

A warning flashed through him. "What's that?"

"Barbecued chicken, roasted vegetables, potato salad, and the best strawberry pie you've ever tasted."

"Wow, I was going to eat leftover pizza."

"You deserve much more than that after all this hard work."

Her inviting smile and tempting menu made Matt's head swim. Why not invite her in and enjoy the food she'd made? But what would Tessa say if she found out? How would he explain having dinner, alone, with an attractive woman like Mallory Willard?

"Let's go inside." She smiled and dangled the basket in front of him.

The scent of barbecued chicken drifted out, making his mouth water. "I guess I can take a break for a few minutes."

He led her to the lodge, fighting a battle with his conscience. *She's offering more than a home-cooked meal, and you know it. It's okay; I'll just eat the food and get right back to work.*

Mallory stepped inside and set the basket on the coffee table. "Why don't you go clean up while I get things ready?"

Matt glanced down at his dirty shirt and hands. "Sure. I'll. . . uh, be right back." He took the stairs two at a time and pulled off his shirt as he hustled down the upstairs hall. After snatching a clean shirt from his closet, he headed for the bathroom. The warm water felt good as he ran it over his hands. Leaning forward, he splashed his face, grabbed a towel, and looked up at the mirror.

Staring at his dripping reflection, a powerful wave of conviction broke over him. He closed his eyes and sighed heavily. Nothing would wash away his guilt if he didn't go downstairs right now and put an end to this. No matter how hungry or lonely he felt, he loved the Lord and his family too much to put himself in a tempting situation with Mallory Willard.

He tossed the towel on the counter and walked out of the bathroom. Verses he'd read in Proverbs that morning came back to him. He couldn't quote them perfectly, but he knew they said he'd pay a high price if he broke his marriage vows and got involved with another woman. The vivid word picture flashed in his mind—*"Her lips drip honey, but in the end her feet go down to death."*

All right. I hear You, Lord.

When he reached the bottom step, he saw her standing by the rolltop desk with the phone to her ear.

"No, he's busy," she said softly. "He can't come to the phone right now."

Matt frowned. Who was she talking to? "Mallory."

She spun around and quickly replaced the receiver. Her lips curved into an unconvincing smile. "Well don't you clean up nicely."

"Who was that?"

She averted her eyes. "Just a wrong number."

He knew she was lying. The call had probably been from one of his kids or, worse yet, from Tessa. Irritation coursed through him, confirming his decision. "Mallory, you need to leave."

"Why? What's the matter?" She crossed the room to meet him.

"I'm committed to my marriage, and inviting you in is sending you the wrong message."

Her eyes widened with false innocence. "But we haven't done anything wrong."

"Exactly. And I want to keep it that way." He strode to the door and pulled it open.

She huffed out a scornful laugh. "My, my, aren't you the noble one."

He hesitated, struggling with the truth, then looked her in the eye. "No, but I've made a commitment to God and to my wife, and I don't want to do anything that would hurt my family or damage the name of Christ." A rush of victory flooded him, and he held the door open wider. "Good-bye, Mallory."

She lifted her chin, and her electric blue eyes flashed. "You're throwing away the possibility of a great relationship. Is that what you really want?"

Doubt tugged at his resolve for a second. He needed a miracle to win back Tessa's love, but this was no time to give up on his marriage or do something stupid. He raised his gaze and met hers. "I made up my mind twenty-five years ago when I married Tessa. Nothing is going to change that."

Flames singed her cheeks, and her lips twitched. "Then you're a bigger fool than I thought." She snatched the basket off the coffee table, leaving the food behind as she strutted out the door. Two seconds later, he heard her car door slam and the spray of gravel as she sped down the driveway and out of his life.

He leaned back against the door and closed his eyes. "Thank You," he whispered. Then he headed down the path to the lake to continue his conversation with the Lord.

Tessa carried the last three bags of groceries into the house, dreading the mess she knew awaited her in the kitchen.

Her selfish complaints about Matt's lack of help taunted her. Since he left she felt like she swam through a soupy sea, barely able to keep her head above water. She'd never realized or appreciated all he did. Now there was no one to share the load. Tonight she had to find some way to dry two loads of laundry, help Evan with his math, and pick up Brie from work, but first she had to put away all these groceries.

Evan looked at her with a perplexed expression as she came in the door. "Something weird is going on."

She sighed and lowered the heavy bags to the floor. "What do you mean, honey?"

"I just called Dad, and some woman answered and said he was busy and couldn't come to the phone."

A chill raced up Tessa's back. "You probably dialed the wrong number. Try again."

Evan shook his head. "I used your phone 'cause the number's programmed in."

Tessa swallowed and clasped her hands in front of her to hide their trembling. *Oh, Father, what's happening? Have*

I pushed him away—right into the arms of another woman?
The image of the tall, blond lawyer rose in her mind, and her
stomach clenched. That woman's interest in Matt had been
obvious from the first day they arrived. Had she been chasing
Matt while Tessa selfishly ignored his pleas to bring the kids
and come to Oregon?

Was he fighting a battle for their marriage, or had he
already given up and given in?

"Hand me the phone, Evan."

"You okay, Mom?"

She nodded, trying to swallow her rising fear. "I'm fine.
Why don't you put away some groceries for me."

Evan quietly pulled a box of cereal from the closest bag
and watched her punch in the number. She ought to take the
conversation into another room, but her feet felt glued to the
floor. Matt's phone rang. Tessa held her breath. What would
she say if that woman answered? After three more rings, the
answering machine picked up. Her heart twisted at the sound
of his voice. Why didn't he answer? What were they doing?

She cleared her throat. "Matt, it's me. Please call. We need
to talk." She could hardly choke out the last sentence.

Evan stared at her and then walked out of the kitchen, his
shoulders slumping. She heard him click on the TV in the living room.

She mechanically put away groceries, anxiety and regret
weighing down every motion. How many times had she
ignored her husband's needs and let her own fears and resentment build a wall between them? Had she destroyed her

marriage with her own willful choices? But didn't Matt have some responsibility, too? Wasn't he the one who'd gone off to Oregon and left her here?

The truth hit her hard. No, she had chosen to hold on to her anger rather than forgive and believe the best in her husband. Her lack of trust in Matt, and ultimately in the Lord, was hurting them all. The weight of her sin and the cost it was extracting from her family felt like a crushing weight on her shoulders.

Father, help me! I'm so sorry. Please don't let it be too late.

Evan drifted back into the kitchen, a worried look in his eyes. "Don't you have to pick up Brie?"

Tessa checked the kitchen clock and snatched her keys off the counter. "Come on, we're already late."

Raindrops pelted the windshield as she backed the van out of the garage. Lightning split the sky, followed by a frightening boom of thunder. She flipped the wipers on high, trying to see through the sheets of rain. She hated driving in storms, but she couldn't leave her daughter stranded at the mall.

As Tessa merged onto the rain-slick highway, her stomach knotted and her thoughts spun into a tangled web. How had her life gotten so out of control? Had she become so absorbed with her problems that she'd drifted away from the Lord and closed her ears to His voice? The memory of Bill's dinner invitation sent a huge wave of guilt crashing over her. How could she have even considered it? The thunderstorm outside was nothing compared to the tempest in her heart.

Forgive me, Father. Please forgive me. Tears rained silently down her cheeks. She choked back a sob to hide her distress from her son, who sat behind her.

Red taillights flashed ahead. She slowed, but a pickup truck cut into her lane, trying to squeeze into the shrinking space between her and the next car. Tessa gasped, slammed on the brakes, and swerved to the left. A horn blared behind her. She frantically jerked the steering wheel to the right. Tires screeched, metal crunched, and Evan's scream pierced the night and tore her heart in two.

Chapter 10

The phone rang as Matt walked in the door of the lodge. It had to be Tessa. He dashed across the room. *Please, Lord, help me straighten this out.* Would she let him explain, or would this be the final blow that broke their fragile bond? No, he'd just turned everything over to the Lord. He had to hold on to the hope he'd been given.

He willed confidence into his voice as he answered.

"Oh, Matt." Tessa's voice shook.

He gripped the phone. "What's wrong?"

"I had an accident." Tears laced her words.

"Are you hurt?"

"No—no, I'm okay, just a little cut on my forehead." She sniffed, her voice still trembling. "But we were hit from behind, and Evan was. . ."

The floor seemed to drop out from under him, and he grabbed the desk chair. "Is he okay?"

"No, we're in the Princeton emergency room. They're taking him to surgery." Tessa broke into jerky sobs.

He closed his eyes and sank into the chair, groaning a heartfelt, wordless prayer.

"I'm so sorry, Matt." Grief choked her voice.

He shuddered and drew in a sharp breath. Was she talking about the accident or the trouble between them? It didn't matter. He could never blame her for any of it. This was just as much his fault as hers. He should've been there to protect his family and prevent something tragic like this from happening.

Sorrow clogged his throat. He leaned forward and rubbed his burning eyes.

"Please come, Matt. We need you."

Her words infused him with new strength, and he rose to his feet. "I'm already on the way." He heard more crying on her end of the line, making him long to be there and hold her.

"The Lord is going to carry us through this. Hold on to Him, Tessa."

"I will, but please hurry," she whispered.

An elderly woman wearing a blue volunteer smock checked the hospital's computer and looked up with a smile. "Your son is in room 127. That's one floor up in Pediatrics on B-1."

Matt nodded and breathed a silent prayer of thanks as he strode toward the elevator. The news that Evan was in a regular room, not in surgery or intensive care, boosted his tired spirit. He followed the signs, rounded several corners, and passed the nurses' station. No one had answered the home phone or their cell phones, so Matt hoped he would find Tessa and the kids here.

His journey from Lost Lake Lodge to the University Medical Center at Princeton had taken only eleven hours and twenty-five minutes. He knew that was nothing short of a miracle since he'd had no reservation, and he'd managed to get one of the last seats available on the only plane flying from Portland to Philadelphia late last night. He'd flown off into the midnight sky and then watched the sun come up and fill the heavens with light, his prayers and hope rising with the dawn. Though the circumstances surrounding his return were serious, he felt an unexplained peace. The Lord was at work.

Matt spotted room 127, and his heart lurched. What if he had manufactured those feelings of hope and peace in his own imagination and they weren't from the Lord? What if they lost Evan?

No, he would not let doubt or fear creep in and steal what he had been given. The Lord would be with them no matter what happened.

The door stood slightly ajar. He whispered one more prayer and walked through. The sight of a sterile, empty bed shook him for a moment, but then he saw a curtain had been pulled to shield a second bed. He braced himself and stepped around the curtain.

His gaze darted from his sleeping son to his wife. She had pulled her chair up to Evan's bedside and sat as close to him as possible with her head resting near his, her eyes closed, her hand covering his small fingers.

Matt stalled, practically bowled over by a powerful wave of love for them.

The tranquil looks on both their faces told him his prayers for their comfort had been answered. He took a deep breath, trying to collect his emotions.

Stepping closer, he leaned down and brushed a gentle kiss across Tessa's cheek. Her eyelashes fluttered, and recognition crossed her sleepy expression. She rose into his embrace. Neither spoke as they held each other tightly. Tears washed his eyes, and he let them fall, unashamed. Oh, how he loved this woman.

"I'm so glad you're here," she finally whispered.

"Me, too." He sighed into her hair, holding her close. Right then, he made a decision. No matter what it took, he'd rebuild his marriage and show his wife and kids how much he loved them. With God's help he'd do it.

Tessa clung to Matt, drinking in the comfort of his strong embrace. She pressed her cheek to his chest, and the soothing scent that was Matt's alone filled her senses. She finally pulled back and looked into his face, wanting to study each line and feature that was so familiar and dear to her.

"How's Evan?" He clasped her hand and glanced toward their son, concern filling his eyes.

"He has a broken leg, but the doctors say he's going to be okay. At first they thought he had a concussion, but they did a CAT scan and ruled that out. He had a three-hour surgery last night to put in pins and repair the fracture. They gave him some pain medication. I guess that's why he's still asleep."

Matt nodded, his serious gaze still fixed on Evan.

Her throat tightened. How could she ever have doubted his love and commitment to her and the kids? She must have been deaf to the truth and blinded by her own foolishness.

He turned to her and tenderly brushed her bangs away from the cut on her forehead. "And how are you?"

Heat raced into her cheeks at his close scrutiny. Did he see the crow's-feet, smudged makeup, and dark circles under her eyes? He smiled, and her fears vanished. His loving look convinced her he saw past all of that into her heart, and he treasured her.

A hot, exultant tear trickled down her cheek. "I love you, Matt. Can you forgive me for being so selfish and hurting you and the kids?"

He reached for her. "Only if you'll forgive me for trying to push you into something you never wanted. That was way out of line."

They spent the next half hour talking about the issues that had put a strain on their marriage and assuring each other how much they loved each other.

"I don't want anything to ever come between us again," he said.

She smiled, awed by his sincerity. "Okay, but you have to promise me one thing."

"What's that?"

"That we'll spend the next twenty-five years together."

Surprise and then understanding flickered across his face. "Today's June sixteenth."

She grinned. "Happy anniversary."

"Wow, twenty-five years." Affection and longing glowed in his eyes. He lowered his head and kissed her, gently at first and then more deeply.

She wrapped her arms around his neck and returned his kiss, wanting to show him he was her first and only love. She didn't care what she had to leave behind. Nothing on earth meant as much to her as this dear, wonderful man and their life together. She'd made a commitment to him and him alone. Everything else needed to take a number and get in line.

Justin swished back the curtain and almost spilled the cardboard tray of fast food in his hands. "Dad!"

Brie rushed to hug her father. "Oh, Daddy!" The delight on their daughter's face gave her a glow Tessa hadn't seen for weeks.

Matt hugged Brie and then turned to Justin. "Come here, big guy." He opened his arms and welcomed his older son with a slap on the back and bear hug.

"Hey, what's going on?" a faint voice asked.

Tessa spun toward the bed.

Evan's dazed expression turned to one of pure joy. "Dad, you're here!"

Matt leaned down and gently embraced his tearful son. "Hey, sport. I'm sure glad to hear your voice. How are you doing?"

"I'm okay. When did you get here? How long are you staying? I want to go back with you." Evan's words tumbled out in a rush, and his chin quivered.

"Hey, slow down. It's okay; we've got plenty of time to talk about that."

Tessa pulled in a deep breath. "No, I think it's time for a family meeting."

They all looked at her, surprise on their faces.

Matt straightened. "You want to call a family meeting right now?"

"Yes. I have some things I need to say to all of you." She turned to Evan. "That is, if you're awake enough to listen."

He blinked his droopy eyes. "Sure, I broke my leg, but my ears are fine."

They all grinned.

"First, I need to apologize—to all of you." Tessa looked into each face. "When your dad and I talked and prayed about going to Oregon, we asked the Lord to make it clear if we should move. He did, but I didn't want to listen. I let selfishness and fear get in the way and make the decision for me, and that hurt us all. I need to trust the Lord to lead us, and we need a full-time dad and mom in this family, so—"

Matt interrupted her. "Wait. Before we make any decisions, I have some things to say, too. The Lord's also been speaking to me, and He's made it clear that keeping our family together is more important than where we live or work. And if that means I need to sell the lodge property and move home to New Jersey, then that's what I'll do. Living in Oregon would be a good choice for us, but it's not the only choice. I love you—all of you." He looked at each of them, and his gaze settled on Tessa. "And you're worth more to me than any piece of property, no matter how long it has been in my family or how much business potential it has."

Tessa smiled. "I love you, too, and I'm ready to move to Oregon if that's where you believe the Lord is leading us."

"But I could get a good price for that property. We could buy a new house here, and you could keep Sweet Something."

"Since you guys can't make up your mind, I think we should vote on it," Justin said.

Tessa and Matt exchanged surprised glances.

"All those in favor of moving to Oregon raise your hand," Justin continued.

Every hand went up, including Tessa's. Laughter bubbled up from her heart. The Lord had made it clear again, and this time she would listen.

"Yes!" Justin pumped his fist in the air.

Brie squealed and grabbed her big brother for a hug.

Evan's sleepy smile spread wider, delight brightening his eyes.

Matt pulled Tessa close. "Are you sure, Tessa? Is this what you really want?"

Assurance washed over her. "Yes, I want to be with you. Wherever you're going, I'm going, too." Then she kissed him again, lingering, savoring the sweetness of their love tested and refined by twenty-five years of marriage and renewed by a miracle of God's grace in their hearts.

CARRIE TURANSKY

Carrie makes her home in Lawrenceville, New Jersey, with her husband, Scott, of twenty-seven years who is senior pastor of Calvary Chapel Mercer County. They are blessed with five great kids, a lovely daughter-in-law, and an adorable grandson. Carrie homeschools her two youngest children; teaches a women's Bible study; and enjoys reading, gardening, and walking around the lake near their home. She has written many devotionals, short stories, and articles. She loves hearing from her readers. Visit her Web site at http://carrie.turansky.com. You may write to her at carrie@turansky.com or c/o Author Relations, Barbour Publishing, P.O. Box 712, Uhrichsville, OH 44683.

A Letter to Our Readers

Dear Readers:

In order that we might better contribute to your reading enjoyment, we would appreciate your taking a few minutes to respond to the following questions. When completed, please return to the following: Fiction Editor, Barbour Publishing, Inc., P.O. Box 719, Uhrichsville, OH 44683.

1. Did you enjoy reading *Wedded Bliss?*
   ❏ Very much—I would like to see more books like this.
   ❏ Moderately—I would have enjoyed it more if _____
   _____
   _____

2. What influenced your decision to purchase this book?
   (Check those that apply.)
   ❏ Cover   ❏ Back cover copy   ❏ Title   ❏ Price
   ❏ Friends   ❏ Publicity   ❏ Other

3. Which story was your favorite?
   ❏ *When Seasons Change*   ❏ *Love Is a Choice*
   ❏ *Reunited*   ❏ *Wherever Love Takes Us*

4. Please check your age range:
   ❏ Under 18   ❏ 18–24   ❏ 25–34
   ❏ 35–45   ❏ 46–55   ❏ Over 55

5. How many hours per week do you read? _____

Name _____

Occupation _____

Address _____

City _____ State _____ Zip _____

E-mail _____